I0519824

ELEPHANT GAS

A Novel

By Ken Graham

Cover Design by Vanessa Heim,
The Heim Company

The Characters and events portrayed in this book are fictitious. Any similarity to real persons, living or dead, is coincidental, and not intended by the author.

Copyright © 2013 by Ken Graham
All rights reserved.
No part of this book may be reproduced in any form or transmitted by any means without the express written permission of the author.

Published by Bolderfish Press
P.O. Box 152
Dayton, WA 99328

ISBN: 978-0-615-98855-9

In memory of Ovella, who encouraged me to write.

Chapter One

I was never actually a writer, but I remember when I first thought I could be one. A few years ago I had a girlfriend named Delores who had two dogs she called Henry and Steve. Delores was obsessed with her dogs, and she treated them a lot better than she treated me. For Christmas that year, I wrote a story about Henry and Steve and gave it to Delores. I didn't buy her anything, because I was broke, but she liked the story. It was about Henry and Steve eating pancakes. Delores liked to cook and she fixed me breakfast a lot, which was an excellent characteristic for a girlfriend. And her pancakes were outstanding, but when she made them, she didn't put on enough syrup. I like pancakes drowned in syrup, and I told her that repeatedly. In the story I wrote, Henry and Steve could talk, and they complained that their pancakes were too dry. At the end of the story, Steve yelled "I'm gagging, I'm gagging," and then ran to his water dish.

When I showed the story to Delores, she actually laughed. She said, "This is really good. You should be a writer." The thought of being a writer – as a job – hadn't occurred to me before. But I knew Delores wasn't just saying that to be nice, because at that point she didn't like me all that well. By March, we were history. After the dog and pancake story, I started to think of myself as a potential writer. This made for a nice transition from being a potential major league pitcher, because I was getting too old for that. You were never too old to be a writer, I decided, so it was perfect. I was doing about as much writing as I was throwing curve balls and change-ups, but at least my new pretend career was more realistic.

I have a friend named Charles, who I knew long before I knew Delores. At some point after I wrote the pancake story, I told Charles about my potential writing career. He was surprised, because we had gone to college together and he knew how I felt about writing back then. Writing papers for classes was a lot of work, and doing a lot of work wasn't how I approached college. Of course, when Charles brought that up, I pointed out that I wasn't actually doing any writing now either. Charles owned a computer consulting business and one of his clients was a small magazine in Seattle called Western Oasis. This was a magazine that had a lot of short articles with big color photos showing people with beautiful houses and gardens. They had ponds in their back yards and expensive appliances and cabinets in their kitchens. Sometimes they traveled to places like Palm Springs and Santa Fe and stayed in expensive and beautiful hotels. And they ate beautiful food. I never knew food could look so good until I saw a copy of Western Oasis. For a while, Charles threatened to get me work writing for Western Oasis. They often used freelance writers, he had said. They pay wasn't much, but I could get my name in print and have something I could show other publishing people, so then I could hopefully get more underpaid writing work. I told Charles that the whole idea of doing research and interviewing people for articles didn't really suit me. I was more of a fiction guy – you know, just writing stuff I made up. He finally gave up and quit bothering me about it, at least for awhile.

I ended up selling real estate in Seattle. It's a job that appeals to people who think they should be able to make a lot of money without doing much work. The job didn't really fit me, but I did it, and I always went for big sales. I was like a scrawny infielder who swung for the fences. The thing is that even scrawny infielders hit home runs once in awhile. About a year after I started, I got my home run. I sold a three-million-dollar apartment building, and that sixty-thousand-dollar commission made the first two years of my otherwise marginal real estate career a modest success. But I was now in my third year and it was time to start swinging like Barry Bonds again.

I had my own office in the Fremont district, a neighborhood north of downtown Seattle, which is considered trendy and hip. Unfortunately most of my real estate clients owned property in much less trendy and hip neighborhoods, but at least I could call myself a Fremont Real Estate Agent.

* * *

On a Friday afternoon in mid-June, I left my office near the Lake Washington Ship Canal and walked north toward Fremont's shopping district. An international music festival was being held that weekend in a giant self-pay parking lot. Groups from all over the world were performing. The crowds were large already at four p.m., and I could hear a steel drum band somewhere ahead. I walked toward the music. The musicians were mostly dark-skinned. The steel drums, congas and a marimba threw a rhythm into the air that hung pleasantly and lingered. The beat sounded Latin, and yet the music wasn't. It was African, and it drowned out the traffic noise from the nearby street. All of the other city sounds I would normally hear were absent now.

The crowd was diverse. The Scandinavians, who had been in north Seattle for many generations, were well represented. So were Asians, many of whom had been in Seattle nearly as long. Other more recent arrivals – Africans and Latin Americans – were scattered in the crowd, though in smaller numbers. There were older people and there were younger people, and there were children. After wandering awhile, watching the people – mostly women – I reached the steel drum band I had heard. A beautiful young black-skinned woman, who was probably about 20, stood in front of the drums with a microphone. She had long dreadlocks and wore a flowing multi-colored skirt that reached her ankles. Her top was tight and sleeveless and showed off her incredible body. I watched this beautiful vision float across the stage like a feather in a breeze. Her body moved flawlessly. She sang a haunting African song, and I froze and stared. As I stood, lost in a beautiful song I couldn't understand and mesmerized by her beautiful voice,

I was suddenly jolted back to reality.

"Keep it in your pants there bubba," said Charles, who had walked up behind me.

"I'm in love," I told him. "This time it's for real."

Charles had on his usual black sweatshirt and black jeans, even though the temperature was pushing 90. "Dude, you don't speak her language, in more ways than one."

"It doesn't matter," I said, barely above a whisper.

"Well think about this, dipshit," Charles went on. "You know damn well she's screwing one of those giant conga players in the back, and it probably matters to him."

Charles had an unnerving grip on reality sometimes, which caused him to miss out on a lot of good fantasies. But he was usually right. "You're right," I said. "What the fuck are you doing here anyway?"

"I'm taking the afternoon off. Let's go get a beer and give your pecker a rest."

"I'll take more than one," I said. "I'm going to dream about her tonight."

The love of my life ended her song and walked back behind a screen with the rest of her band. I would never see her again. Charles and I began walking through the crowd, listening to some South American music from another band. The crowd was getting bigger now, and lines were forming at the food vendors. We passed them all and headed to Max's Tavern. At the edge of Fremont's shopping district, we walked past the hulking image of Vladimir Lenin, leading his comrades forward. The giant bronze statue was moved Fremont a few years after it was toppled from its previous perch in Slovakia at the end of the Cold War. "I hope it doesn't get knocked over again," I told Charles.

"Yeah, that would really mess up traffic," he replied.

Max's was probably the least hip place in Fremont. It was a long, narrow, dark biker bar where Charles liked to hang out. He didn't fit in there at all – and neither did I – but the people with the leather and tattoos behind the bar tolerated us. Max's was in an old converted warehouse on a side street. On the outside it was kind of gray with a low flat roof, and it had little windows above eye level with little neon beer signs hanging in them. Charles and I came here regularly, which at our age, meant every couple of months. Max's had been one of our hangouts in college, back when, "regularly" meant daily. It was the only bar from those days, more than 20 years before, that was still in business.

When we walked in I saw a really ugly woman sitting by herself near the door. We walked toward the bar and her face stuck in my brain. Charles ordered a pitcher of the only non-light beer they had, which wasn't very good, from a bartender who was about 80. Charles waited for the pitcher and I sat down at a shiny rectangular wooden table that looked like it was made from a bowling alley lane. I looked around and saw the ugly woman staring at me. At the table next to me, a skinny greasy-looking biker in full leather was talking to an incredibly hot girl who looked like she was about 18. Even with all the background noise I could hear him telling her something about riding to Mexico. They were both laughing and she was definitely into him. She had to be a teenager. If she was 21 I was 100. She was blonde and thin and built. Everything she wore fit tightly. She reminded me of college, and the dorm, and smoking dope, and all the girls I had fantasized about from a distance. I should have become a biker, I thought. Holy crap, what a moron I was then.

"Holy crap, what a moron you are, Smith." Charles showed up with the beer while I was eyeing the child goddess. "What's the matter with you?" he whispered. "That girl's not even legal. Let's get a table on the other side. It's not so bright over there." It wasn't so bright over here either, but we walked through a slalom of bowling-alley tables, past the biker and the goddess, who ignored me, and found a tiny table in the corner with a dim yellow spotlight aimed directly at its center from overhead.

"You really need to get laid, man," said Charles. "But you've got to be realistic about your prospects. I mean look at yourself." He proceeded to lecture me about how a 44-year-old slightly flabby white guy wasn't going to be turning the heads of any gorgeous African singers or tight-bodied blonde college girls less than half his age, and that I was completely wasting my energy. Then he asked, "Did you see that woman over by the door? She was checking you out."

I looked at Charles in disgust. "Very Funny. She's a total scud, man."

"You've got to take what you can get," he said. "You're a scud-magnet. Have a couple of beers and she won't look so bad."

"Look at her nose. She looks like a dolphin," I said. "Does she have teeth? I can't even tell."

Charles started laughing hysterically. He said, "Hey, you know what they say about girls with no teeth."

"She would definitely come in at the bottom of the list," I said.

"What do you mean?"

"You know, my hot date list."

"Oh yeah, your ranking of all the women you've ever gone out with, based on how good looking they are. You've never dated a woman that ugly?"

"Are you kidding? I'm much too shallow for that."

"So who's number one now?"

"Still Delores," I said. "She's going to be hard to beat. Your sister's definitely in the top five though. And she gets bonus points because she doesn't look anything like you."

"Very funny."

Charles's real name was Chuck Roberts. It made him sound like a cowboy, which he definitely wasn't. He was a geek. His parents named him Chuck, but he used Charles as his nickname. He was a hair machine. Actually, he was a hair factory – except for the top of his head. I saw him once standing in his yard without a shirt. He looked like some kind of freaky bonsai shrub with a white dome on top. His wardrobe was designed for winter in Seattle, and he wore it no matter what the weather was. He didn't like the sun, and he spent as little time as possible outside. So he saw no point in buying summer clothes. Even though he was a geek, Charles had the gift of gab. He was several years into his second marriage, and he had lots of friends besides me. He was self-employed, and he was very good at finding work.

Once we were settled at the table with our beers, Charles looked at me seriously. "Speaking of my sister, I need to talk to you about something."

"So how's Ramona doing?" I asked.

"That's what I need to talk to you about."

A couple of months earlier I started dating Charles's older sister Ramona. Ramona had moved back to Seattle after her latest divorce and she told Charles she thought I was kind of cute. At least that's what he said that she said. He also had told me that she used to be a cheerleader at UCLA, which turned out not to be true. She didn't even go there. Charles had also assured me that Ramona didn't look anything like him, and on that basis, I agreed to go out with her. He was right about that. She was pretty hot, considering that she was four years older than me. We went out a few times, and as far as I knew things were going pretty well.

"Setting you up with a relative was a bad idea," Charles said.

"You're kidding! You think she wants to stop seeing me?"

"She told me to tell you that."

"You're kidding!" I said again. "You mean your sister sent you to break up with me for her? You're fucking kidding me!"

"No, I'm not kidding you."

I couldn't think of anything to say for a few seconds. "OK, no problem," I finally said. "I'm sorry you had to do this. So what's the deal? Am I too old for her?"

I was joking, but Charles wasn't laughing. "Well, actually, yeah."

"What?! You're kidding!"

"I said I'm not kidding. And quit saying that. I guess she just likes men under 40."

"She's almost 50." I was yelling now. "Are you nuts?!"

"No, I'm not nuts, and I'm not kidding."

I took a moment to regain my composure. "Look at me. I'm in pretty decent shape. I'm sure I don't look like I'm over forty. And I don't think I'm so bad looking, am I?"

"Whatever you say, Smith," he replied. "You act like you're 19 most of the time, so I'd have thought you'd be perfect for her."

"Well I'll be fucked," I said. "Oh well...I get the hook again." Then I looked at Charles and raised my eyebrows. "The sex was great, you know."

"I told you not to talk about my sister that way. I don't want to hear it." Then he changed the subject, and Ramona was history. Just like that.

"Listen, Robert my boy, here's how I'll make it up to you," he said.

"You don't have to make it up to me. In fact, I don't want you to make it up to me. Are you going to tell me you have another sister who can mess up my life even more?"

Charles ignored that. "You know how you're always going around saying you're going to be a writer?" He was smiling now.

"Oh, not that again. I don't go around saying that," I said. "I told you that once, and I'm really sorry I did. I'm pretty sure I was drunk at the time."

"I've seen some of your writing," he said. "You write really good."

"Well I write better than you talk."

He ignored me again. "I might have a job for you."

"Look dickhead, just because I'm too old for Princess Ramona doesn't mean you owe me anything. I can manage my own pretend writing career just fine."

"Relax Hemingway," he said. "I was talking to the Oasis editor the other day. She needs a piece on some little town in Oregon. And she asked me about you again. She said none of their real writers are willing to go there. "

"You were talking about me to Agnes again? I asked you not to do that. I told you, I write fiction."

"She asked about you. And her name's Angela."

"Well, she looks like an Agnes," I said. I had met Angela once, and the only sexy thing about her was her name.

"Well maybe she thinks you're cute. Like scud-woman over there" said Charles. "She told me this would be the perfect opportunity for a hungry young rookie. Or, in your case, a desperate old rookie."

"Yeah, wonderful. Tell her no."

"And guess what it's called," he said, ignoring me once again.

"What what's called?"

"The town. In Oregon. This will crack you up."

"OK, I give up. What's it called?"

"Elephant."

"What do you mean?"

"The little town in Oregon that you're going to write about. It's called

Elephant."

"You mean the one I'm not going to write about." I said. "What a stupid name."

Charles explained that Angela needed an article for the magazine about Elephant, Oregon, because of the publisher's brother-in-law, an old guy named Ralph something. He grew up there, and her boss owes Ralph a favor. He was going back for his 100th high school reunion or something, and he wanted to impress the folks back home. So now Angela needed to find someone willing to go there and write something warm and fuzzy, so Ralph could take copies to his reunion.

"You know," he said. "Find something cute, or historic. Or just strange. Something that will make some of the bored people who read the magazine want to drive three hundred miles to go see it."

"Three hundred miles? Are you out of your mind? Where the hell is it?"

"It's out in the east – near Montana, or Nevada, or something."

"Shit, you're crazy. You want me to drive halfway across the country to spend a week talking to a bunch of hillbillies in a little town with a stupid name?"

"It would just be a couple of days."

"No thank you."

You should think about it," Charles continued, not giving up. "Look at yourself. This real estate gig is getting you nowhere. When was the last time you made a sale?"

"I'm getting real close," I told him, and he started laughing.

"You're like a gambling addict," he said. "You're sure you'll get the big payoff any minute. Why don't you just go to Vegas and hang out in casinos. At least the drinks are cheap and the women are better looking."

"You're funny."

"So are you going to finish the deal with your client from hell? What's her name?"

"Doris. Yeah, we actually have a buyer for her apartments. We should close the sale in a couple of weeks."

"I've heard that before," said Charles. "And how many other clients do you have?"

"None. Doris is it. I have one million-dollar listing, and when it sells I'm going to the Caribbean." And I wasn't joking.

"Well, it's your funeral," he replied. I wasn't quite sure what that meant, but right then Charles pulled his vibrating cell phone out of his pocket, spoke into it for a moment and then closed it. "Darlene's meeting us here," he said.

"Uh, this has been loads of fun, but I gotta run," I said. "I just remembered I've got to meet someone. I think I have a new client."

Charles's latest wife, Darlene, was a young female Hitler, and around her, he was like a German army private. I was embarrassed for him, even if he wasn't. "Why don't you like her?" he asked, as he always did. I just smiled and waved and didn't answer.

When I walked out of Max's, the goddess was long gone and I saw the skinny biker punching his thumbs on a BlackBerry. Thankfully the ugly woman had been joined by an equally ugly man. I could feel her staring at me as I went by. The sunlight blinded me when I got onto the sidewalk and headed south through the growing Fremont crowd, past the bronze Lenin and toward the Ship Canal and my office.

Chapter Two

The Fremont neighborhood lies along the north edge of Lake Union and the canal that leads out to Puget Sound. A beautiful century-old drawbridge crosses the canal and connects Fremont to Queen Ann hill and downtown Seattle. The giant arch of the Aurora Avenue Bridge hovers high above the neighborhood. Fremont is home to the Seattle offices of Adobe and Google, and a lot of very expensive condos, but yet it has a bohemian feel. Besides the Lenin statue, Fremont is home to some other strange pieces of public art. A giant troll skulks underneath the north end of the Aurora Bridge, crushing a Volkswagen Bug in its gnarled fingers; the four figures in the famous "Waiting for the Interurban" sculpture often get dressed up by the locals for special occasions; a fifty-foot 1950s cold war rocket sits upright, waiting to launch.

Fremont is like a little town in the middle of the City, with narrow neighborhood streets, where cars constantly have to stop for pedestrians and bikes. Second-hand stores and grubby-looking coffee shops mix with small shiny designer clothing and furniture stores and expensive restaurants. Banks sit on some of the corners, and insurance and other small professional offices take up the higher floors. I liked working in Fremont, even though I hardly fit in.

Many of the buildings in Fremont are old, but their owners keep them in good repair. A lot of the buildings, new and old, are painted in bright colors. Whenever I was on the sidewalk in nice weather I saw people washing windows and painting trim and planting flowers in boxes. Workers and their trucks were almost always around, keeping up maintenance on the buildings and businesses. There was rarely an empty storefront. New businesses seemed to show up constantly, and whenever one would fail and close another was ready to step in and give it a try. Needless to say, real estate prices were high here.

I had opened my Fremont office two years earlier, because I didn't want to have to share commissions with a broker anymore. Now I was sharing my commissions with my landlord, and the phone company and Office Depot. I had a better deal financially before, but I liked working on my own, and being in Fremont. I worked mostly with clients who were buying or selling apartment buildings, which are known in real estate jargon as "multi-family residential" properties. There were lots of apartment buildings in the Fremont neighborhood, ranging from houses converted to duplexes all the way to multi-million dollar high-rises. My plan had been to be like the neighborhood grocer or shoe repair guy. I could just chat with people in the neighborhood who had money to invest and help them see their dreams come true through ownership of part of the neighborhood. But the real estate business is not quite like the shoe repair business. And the people I got to know in the neighborhood were all struggling and had no money to invest. They were either renters or employees. The building owners and investors lived somewhere else, and they did business with high-level brokers who also lived and worked elsewhere. When it came to real estate investment, Fremont definitely wasn't a little town.

I had no client prospect waiting for me when I got to my office, but as I unlocked the door, my cell phone rang. "Hello Doris," I mumbled into the phone, after glancing at the caller ID and taking a deep breath.

"Robert, it's Doris Ellington," she said, ignoring my greeting.

Doris Ellington was my sworn enemy. Hearing her voice on the phone made my head hurt. Spending an hour with her in person was like spending a month at the dentist. But Doris was my only client at the moment, and so I was as cheerful as I could force myself to be. "Did you see the letter that attorney fellow sent about the landscaping at the apartments?" Doris asked.

"Yes, Doris, he wrote it to me," I replied, as my jaw stiffened. "You just got a copy."

"Well, if you had just gone and looked at those trees, you'd have known they didn't need spraying, and you could have told him that."

"Doris, I have no idea when a tree needs spraying. Landscaping isn't part of my job."

"Well, I don't blame him for being upset, and I don't want to get sued," she said.

"Well then, maybe you should have the trees sprayed like you said you would in the contract."

She was being surprisingly patient with me. "My nephew looked at them and he said they didn't need it," she said. "You should have told that lawyer man that yourself."

I grabbed the edge of the door and swung it toward my head, reluctantly stopping it at the last possible instant. "Doris, your nephew fixes flat tires for a living. He doesn't know anything about trees either. Besides, last week you told me he was an idiot," you fucking bitch. The last three words I only said silently.

"You tell that lawyer that those trees don't need spraying," she ordered me. "That's part of your job."

"Doris, you signed a contract that said you'd spray the trees. Now you want me to tell the guy who's buying your building – a Southern California attorney – that you're not going to live up to your agreement?"

"I only meant that I'd spray the trees if they needed it," she said. "Since I'm sure they don't, I'm not paying for it."

So here I was in my latest version of real estate hell. If and when the L.A. lawyer finally closed on the purchase of Doris's apartment building, I would receive a commission check for around $30,000 – the commission that would once again get me out of debt and give me my first time off in two years. But it meant that I was completely at Doris's mercy, and she pretty much knew it. I had no other income on the horizon, and I had a mortgage payment and three credit cards with balances increasing rapidly.

When our conversation was over and Doris was finally done explaining her absolute refusal to spray the trees, I sat down at my computer, took a deep breath, and composed an email to Richard Lane of Breech and Lane,

PC, in Los Angeles, California: "Mr. Lane, I'm just writing back to confirm that the tree spraying will be taken care of promptly. I'm sorry for the miscommunication about that." With the email sent, I got out the yellow pages and looked up tree sprayers. And I watched my commission shrink by a few hundred dollars.

Waking up from that nightmare, I sat in my office and looked out the window at the streets full of people. I pulled my phone out of my pocket and turned it off. As I walked down the stairs to the street I tried to put Doris and Ramona and Elephant, Oregon, and another condo payment that would have to be paid with my credit card, all out of my mind.

* * *

The next morning, which was Saturday, I parked my faded maroon 1994 BMW in front of Ugly Al's Coffee Emporium. It was shortly before eight o'clock. The sky was clear again and the sun was already well up. I looked back for a moment at the Beemer with its blotchy paint and sagging springs. The streets were nearly empty and screeching seagulls were the dominant sound. Ugly Al's was one street over from Max's Ale House, and down a block. And it wasn't exactly an "emporium", though I'm not even sure what that is. It was actually a hole-in-the-wall coffee shop with four tables, a couch and an industrial, well-used espresso machine that dominated the back corner of the shop. An old-fashioned spring-loaded screen door on the front squeaked and banged shut loudly when you let go of it.

Ugly Al's was owned and operated by Jennifer something. I was in love with Jennifer, even though she had a last name I could never remember. Unfortunately, Jennifer had a rather large husband – from whom she got the last name, which is probably why I couldn't remember it. She also had a young son. She was thin with light brown hair. She had long arms and legs and was kind of gangly and seemed a bit uncoordinated, even though she wasn't. Her face was bony and her nose was a little too big. Sometimes she wore glasses and sometimes she didn't, and she didn't wear makeup. She wasn't ugly, just not a natural beauty. The understated elegance and creativeness in how Jennifer had set up her shop fascinated me. I liked to think she sensed our chemistry, but her friendliness probably had a lot more to do with over-tipping on my part. Or maybe it was just pity on her part.

"So where's Al today," I asked Jennifer when I walked into the shop. Even though there was actually no "Al", I had asked her that question many times before, and once again she laughed politely and smiled.

Jennifer had made up the name of her shop. The first time I asked her about it, she told me she hated cute coffee shop names. "Hava Java? The Buzz Stop? Happy Go Latte?" She said them all with a sneer. "Gimme a fucking break!"

"I know a couple more," I had said. How about "Espresso Chang-O?"

"Yuk."

"Perkatory?"

"Hmmm. I kind of like that one," she laughed.

This morning she made me a double iced mocha and told me about Christopher's new habit of wearing her bras on his head.

I asked if she was referring to Christopher Senior or Christopher Junior.

"Very funny. You're cute." That earned an even bigger tip.

I sat down at a window table with my mocha and tried to get the image of Jennifer's bra out of my mind. A woman came in with a stroller containing a small child. She and Jennifer did the co-mommy thing, asking excited questions about each others' babies. A copy of a weekly underground newspaper called The Ditch was lying on the table and I picked it up. I looked through the ads in the back for escort services and nude models and thought about Ramona. "What a bitch," I mumbled to myself.

"What?" Jennifer yelled over to me.

"Oh, nothing," I said, not realizing my comment had been audible. "Just talking to myself. Don't worry, I'm just slowly going insane."

"OK, good," Jennifer replied with a straight face. I hoped that just meant that she hadn't heard what I said. I went back to the newspaper and my dark thoughts. Well, it's Ramona's loss, I thought, trying to convince myself that was true. Then I sat back and looked around the room. The old wood floors and beat-up wooden bar made the place feel like an old ship.

Jennifer had the milk steamer going full blast now for her new customer. She was wearing a black low-cut top and tight jeans. She had her hair in a pony tail and her glasses on today. This was my favorite look – not that it mattered. I watched as Jennifer worked, with her intense focus and her arms always moving. She had the perfect temperament for her job – the appearance of patience and no stress. She was good at faking both, I thought. She would focus all of her attention on the person she was talking to and make them feel like the most important person in the world. I was even more infatuated.

Being barista is like being a combination bartender and train engineer. You have do have great social skills and mechanical skills and, most importantly, you have to be fast. Jennifer had been a bartender before she opened Al's, and she told me once that serving coffee had many advantages. The most important one is that the customers are sober – at least mostly. And you get to bed at a decent hour. "Sober people don't tip as well," she had said. I told her I'd always tip her as if I were drunk.

"Is this a work day, Rob?" Jennifer asked a few minutes later, after the other mommy had left. She was hauling a load of cups and plates in from the sidewalk tables.

"No way," I mumbled, as she headed behind the counter to unload. I thought about how nice it would be to have a job like Jennifer's. You'd have lots of different customers, and you could afford to piss one or two of them off if you felt like it. If Doris Ellington came in and started whining about her latte, I could just quietly tell her to go fuck herself and buy her latte somewhere else. It wouldn't cost me more than one or two coffee sales a week. Probably less, as tight as she is

On a Saturday morning with a great cup of mocha and nothing important to do, I could sit back, relax and pretend that life was wonderful. It really wasn't that bad. I could sit here in this huge city, among all of these people. And none of them knew a thing about me. Even Jennifer didn't know anything important about me. Although I wished she'd ask, she didn't. With a few exceptions, nobody in Seattle knew that my career and my love life both sucked. The woman who just left Jennifer's shop probably thought I was a prosperous businessman. Maybe the ugly woman at Max's the night before thought I was a software billionaire taking a break from working on his foundation that helped African children – or something. Many successful people, much younger than me, sit in coffee shops in Seattle on Saturday mornings and read The Ditch.

Just as the caffeine was starting to kick in and I was deep into an article about an all-girl grunge revival show in The Ditch, my pants began to vibrate. "Shit," I said out loud. Why did I have my phone with me? And why was it on? I had forgotten to take it out before I left the condo. I reached into the cargo pocket of my shorts and quickly hit the cancel button without taking the phone out. I slowly removed the phone and glanced down at the little screen. There it was – the dreaded word, spelled out in plain English on the caller ID. "DEATH." This was the name I had programmed into my cell phone for Doris. I had entered her initials at first. Later I added three more letters for emphasis. I slipped the phone back into my pocket and felt the pleasant, relaxed feeling I had a few moments before get sucked right out of the room. I could almost hear it whistle out the door. When I pulled the phone back out a couple of minutes later I saw that there was a message on my voicemail, as I knew there would be. I slowly dialed star-eight-six and then listened.

"Robert, this is Doris Ellington," the voice said. Doris was always careful to identify which Doris she was. It never seemed to occur to her that I knew no other Dorises. "Robert, I need you to go over to the building and check on something. Manuel got a message on his cell phone that water is leaking out of the office door. He's in California, so go look around and see if you see any water. Then call me back. I'd do it myself, but I have ladies coming over this morning. And hurry." No "please", no "thank you", no "yes I know I'm the skank bitch from hell." Just "click."

First of all, Doris would never ever do it herself, ladies or not. And second, she had an apartment manager who liked to travel. Not a good qualification for an apartment manager. But lucky for her, she had me: her Real Estate Slave. Another Saturday morning ruined by Doris. It was becoming routine. I put the phone back in my pocket. I sat and drank my mocha and watched while Jennifer steamed some milk for another customer. She didn't let even the biggest asshole customers bother her at all. She just smiled and said pleasant things and otherwise ignored them until they walked out of the shop.

"Did you get some bad news, Rob?" Jennifer asked after she had finished serving her other customer. I must have had a pained expression.

"Just another day in Real Estate Paradise." I said goodbye to Jennifer and walked slowly out the door. I got into the BMW, which, 15 years ago, was a desirable car. I'd have been a well-thought-of Yuppie driving this car. Now, at beyond 180,000 miles it was the car of a wannabe who wasn't. The body was still nice, even with its faded blotchy paint, but the look was dated. The tires were almost bald. The leather seats though, were like an old and very comfortable couch, including a couple of small tears. The car ran like a trooper, but who was I kidding. I might as well put a bumper sticker on it that says "I can't afford a decent car."

I scrolled down the contact list on my phone until I got to "DEATH", and then pressed it. Doris answered right away. "This is Robert Smith," I said, pretending that she knew lots of Roberts. Who knows, maybe she did.

"Are you at the apartments yet?" she asked. "Did you find any water?"

"Doris, you just called five minutes ago. I had to finish my coffee." I knew that would piss her off.

"Robert, there's no time for coffee. This could be an emergency."

Then why don't you call the cops? I felt like asking, but I didn't. "Why is Manuel out of town?" is what I did ask. "Can't you find a backup manager?"

"He almost never leaves," she lied.

CHAPTER THREE

Doris's apartments were located in Bothell, a Seattle suburb which is nowhere near Fremont. I fired up the Beemer and headed toward I-5 northbound. At least on Saturday morning there should be little traffic and I could get this trip over quickly. Water from the sprinkler probably ran toward the office and someone got panicky. Or maybe a pack of dogs came by and all peed on the office door. After 20 minutes of driving and trying to think of all of the stupid reasons there could be a puddle in front of that office door, I arrived at the entrance to the Victorian Manor Apartments. The trees in front looked kind of droopy and sick, like maybe they needed spraying. Then I, too, began to feel sick as I looked toward the office and saw water cascading over the curb and down the driveway, a hundred yards from the building. The sky was blue and cloudless and the sprinklers were off. As I drove into the parking lot, I could see that the water was coming from the laundry room. I saw two women, one with small children, doing their wash and completely ignoring the flooded floor.

"Doris, you need a plumber over here right away," I yelled into the phone, after I had quickly announced myself with my first and last names. "Right away!" I repeated.

"Can't you just turn the water main off for now?" she asked calmly. "It's so expensive to hire a plumber on Saturday. Besides, my guests are here and I don't have time to worry about that."

"I can't turn off everybody's water for two days!" I felt my blood pressure escalate and I needed to calm down. The worst thing I could do was continue to discuss the situation with Doris. "Look, forget about it, I'll take care of it," I said. "I heard her start to say "good" and then something else, as I hit the "end" button on my phone and made her go away.

"I'm sorry ladies," I said as I walked into the laundry room. "We have a leak and we have to turn off the water and the power. I can't risk anyone getting electrocuted."

The thin brunette with the two toddlers gave me a blank stare for about five seconds and then slowly began unloading dripping clothes from her machine, without saying anything. The stocky redhead whose face was covered with freckles wasn't going to make it so easy. She was wearing a very long T-shirt, and I couldn't tell what else. She was average height and had very thick, muscular legs. And she was pissed. "No way, man," Freckles said threateningly. She took a step toward me and I instinctively stepped back. "I'm not taking these clothes out now. They're full of soap. What the fuck?!"

"Look," I said, in as calm a voice as I could. "You're standing in water. If one of these machines has a short in it, you could get electrocuted." I didn't really know how likely that was, but I needed to say something to change her mind. I took out my wallet and pulled out two five-dollar bills. Only two singles remained. I gave one of the fives to the redhead and said "here, you can go into Bothell and finish your wash at a laundromat. And get a coffee while you're there." Then I walked toward the brunette with the children and handed her the other bill. She took it silently.

"Fuck that!" the redhead yelled, after she had taken the money. "My boyfriend has my truck. Am I supposed to walk? Carrying these clothes? Fuck that!"

I could see water flowing under the door from the back room, and I needed to go find the main water valve and the breaker panel. "Look, go take your clothes and set them next to my car. I'll be there in a minute, as soon as I turn off the water and power, and I'll give you a ride to laundromat."

I used the key Doris had given me to open the door to the storage area behind the laundry room. I found a water cutoff valve for the laundry room and closed it. Then I found the breaker box and began flipping the switches off. When I heard the redhead yell and start cursing, I knew I'd turned off the overhead lights, so I turned them back on. When I finished and walked back out into the laundry room, the redhead was just walking over to the car. She opened the back door on the driver's side and dropped the soapy dripping plastic basket onto the leather seat, before I could direct her to the trunk. She then walked around the car and sat down in the front passenger seat. I stopped and took a breath and imagined the soapy bubbles filling up the back seat of my car. I got in the driver's seat and silently drove out of the parking lot. The redhead angrily gave me directions for the Crazy Bubble Wash and Go. We drove there and I pulled into a parking spot directly in front of the laundromat. The redhead silently got out of the car. I also got out and pulled the sopping basket of clothes out of the back seat and gave it to her. She walked toward the door of the laundromat, saying nothing.

"You're welcome!" I yelled to her, as I got back into the driver's seat.

The redhead stopped and froze for a second. She set her basket down on the sidewalk and turned around, slowly walking back toward the car. She went to the driver's side and I thought she was going to open the door and try to pull me out. I was too startled to do anything. When she got directly next to the door, she suddenly lifted her right leg and thrust it forward as hard as she could, like a TV cop kicking open an apartment door. The car shook violently. She then turned and walked back to her basket, picked it up, walked to the laundromat door and disappeared inside.

I sat in the car for at least a minute, too stunned to move. Finally, I slowly opened the door, which made a strange squeak I'd never heard before. I stepped out and swung the door so I could see the outside of it. The door panel was caved in. I kneeled down to look closer and saw bits of the blue paint flaking away from bare metal. Bent bare metal. I looked over at the laundromat door, but it was dark inside and I could see nothing there. I looked around to see if anyone had witnessed what happened, but if they did, they were gone. The idea of suing the redhead for damages crossed my mind, but that was silly. She obviously had no money. Even if she had car insurance, it was unlikely to include whatever category of coverage would be needed for this. The only comfort I got from the situation was that hopefully she would have to walk home. With that thought, I got back in the car and pulled out of the parking space before she could come back out and kick in the other side.

At about noon I sped the damaged Beemer into its parking place underneath my condo, hitting the brakes hard suddenly to avoid smashing into the concrete wall ahead. The choice of not applying the brakes right then was one that I strongly considered. I lived on the middle floor of a three-unit building at the edge of Fremont. It was built on large steel poles, like stilts, with three open parking spots under it. A stairway crisscrossed its way up the left side of the gray wooden building. I climbed slowly to the second landing and entered my dingy home. A Seattle Mariners baseball game was about to start, so I turned on the TV and collapsed on the futon couch. The M's were down by two to the Angels in the fourth inning when my cell phone began to vibrate. Since I knew it was Doris, I didn't answer, but let it continue to buzz, not having the energy to reach in and cancel it. Soon the phone in my apartment rang. Boy is she relentless, I thought as I let the machine pick it up.

"Where the fuck are you?" Charles' voice yelled on the answering machine. "I need my monitor back. Call me."

Charles owned more than a dozen working computer monitors, and probably a hundred that didn't work. He was a big believer in not throwing broken computer equipment away, but recycling it instead. In practice, he accomplished the first part, but not the second. About a month earlier my computer monitor at home had expired, and I quickly threw it in the trash without telling Charles. I told him I had recycled it and he kindly loaned me one of his until I could buy a new one, which I hadn't gotten around to doing, and couldn't afford anyway. After a three-run Angel homer in the fifth inning, I turned off the TV and called Charles to tell him I was on my way over. I had a little room on one credit card, so I would apply it to a new monitor that afternoon at the computer store.

The basement in Charles' house was stuffed almost completely full of junk. Narrow corridors meandered through stacked broken printers, monitors and CPUs, along with empty boxes. At the far end of the basement was the nerve center of Charles's computer consulting empire. It was a large former family room with exposed studs and walls lined with monitors and cables and other black and beige-colored computer equipment. I thanked Charles for the loaner and asked him what he was working on.

"OK, I'll show you," he said. "I've been designing this killer game program. It's a Corvette chase game. The cars actually race around the room on the screens. Can you believe it? I can't believe no one's ever thought of this!"

"But . . ." That's all I could get out of my mouth before I started laughing.

"But what?"

"But . . . anyone who buys your game will have to buy, like, 20 monitors."

"That's doable."

"For who? Someone like you?"

Charles ignored me and sat down at one of the monitors and typed in a few instructions. Suddenly a yellow Corvette began circling the room on the computer monitors. "I had to build a special box to hold all the video cards," Charles said. To begin with, the car slowly crept around the room, moving from one monitor to the next. A cartoonish background in all of the screens looked vaguely like a crowd of people sitting in bleachers.

"Here, watch this," Charles said. "I can speed it up." He tapped the keyboard a couple of times and the car began racing around the room faster and faster. And the fake sound of the engine noise got higher and higher.

"OK, man, I'm getting dizzy now," I said. "I gotta go. I know you'll sell a ton of those."

I thanked Charles again for the monitor and we walked back upstairs. "What happened to your car?" he asked. He could see the Beemer sitting sadly in his driveway out the living room window.

"You won't believe it," I said, and then told him about my trip to the apartments that morning and the water leak and the redhead with the soapy clothes who kicked my car.

As I went on, Charles started laughing. "What is it with you and women?"

"I don't know, but they're ruining my life." I started to go down the list of women who had recently treated me badly. It was long, and soon Charles was off on another thought.

"You know what I think?" Charles asked.

"What do you think?"

"I think that girl must have a hell of a leg. That's solid German steel in that car. Maybe she's one of those girls who kick field goals for the boys' football teams."

I laughed. "Could be. She definitely had good form."

As I was leaving, Charles suddenly turned to me and said "By the way, Angela needs that article about Elephant by mid-July. "You want her number?" I didn't even answer him. I just gave him a look that made clear that I didn't.

* * *

Sunday morning was pretty much like Saturday morning, except that my car was now dented. I parked a few spots away from the front of Ugly Al's, and then I bought a copy of the Seattle Times from the box and went in and ordered my mocha. Jennifer was unusually friendly, and no one else was in the shop. "You're my favorite customer so far today," she said. "You're also the only one so far."

"Thanks a lot."

I sat down and opened the paper, and soon another regular Al's customer came in. His name was Steve something. He was a lawyer who was younger than me and drove a new Porsche. "Smith, what the hell happened to your car?"

I cringed and saw Jennifer looking at me. "Uh-oh, Rob, did you have an accident?"

"Yeah, well, my life is just one big accident these days," I said. I proceeded to tell Jennifer and Steve about the redhead with the laundry who kicked my door in. They both laughed.

"I didn't know you could do that," Jennifer said. "You can dent a car with your foot?"

"A girl did that?" Steve asked, incredulously.

"Yes, and yes," I replied to both of them. "And you know what I think? I think maybe she was one of those girls who kick field goals for the boys' football team." That got barely a chuckle from either of them. "I thought that was funny. You might as well try to find humor in it." Steve left with his latte and I went back to my paper. No one else came into the shop, and after a few minutes, Jennifer came over and sat down across from me.

"So what are you going to tell the insurance company?" she asked with a big smile. "Tell them it got kicked in by a football player. You don't have to say it was a girl."

I told her I wasn't sure the insurance would even cover it, and I didn't want to think about it right now. We sat there awkwardly for a few moments, and then I thought of a question. "Have you ever read Western Oasis Magazine?" I asked.

"Oh, I love Western Oasis," she replied, her eyes lighting up. "That's a totally cool magazine."

"Really? You like it?"

"Yeah, they have some totally cool stuff in there. They had this thing on New Mexico?" she said, like she was asking a question. "It was just beautiful. It made me want to go there so bad."

"Really?"

"Yeah, and I'm going to go there someday." Then she laughed. "I'll probably be old and almost dead."

"What other stuff do they have?" I asked.

"Well, there's a lot of pictures of how gay guys decorate their houses," she said, laughing.

"Oh Great."

"So why did you ask about Western Oasis?"

"Well, they might want me to write an article for them."

"Get out! That would be so cool!" Jennifer's face completely lit up. "I didn't know you were a writer. That's awesome! What are you going to write about?" She was leaning over the table now, staring directly into my eyes.

"Well, I'm not sure I'm going to do it." I didn't tell her that I'd turned it down flat. "They want a story about a little town in eastern Oregon. It sounds like kind of a hassle, and I'm sure it doesn't pay much."

"Oh, you've got to do it, Rob," she said, excitedly, putting her hand on my arm. "That would be so cool! After that maybe you could do an article about my shop. I would just die if Ugly Al's could get into Western Oasis."

"Well, Okay then. I'll see what I can do," I told her

"That would be so cool!" she repeated.

I sat motionless for a moment as Jennifer smiled and daydreamed about her magazine debut. Suddenly I told her that I had to go and left her a big tip. I walked out the door and quickly found Charles' number on my cell phone and hit "send."

"I'm doin' it!" I shouted into the phone, when he answered.

"Doing what?" He sounded like he was asleep. "What are you talking about?"

"The article. I'm doing it. Tell Agnes I'll go to Elephant."

"What? Wait a minute. Why?"

"It's a long story," I said. "Just give me Agnes's number again."

"Her name's Angela. And why did you change your mind?"

"Why do I do anything? Because of a woman."

"Calm down cowboy. I'll have Angela call you tomorrow. Now tell me about this woman."

"It's just Jennifer. She thinks the Oasis is a totally cool magazine. I had no idea."

"Jennifer? From the coffee shop? You're still getting your pecker hard over her? She's completely out of your reach, man."

"I don't care. She was totally impressed when I told her I might write for the Oasis. That means other women will be impressed too."

He just laughed and said "yeah, whatever you say, Robbie Boy."

"So you'll call Agnes?"

"Angela. Yeah, I told you I would. Tomorrow."

"Why not today?"

"It's Sunday, dumbshit.

"Oh yeah."

"You'd better be nice to her," Charles said when he called Monday afternoon to tell me that I'd soon be hearing from Angela, the editor of Western Oasis Magazine. "And if you call her Agnes, you won't get the job, and Jennifer will think you're even a bigger loser than she thought before."

"Not to worry," I said. "I'll treat her like a queen. An ugly queen."

* * *

Angela Arness was clearly too important to spend much time talking to me when she called my cell phone on Tuesday morning. "You can have this if you want it," she said coldly.

"Thank you, ma'am," I replied. "Do you have any, like, guidelines or anything?"

"Twelve hundred words, including one or two sidebars. We'll send a photographer after you get back. I need it by mid-July."

"Uh . . . OK. Is that it?"

"Look," she said, suddenly giving me her full attention. "Let me be straight. We probably won't even run this. That little town doesn't fit our profile at all. But ownership has made the request and we have to go through the motions. If you produce the piece and it's accepted, you'll get paid whether or not it runs. The best way to see what kind of piece we're looking for is to read the magazine. That's all I can tell you."

"OK," I said. Time was up and Angela said her quick goodbye and hung up.

That was my one and only conversation with Angela. One of her assistants, who sounded like she was 12, explained to me what expenses were allowed and how to file an expense report. I'd get reimbursed for gas and meals and a room for up to three nights. And I'd be paid $300 for the article. And with that, my writing career began.

CHAPTER FOUR

The following Thursday I went to Kmart. I knew the eastern parts of Oregon and Washington were hot this time of year, so I bought new flip-flops, a couple of pairs of cargo shorts and new sunglasses. I also bought three small spiral notebooks and a box of pencils, so I could carry them around and look like a writer. In the automotive section I bought motor oil, an oil filter and jumper cables. I also bought an "emergency road kit", which contained flares, a couple of big plastic reflective triangles, a flashlight and a blanket (so I could sleep in my disabled car?). It included a big piece of cardboard folded accordion-style that, when you stretched it out in your windshield, displayed large red letters that spelled "SEND HELP." Somehow, this seemed like a good thing to carry in my BMW. Most importantly, I bought a giant package of D cell batteries. Earlier in the day I had extracted my dusty 1990s-era boom box from its closet. I had long since lost its adapter that plugs into the car's cigarette lighter, but it would play CDs for a few hours on six batteries. The boom box was made necessary by the fact that the custom stereo system I had put in the BMW five years earlier, right after I bought the car, had ceased operation a year later. Since most trips I made in the car lasted less than ten minutes, and my bank account could never handle the repair, I had driven without music since. The boom box, along with a glove-box full of spare batteries and a box of '90s grunge CDs would provide the soundtrack for the ten or more hours I would spend driving this weekend.

Even though the Beemer's maintenance had been mostly neglected otherwise, I was an obsessive oil changer. I had all the necessary tools stored in a little closet next to my parking space under the condo. I finished that job and had my bag and the car packed by eight o'clock Thursday night.

A couple of days before, an internet search had gotten me the phone number of the Greater Elephant Chamber of Commerce and its Executive Director, Stacy Armbruster. When I called her I was surprised that she sounded quite young, and nothing like a hillbilly. When I told her the reason for my call, she spoke excitedly and she put a question mark at the end of many of her sentences, like she was from Southern California. "Mr. Smith, we're delighted that you want to come and visit our beautiful town," she said. And then she went on with her Chamber of Commerce speech: "Our historic town has beautiful restored buildings? And half the town is on the historic register?" She continued for several more sentences and then finally stopped to take a breath. "I know your readers will love Elephant." was how she ended her speech. I asked Stacy if she had ever heard of Western Oasis Magazine, and she said, "Oh yes, it's like Sunset, only smaller. We were in Sunset once? And we've been in the Seattle Times and the Oregonian? But never in the Oasis." She was definite about this, and had obviously been keeping track. We agreed that I would come to Elephant the following Friday, and I told her I didn't want any special arrangements made. I wanted to see the town as it normally was. She laughed and said it would be our little secret.

* * *

I was bored with Nirvana and Alice in Chains by the time I reached Lake Sammamish on Friday morning, ten minutes out of Seattle. The music had spoken to me a couple of decades earlier, but now I didn't have the energy to be that angry. I reached back and shut off the boom box and began studying the other cars and trucks on the freeway. Lines of semis snaked their way into the foothills of the Cascade Mountains. I passed them easily while the freeway climbed gently. At one point a large Mercedes roared past me, driven by a silver-haired executive in a dress shirt with his jacket on a hanger against the back-door window. A Spokane attorney late for court perhaps? Or a real estate developer planning a new ski lodge at Snoqualmie Pass? Not long after that, I passed a librarian, or at least that's what I decided. She was young and homely with thick black glasses and straight black hair, driving a ten-year-old Ford Taurus. She didn't look happy. I passed young families with kids and dogs in minivans and old couples in Oldsmobiles. As I traveled deeper into the mountains, the freeway turned upwards. Giant rock crags pointed to the sky like witches fingers. I could easily tell the loaded semis from the empty ones by their speed, or lack of it. The Beemer didn't like the climbing, and began to feel like a loaded-down truck. In fifth gear, with the accelerator to the floor, my speed topped out at 70 and began to drop. I shifted down and regained some of it, while the engine screamed. Again I couldn't get the speed past seventy and the temperature gauge was creeping dangerously upward. Any BMW should fly up this hill, but mine didn't. A few minutes later, something appeared suddenly in my rear-view mirror. It was a white BMW roadster that looked brand new. Its top was down and it was driven by a blonde in giant sunglasses. Her hair was in a bun and, as she glided by, she gave me a look that the head cheerleader would give to the captain of the chess team. This woman definitely didn't work, I decided. Maybe she was having an affair with the Mercedes guy. Someone else was definitely paying the bills. Had to be. The first of several semis passed me when I was three miles from the top of the pass. The temperature gauge was just below the red zone and I backed off. I got off the freeway at the summit.

The view here was thrilling. The sky was deep blue, and what looked like moss on the sides of rocks was actually blue-green fir forest climbing the steep hillsides. I saw a couple of idle chair lifts cutting thin gashes through the trees, but I could hardly enjoy any of this, faced with a sluggish BMW and four hours of hot desert driving ahead of me.

Cruising downhill toward the eastern Washington desert after the motor cooled, the temperature outside got hotter. But the car's cooling system held its own when it wasn't climbing. I drove for another hour among the semis and SUVs and the occasional hillbilly pickup truck. A few miles before I reached Yakima I saw the flashing blue and red lights of a

Washington State Trooper. As I got closer, I moved into the left lane and saw the officer in his wide-brimmed ranger hat standing next to the driver's door of the white roadster, his hip resting against it. One leg was cocked casually behind the other, knee bent and toe pointed down. I could see the broad smile on the blonde a hundred yards away. Her sunglasses were on her forehead now. She was definitely working him, and it might have been working. On I went, incapable of speeding even if I wanted to.

An hour later, as I got closer to Oregon, I stopped for a cold drink at a run-down store and gas station. I bought a cup of Pepsi with ice and a bag of peanuts from an overweight woman in her thirties missing half her teeth. The other half were heavily tobacco stained. She was wearing a T-shirt a couple of sizes too small that had a bucking horse on it. She gave me a big smile and wished me a good day and then coughed onto the lid of my Pepsi as I turned to leave. I wished her the same. As I walked to the car I looked up and saw the blonde in the white roadster pull into the dusty gravel parking lot. I didn't open my car door far enough, and as the blonde pulled up next to me, the dented door closed on my arm and knocked my drink into my chest, popping off the lid and spilling half of it down the front of my shirt. I could tell she was trying not to laugh as she stared at my shirt and then at the dent in the door. After she turned and walked into the store, I quickly peeled off my shirt and then peeled gravel as I left the store and headed back to the freeway. It was too hot for a shirt anyway, since the Beemer's air conditioner had given up the ghost years ago.

In another half-hour, just before I crossed the state line, the blonde flew past me at an even higher speed than the first time. This time she ignored me. Soon after crossing the big bridge over the Columbia River at Umatilla, Oregon, I saw the sign for the exit to Elephant. Going east now on a winding two-lane road, the desert turned greener as I slowly climbed into the foothills of what my map said was the Blue Mountains. Barns and fences and cattle became more numerous. So did abandoned trucks and farm equipment.

A few miles later, a small green sign next to the road told me I was entering Elephant. It claimed the town contained 993 citizens, though I saw none of them from here. I soon passed a large junkyard for logging trucks on my right. Across the road, several old cars and piles of abandoned equipment were scattered around a couple of rundown barns. After the junk piles, the road made a bend, and now a huge gray, round, bulbous monstrosity loomed in front of me. It looked like some kind of creature from a Japanese horror movie. I slowed the car as I approached it. Suddenly it made sense. It was an elephant. It had a head, and the head had ears. It had a trunk that curled and wrapped around next to its head. I could see where a small tail had broken off, and it stood on long thick legs. Each leg was at least ten feet high and the elephant was probably three or four stories high at the top of its head. I pulled over and studied the great gray creature. It was even taller than the giant Lenin statue in Fremont.

One of the elephant's legs had a door, which made it look like a leg-shaped outhouse. It appeared that this had once been a gas station. The elephant straddled a raised island where gas pumps obviously once stood in the middle of the big asphalt lot. A non-descript white building with a flat roof sat away from the road, 20 or 30 feet beyond the big elephant. The building had two large roll-up doors with a plain rectangular sign attached to the top of the building above them. The sign had faded letters that were hard to make out but obviously spelled the words "Elephant Gas." My first thought when I saw the big elephant was relief. I'd actually have something to write about. Western Oasis might be the first lifestyle magazine to feature a big fake elephant.

Beyond the giant beast that greeted visitors, the town of Elephant spread out in a wide valley with hills on three sides. I could see homes scattered on the lower hills. The hillsides above were greenish gold, covered with wheat almost ready to be harvested. Clumps of trees stood here and there. I saw one older pickup moving away from me on the main road into town; otherwise, the town was motionless. Across the highway from the big elephant was a park: big and unnaturally green. From where I sat, I could hear the "chucka chucka chucka" of the sprinklers, like giant fire hoses, rotating robotically in full circles. A blue cinder-block cube-shaped hut stood near a large parking lot – obviously the real outhouse. No one was around.

When I looked back up at the elephant, it hadn't changed its expression.

It seemed quite happy, even in its dilapidated state, to be presiding over this quaint little place. Like the bronze Lenin, it was half a world away from its native environment. The afternoon sun was shining on the elephant's butt and, when I looked closer, I could see wrinkles that had actually been sculpted into the sides of the body and the legs. This was no cartoon elephant. It was a real sculpture. When I finished gazing up at the elephant and got ready to drive on into town, I saw a car coming toward me. It was a non-descript white American car with a young woman driving. She slowed as she got close and pulled up next to me.

"Are you the writer?" the woman asked.

This caught me by surprise. "I'm sorry?" I blurted.

"You're from the magazine, right? You're the writer doing the article?"

I had to think for a moment. That's right, I'm a writer. "Oh, yeah. That's me," I said after a moment.

"They said you had a BMW. That's cool!"

"What? Who said that?"

"They told me to watch for a BMW. So I knew it was you. Nobody here has one. I really like it." I think she actually meant it, even though she was looking directly at the big dent in the driver's door.

We stared at each other silently for a moment, waiting for the other one to speak. I finally blurted the first thing I could think of. "Nice elephant."

She looked embarrassed and laughed as she glanced upwards. "You know, when you live here, you almost forget it's there?"

"Really?"

"Well no, not really," she replied, giving a forced smile. "But I try."

I looked up at the elephant again and tried to think of something nice I could say about it. "It's different," I said, immediately realizing that that sounded dumb. "But I like it." That probably sounded dumber.

"Yeah, it's different all right." The smile was gone now.

I could come up with nothing further to say, so I just stared at her.

"I'm Stacy," she finally said. She started to reach her hand out the window, but then realized that our cars were too far apart to shake hands. So she just smiled again and waved and pulled her hand back.

I waved back and said "Oh yeah, Stacy." This was the woman from the

Chamber of Commerce I had spoken to on the phone. The one who spoke in questions. "It's nice to meet you."

"Do you want to come to my office?" she asked.

"Uh...sure." I looked down and suddenly realized that I wasn't wearing a shirt. "Oh...Shit!" I blurted, before I could stop myself. "Sorry about this," I said, motioning to my bare chest with an embarrassed smile. I stumbled for an explanation. "My air conditioner doesn't work. It was hot. And I spilled my drink."

Stacy shrugged and smiled and looked embarrassed. "It's ok. Follow me." She made a U-turn and I followed her into town. I looked up and ducked my head slightly as I drove under the giant elephant's head. I started to put on my stained T-shirt while I drove and then decided against it. I put on the hoodie sweatshirt instead, with nothing underneath.

Elephant's Main Street was lined with old brick storefront buildings with common walls. Most of them were probably built in the 1800s. They looked like they could be in one of those old movie sets where they shot westerns. Some of the buildings were nicely restored to their original condition. Others had been "modernized" at some point: big aluminum-framed windows had been installed and all of the detail in the brick fronts had been removed. Several of the other buildings were original, but run-down. Downtown was three blocks long, and in that span there were only a couple of breaks in the otherwise solid walls of building fronts. One was a parking lot next to a bank. Another was a vacant lot. Beyond the downtown buildings I could see the trees of the residential neighborhoods. The rolling hills behind them were being farmed, and there were tree-covered hills in the far distance.

Right in the middle of downtown Elephant was the office of the Greater Elephant Chamber of Commerce. It was in one of the buildings that had been restored. An antique-looking wooden sign, which was obviously new, hung from a wrought-iron standard that extended straight out above the entrance. The street was lined with angle parking and all of the spaces in front of the office were empty. Stacy pulled her car into one of the spaces and I pulled into the one just to its right, hoping to obscure the BMW's driver's door as much as possible.

As I stepped onto the sidewalk I was startled by a human form that suddenly appeared directly in front of me. It was a skinny man with hair halfway down his back. He wore a bright blue baseball hat with white lettering that said "Arctic Circle" on it. His gaunt face was very tan and had deeply set wrinkles. "Hi Billy," Stacy said casually as she passed him on the way to her office door. Billy nodded at her silently. I told him hi also, and he gave me a similar nod and kept walking. Billy was thin and looked almost malnourished. He had a huge ring of keys hanging from a belt loop on his loose-fitting jeans. Even though the temperature was over 90, Billy wore a powder-blue windbreaker with a white logo that said "Arctic Circle Bowl" and depicted three bowling pins and a white bowling ball. Billy walked on unfazed as Stacy and I entered her office.

The desk in Stacy's office sat in the middle of a big room looking out onto the street. Inside, the building had been restored as nicely as the outside. Oak wainscoting lined the walls, with tasteful beige wallpaper above it. The front door and the two doors in the back of the room had heavy woodwork around them. The floor was old wood that had been refinished. Stacy sat at her desk and I sat across from her. She was wearing a dark gray business suit with conservative pumps and nylons. She had on a thin gold necklace and stud earrings. Her hair was straight and dark brown and stopped just above her shoulders. She was a little plump, but she had a pretty face. She was trying to act older than her face looked, which was about 20. Everything about Stacy and her office meant business – she clearly took her job very seriously.

I, on the other hand, was well over forty and didn't appear to be taking my job seriously at all. My left ankle rested on my bare right knee, just below the cargo pocket of my shorts. A flip-flop dangled from my toes and a worn-out Seattle Mariners baseball cap perched on my head. My faded black hoodie had frayed and ripped cuffs and a big hole in one elbow, and it had more than a couple of stains. Stacy was rearranging the top of her desk and I was sure she was disappointed. I apologized for the state of my clothes and assured her that nicer clothes awaited in my luggage. In reality, the ones there were cleaner, but not much nicer. I had packed a pair of sneakers though.

Stacy forced a smile and mumbled something about me not needing to worry. About then I excused myself to go the restroom, using the long drive as an excuse. Mostly, I just wanted to see how bad I really looked. Stacy cheerfully pointed me to the rear of the building and seemed relieved for me to leave, even for a moment. I stood in front of the mirror in the small, spotless bathroom and tried to straighten out my hair. It was no use. The hat had left a permanent impression, so I put it back on.

When I came back into Stacy's office I saw three pairs of eyes staring back at me through the front window. Three women, carrying handbags and obviously much more dressed up than they would normally be on a Friday afternoon in the summer, stood on the sidewalk just to the left of the front door to Stacy's office. Stacy noticed them at the same time I did, and she had a frightened look on her face. "Oh, no," was all she could utter before the three opened the front door and entered. The woman who appeared to be the oldest did the talking. She was tall and thin and wore a pink and white flowered print dress. Her hair was unnaturally black, but nicely kept. She looked directly at me and asked, "Is that him?"

"Gladys!" Stacy said sharply.

"Happy to meet you Mr. Smith," the woman said, suddenly rushing up to me and reaching out her hand. "I can't wait for Ruth to meet you."

"Gladys!" Stacy repeated.

Nice to meet you, uh, Gladys," I said, wiping my hand on my shorts and then shaking Gladys's hand. "And I'm looking forward to meeting Ruth too." Then I looked at the other two women and introduced myself.

"Mr. Smith is from Western Oasis Magazine," Stacy informed them.

"Yes, we know," they replied simultaneously.

"He just arrived from Seattle." Stacy then proceeded to repeat the apology I had given her for the state of my clothes.

Gladys ignored all of that as she introduced Bea, a slightly younger and much heavier woman, who wore a big smile but said nothing. Gladys told me that Bea owned a gift shop on Main Street. Gladys then introduced Beverly. I asked Beverly what she did and Gladys immediately said "Beverly works at the drug store."

"Gladys!" shouted Stacy. "Let Beverly talk for herself."

"So what do you do, Gladys," I asked. Gladys looked about 70, but somehow she didn't look retired.

"Oh, I have a little ol' hair salon just down the street," she said.

"It's the best beauty shop in Oregon," said Stacy, now smiling. "Right Gladys?"

"Gladys got embarrassed and then replied. "Young man, you can come in for a haircut any time."

"Well, I . . ."

"I don't know how the young people in the city wear their hair," she said, "but around here, you could use a haircut."

"Gladys!" Stacy shouted.

"It's OK," I said to Stacy. Being lumped into the category of "young people" made it OK.

"I'm 84 years young," said Gladys, "but I can still give a young man a proper haircut." I was starting to like Gladys.

"Well he can't do it now Gladys," said Stacy. "He has to sit here and talk to me. And you ladies need to go back to work. Look at you, in your fancy dresses."

"You've got a deal," I said to Gladys. "Do I need an appointment?"

"Ha! This isn't the big city, young man. You just come on into the shop any old time and I'll do you."

She has cookies," said Stacy.

I smiled. "I love Cookies."

CHAPTER FIVE

As the five of us stood in Stacy's office, the front door opened slowly again and a small gray head poked through.

"Come in!" said Gladys, almost hopping up and down with excitement. "Come in Ruth!"

"Hi," was all Ruth could say.

"Hi," I replied. I looked at Stacy and she smiled weakly and shrugged her shoulders, obviously annoyed by the intrusion.

"Mr..." For the first time, Gladys was stumped.

"Smith," Stacy and I said, in unison.

"I'm so forgetful," said Gladys. "Mr. Smith works for that magazine I was telling you about. He's a well-known writer who's going to write an article about Elephant. Aren't you Mr. Smith?" Bea and Beverly nodded their heads and smiled.

After a short pause I said, "uh ... oh, yeah." It was all I could come up with.

"Every time one of those big-city writers writes about Elephant we get a few strangers here," Gladys explained to everyone in the room. "Then they stop coming after a month or so.

"That's not true, Gladys," said Stacy. "I had people come in a year after the Sunset article."

"But do they ever come back?" Gladys was glaring at Stacy now.

"Let's not argue in front of our guest, Gladys. Yes, some of them come back."

"Not very many!" Gladys seemed quite sure.

So far, Ruth had said only one word. "So Ruth, what do you do?" I asked her. Ruth was probably as old as Gladys, but I figured I'd give it a shot.

"Oh, Ruth doesn't do anything," Gladys blurted before Ruth could reply.

"Gladys!" yelled Stacy. "That's not true. Ruth does many wonderful things for Elephant." Then she turned to me. "She does lots of volunteer work."

"I thought we weren't going to argue in front of our guest," Gladys said, glaring at Stacy once more. Stacy glared back while Ruth, Bea and Beverly stood silently.

Stacy looked at me. "These four ladies are all on the historic preservation committee for Elephant," she said. "They're making sure that the history of Elephant is preserved for future generations to enjoy. It's a very important job. Right ladies?"

Beverly spoke up now. "Yes, much of Elephant is on the historic register," she said. "So the city has a committee to make sure everybody stays within the guidelines. That's us."

"Yes," added Bea, with a smile. "We have the force of the government behind us."

Stacy objected to Bea's statement. "Force is a pretty strong word," she said. Bea just smiled some more.

Just then, a brand new Chevy pickup the size of a parade float pulled up next to the BMW. It had four doors, a very long bed and dual rear wheels. It was more than twice the size of my car. The driver stepped down out of his truck and stopped and stared at my car for a moment. Then he walked toward the door of Stacy's office. He was an older gentleman who could only be described as a farmer. He wore a blue plaid work shirt and blue denim bib overalls. He was short, but not overweight, and he had dark gray hair under a bright green and yellow John Deere baseball cap.

"Oh, my," said Gladys, with a sudden look of concern when she saw the new visitor. "Now what in the world is Gustav Reimer doing here?" she asked, not very sweetly.

Stacy glared at Gladys again. "He's here to see me," she said.

Gustav Reimer came through the door silently and in a businesslike manner. The three quiet ladies moved out of his way, and Gladys stepped backward, staring at him, but saying nothing. He looked around the room for a moment with no expression on his face, and then walked toward Stacy, ignoring the rest of us.

"Hello Gus, how are you today," said Stacy, in her friendly, professional voice.

"Fine, thanks."

"Here's the tourism report," said Stacy, handing Gus some papers. "I can answer questions for the board at the meeting next week."

"Fine," replied Gus politely, turning to walk out of the office.

"Gus, I'd like you to meet Robert Smith," Stacy said suddenly. "He's the writer from Western Oasis Magazine that I talked about at the last meeting." Then she turned to me. "Gus is on our chamber board of directors, and he's a retired farmer."

Gus held out a thick calloused hand and gave mine a firm but disinterested shake and nodded.

"It's very nice to meet you sir," I said. "You have a very fine town here." That sounded stupid, but Gus just nodded again and smiled, and then headed for the door.

Gladys's silence set a new record, but it ended the moment Gus closed the door. "I declare. That man . . ." She was suddenly angry.

"What's the matter, Gladys?" asked Stacy.

"I don't think Gus Reimer even knows I exist."

Stacy stared at her almost in disbelief. "Gladys!"

Ruth suddenly spoke for the second time. "Gladys and Gus were high school sweethearts," she said, looking at me. This was obviously news to Stacy, who now got a huge smile on her face.

"Gladys, I had no idea!" Stacy exclaimed.

Then Beverly spoke. "Elephant High School, class of '44," she said, with a proud smile.

Stacy leaned against her desk and shook her head slowly. "Oh...my...God, Gladys. You're kidding. Gus was your boyfriend?!

Gladys glared at Beverly. "He wasn't my boyfriend. Not really. I saw lots of boys."

"Oh really?" replied Stacy. "And I'll bet you didn't have to chase any of them?"

Now it was Bea's turn. "They went steady all through high school," she said. "Then he went off to the war after graduation and broke up with her in a letter. They haven't spoken since."

I looked over at Ruth, who was grinning broadly. "You're quite the troublemaker, Ruth," I said. Stacy burst out laughing.

Gladys was furious. "Why that man …" She started to say something about Gus but then stopped.

Now Stacy got serious and shifted into her best chamber of commerce voice. "So, Rob," she said, "If you'd like to sit down, I can tell you a little about Elephant." This was an obvious hint, but the four ladies were having none of it. They were all staring at me now, and making no move to the door.

I looked down at my ragged sweatshirt. My flip-flops were feeling kind of greasy under my feet. "You know Stacy," I said, "I think I'd like to clean up a little."

Stacy looked disappointed in her business suit and pumps and perfect makeup, but she didn't argue. Then her face brightened. "Would you join me for dinner?" she asked. "The Moss Creek Café will be open. We can talk about Elephant then."

I told Stacy that I'd love to have dinner and she started to tell me where the café was, but I held up my hand. "I'm sure I can find it. It's not that big a town, right?"

"Right."

The other women were staring at me now. "Are you ladies going to join us?" I asked.

A look of panic came over Stacy's face. "Oh, no," said Gladys, "we couldn't." She obviously hoped Stacy would disagree with her, but she didn't.

* * *

I walked out of Stacy's office, backed the dented Beemer out of its spot and headed east toward the Moss Creek Motel, which I could see from where I was. It sat at the opposite end of Main Street from the big elephant. At 5:30 on Friday afternoon, most of the businesses on Main Street were closed. I saw only five or six people and three or four cars on the street. There were a couple of cars parked in front of the Eastern Oregon Bank branch. Across the street from Stacy's office, Billy walked silently along the sidewalk in the opposite direction from when we had seen him earlier.

As I drove down the street I could see someone inside a large two-story brick building on a corner. It had an old worn-out sign painted on the brick on the side of the building that said 'Muriel's Hardware and Coal Company'. The sign had old-fashioned yellow block letters outlined in white, and it showed a simple drawing of a yellow elephant with a bucket of coal hanging from its trunk. On the opposite corner from the hardware store was a well-kept small storefront. The name of the business was spelled out on a sign above the door. It said "GUNS-N-THINGS." In the window I could see a bright orange camouflage jacket with a matching hat above it. A well-tended and colorful flowerbox hung below the window.

Once I saw "GUNS-N-THINGS" I decided to stop the car and walk around. I parked on the side street next to the gun store and got out and looked across at Muriel's. The building had a wide cornice across the top and tall arched windows in the second floor. Above the inset entrance to the store, the words "Stubbs Building" and the number "1879" were inlaid into the brick. The painted bricks and trim were faded and peeling. Below that, a sign that was probably put up in the 1960s stuck out at a right angle from the front of the building. It said "Muriel's Hardware" and then below that "Everything You Need In One Place." The large windows on either side of the entrance were obviously not original – they were large aluminum-framed display windows.

I opened the heavy wood door and a little metal bell rattled loudly against the top of it. This wasn't Wal-Mart, but the store was crammed full of stuff. The four people in the store all stopped what they were doing and stared at me. It was dark inside and smelled like cigarettes. The floor was old dark wood that hadn't been refinished in many years. I smiled and made a little wave with my hand, and everyone kept staring. Finally the middle-aged woman behind the counter had a sudden realization. She got a big smile on her face and rushed around from the counter and extended her hand in my direction long before she got to me.

"Hello, you must be the man from the magazine. Welcome to Muriel's."

"Oh. Yes. Hi. I'm Robert. Thank you." I sounded like a robot. "Word gets around quickly here doesn't it? I've been in town less than an hour." I tried not to sound annoyed, but I probably did.

"Oh, Stacy's been getting us ready for your visit all week," the woman said. "We've heard all about your car. Is it here?" She looked out the front window and craned her neck both directions, without success.

"My car? It's parked around the corner, but it's not much of a car," I said.

"Well she told us you were an important writer with a fancy car, and we should be sure and spiff up our shops." That was the word the woman used. Spiff.

I tried to make a joke, but screwed it up. "So, does that mean your store is usually a bigger mess than this?" The woman's feelings were obviously hurt. I tried to laugh and tell her I was kidding. Then I changed the subject.

"You're not Muriel then," I said. Now she laughed and put her hand on my arm.

"My goodness no, Robert. I'm her great-granddaughter. Helen James. Muriel died in '42." Everyone in the store was now smiling at my ignorance.

"Oh, Okay. How long has the store been here then?"

"Muriel bought this building from Dr. Stubbs in 1916," Helen said. She started her store over on Standard Street back in '96. 1896," she corrected herself.

"Wow. This store's over 110 years old?"

"Yes it is," she said proudly. "And still going strong, even if it's a mess."

I apologized again for my comment and I told her that her store was wonderful. But I don't think I convinced her. Muriel's was like an old fashioned general store. It had tools and paint and clothes and dishes and pots and pans and motor oil and gifts, and more clothes. It had everything but food. I didn't see any coal either, but it might have been there. The shelves were full of merchandise. Paint was peeling off the walls and ceiling, and old fans and school lights hung from the 30 foot ceiling. It was dark in the store, as if Helen was trying to save electricity by keeping the lights low and making the merchandise hard to see. I walked around while Helen followed me from a distance. Then I told her I'd probably stop back later in the weekend, and I went out the front door.

I looked across the street, examining the businesses behind the century-old store-fronts. There was Roach's Insurance, The Moss Creek Farm Cooperative, an attorney's office and a laundromat that seemed to be permanently closed. It occurred to me that the architecture of the buildings seemed similar to many of the buildings in Fremont in Seattle, but the town felt very different. This was like a cross between Fremont and an old west ghost town.

I walked across to GUNS-N-THINGS. The store was closed, but in the window past the orange camo jacket and hat I could see T-shirts and children's camo hats and camp stoves and, under a glass counter, four or five rifles or shotguns. There was also a couple of handguns and, next to those, many small colored boxes of ammunition. In another glass case near the window was a light silver colored semi-automatic rifle. It looked like a machine gun to me.

"SHIT! Jesus Christ!" That was me. As I was studying the machine gun, I was tapped on the shoulder without warning. I jerked forward and spun around to find Ruth standing behind me, looking as startled as I was. "Oh, Ruth, it's you," I said as soon as my breathing started up again.

"Oh, I'm so sorry Mr. Smith. I scared you."

"That's OK Ruth. I was just looking at the guns. I was a little nervous."

She tried to make me feel better. "Everyone has guns here, Mr. Smith," said Ruth. "But don't worry, they won't shoot you."

I smiled. "Well, they haven't seen what I'm going to write yet."

She smiled too, but didn't seem to get the joke. "We'd like to talk to you about the elephant," Ruth said, and then stood silently, waiting for my response.

"That would be fine Ruth. That's why I'm here. To talk to people about

Elephant."

"I mean *the* elephant," she said. "The historical committee thought you might want to learn more about its history and the history of the town. The elephant has a very interesting history, and we're trying to make sure it gets preserved. We'll tell you all about it if you'll meet with us tomorrow."

"That sounds perfect, Ruth," I said. I told her I was going to Gladys's salon the next morning and suggested they meet me there. Ruth agreed to tell the other ladies about our meeting and then walked quietly away. As quietly as she had appeared.

I looked back into the gun store and noticed a rack of greeting cards. I could see photos of men with guns and animal carcasses hanging upside down. Perhaps they said something like "Thinking of you, deer" on the inside, I thought

I continued down Main Street, passing a real estate office with dozens of 3x5 cards in the windows describing properties of all shapes, sizes and prices. I stood and studied them for awhile, glancing occasionally over my shoulder. The prices didn't seem right. A large Victorian home in Elephant cost about the same as a vacant lot in a bad Seattle neighborhood. I wondered how these real estate agents could make a living.

As I faced the window of property cards, I heard the rumble of a large engine behind me. I looked around and saw a shiny maroon Corvette Stingray from the 1960s rolling slowly down the street. The car was beautifully restored. The driver was probably in his 60s, and definitely male. He had bushy gray hair tied back in a ponytail, and he wore a goatee. He had on a Hawaiian shirt and black-rimmed sunglasses and was staring straight ahead, without so much as a glance to either side. He drove very slowly and the half-dozen people on the street watched as he passed. It was a one-car parade. I watched the car drive to the end of Main Street and then turn into the lot next to the big elephant.

I finally walked on down to the Moss Creek Motel. My car was still parked three blocks away with my bag in it, but I figured I'd start the paperwork as long as I was in the neighborhood.

CHAPTER SIX

As I approached the motel I saw a woman on a ladder to the right of the entrance to the office. She had long blonde hair in a ponytail and wore tight jeans, a tight top and work boots. Even from a block away she was a babe. She had a paint brush in her hand and was stretching upward, painting the motel's gutter. I stopped and stared and felt my heart speed up. Then, as I walked on, she turned and saw me. She gave me a big smile and waved me over, putting her brush down on top of the can that was hanging from the ladder. "Hello Mr. Smith," she said cheerfully. "We've been expecting you." I watched her descend the ladder. She looked like she belonged in a magazine.

"Oh, thank you," is what I think I said.

I must have asked her how she was, because she replied confidently, in a schoolgirl voice, "I'm super!" She reached out her hand and grabbed mine. I tried to swallow, but I couldn't. "Come on in. I'm Sarah. Your room is ready." She whipped open the door and led me into the motel office without losing her smile. As we entered, I saw another vision behind the counter. "This is my little sister Andrea," Sarah announced. Andrea was brunette, and as beautiful as Sarah. She was thin and her clothes fit as tightly as her sister's. I was in shock. Here I was in a little motel in a hillbilly town in the middle of nowhere with two of the most beautiful women I'd ever seen. They both appeared to be in their 20s, and they obviously were sisters. I tried not to stare, but it was no use. They didn't seem to mind.

The motel office was clean and decorated tastefully. A leather couch and a matching easy chair sat in the small room that served as a lobby. It was like a doctor's office, with beige walls and a beige carpet. The room was spotless. Just as my mind began wandering with fantasies of a weekend sex orgy in my motel room, a loud screech brought me back to reality. A door behind Andrea was suddenly flung open by a three-year-old boy running at full speed. The screech turned into a long howling scream from the back room, accompanied by the yapping of what sounded like a herd of tiny dogs.

"Taver, what did you do to your sister?!" yelled Andrea excitedly.

Sarah was calmer. "I'll take care of them," she said to Andrea. "Go ahead and do Mr. Smith's paperwork." Then Sarah turned to Taver and said "Come here honey." He calmly walked over and grabbed her hand as she led him back through the doorway.

"Sorry about that," Andrea said nervously. "Aunt Sarah's way better with my kids than I am. You have a BMW, right?"

What was it with the car? "Yup," I said. Andrea craned her neck, looking for the car in the parking lot. "It's still parked down the street. I was walking around downtown and I ended up here. I'll get it later."

"It's not much of a walk, is it?" Andrea said. "Oh, I guess I shouldn't say bad things about Elephant. We're supposed to be trying to impress you." She smiled.

"So I guess you've been talking to Stacy?"

"Well, she's been talking to us. She has a good heart."

"Face it, this ain't exactly Vegas," said Sarah, entering from the back room, still with her beautiful smile. "Stacy means well, but if she thinks she's going to turn this Hooterville into Disneyland, she's dreaming." Andrea glared at her sister, but didn't say anything.

"It's a nice town," I said, trying to sound convincing.

"We like it here," Andrea said, without sarcasm. "It's a great place to keep the kids out of trouble."

"Yeah, everybody knows everybody else's business," said Sarah, "so when the kids get into trouble, we hear about it fast."

A new round of screaming escaped from the back room now, and two toddlers emerged, accompanied by two tiny animals that appeared to be dogs, even though they were smaller than many cats. This group was closely followed by a teenage girl yelling at them all to come back.

"It's a daycare center here sometimes," Andrea said to me. "I'm sorry about that." She was glaring at Sarah now, who calmly addressed the teenager.

"Kenzie, you have to keep the kids and the dogs in the family room," Sarah said.

"I know mom," Kenzie said. "I can't get them to stop running." Kenzie and Sarah succeeded in rounding up the smaller creatures and herded them back through the door.

"So what are you going to write about?" asked Andrea as she handed me a key to room 208.

"Well…" I thought about the question for a moment and then said, "I'm supposed to write something that will make people want to come here to visit. Any suggestions?"

Andrea kind of laughed and Sarah emerged through the door again and said "Boy, if you can do that, you're a genius. You might win a Pulitzer Prize."

"Sarah!" Andrea admonished her older sister. "It's not that bad."

"Visitors must come here," I said. "You guys are in business." The girls looked at each other and laughed.

"What about the giant elephant?" I asked. "Maybe people would come to see that."

Andrea got serious. "You're not going to write about that are you?"

Before I could answer, Sarah said: "Oh, you should, Mr. Smith. It's our biggest attraction." She had her beautiful smile back now, as her sister stared at her. "It's our claim to fame. Why hide it?"

"I just talked to a lady who says there's a group trying to save the elephant and restore it," I said.

"The hysterical society!" Sarah and Andrea said in unison, and then started laughing.

"We know those bitches," Sarah continued.

"We don't like them," Andrea said with a grin. "We'll tell you about it sometime."

"They don't like us either," said Sarah, "because we're pretty."

Andrea smiled and said, "I think there are other reasons too. Sarah yelled at them."

"Well, they deserved it. I'll show you your room, Mr. Smith," Sarah said as she pulled the key out of my hand. I followed her out the door. "My brother-in-law will be here soon to take all those kids. It's not normally like this around here."

I asked Sarah if Stacy had alerted every person in town that I was coming and she said she was sure Stacy had. "Everybody's running around like crazy, washing windows and scrubbing and polishing," she said. "I think it's hilarious."

"You mean you didn't do that?"

"We try to keep the motel nice all the time. We figured you should see it like it always is."

I followed Sarah as she jogged up an outside metal set of stairs. When we got to the top I asked her if she and Andrea owned the motel, and she told me her mother and stepfather had bought it about three years before. "It's a family operation," she said smiling. "Mom runs it and us girls help out. I'm a contractor. That's my main job."

"Really. What kind of contractor?"

"I do small remodeling jobs and repairs," she said. "I'm like a handyman. Or a handy-woman, I guess."

"Sort of like painting those gutters?" I asked. "Is your mom a client?"

"Yup. She's my best one," Sarah said. "Keeping this place up is almost a full time job. But I have other clients too. I'm going to do some work for the owners of the big elephant soon."

"Are you going to help save it?"

"Oh no," she replied. "They need to blow that thing up. A lot of people want to get rid of it, but the hysterical society is fighting it. I think it's all hilarious. I'm going to paint the garage."

"So how come you and Andrea don't like the historical society?"

"A couple of years ago they told us our motel is historic and they stopped us from making changes. Can you believe that? Does this place look historic to you? It's ridiculous. It seems like everything I do to this place I have to get their permission."

The Moss Creek Motel was a classic 1950s-era highway motel. It was a dull dark yellow with white trim. It had two wings, with slightly pitched roofs. The one we were in had upper and lower levels and the other, including the office, was one-story. It had a large parking lot, with parking spaces directly in front of all of the lower level rooms. I mentioned to Sarah that the motel seemed very well maintained. And she smiled at me and said, "Thank you Mr. Smith."

"You can call me Rob," I replied.

"Thank you Rob."

Sarah unlocked to door to room 208 and opened it for me. It was a typical small motel room, but it looked and smelled very clean. It was dark until Sarah turned on a lamp and opened the drapes covering the room's single front window. Then I saw orange. The room had light orange walls and a darker orange shag carpet. The bedspread was orange and brown and the room had a brown desk with an orange lamp on it.

"Orange," I said.

"Yup. All the rooms are like this. Either orange or olive green. Ugly, huh?" Sarah explained that the motel had been remodeled in the 1970s. "We couldn't afford to change the décor in all of them," she said. She was perfectly cheerful about the unfortunate colors.

"Hey," I said, "when you're sleeping, it doesn't matter what color the room is, right?"

She agreed. "Well, I'd better go rescue Andrea from those kids. Bye." And she was out the door and down the stairs before I could reply. I sat down on the side of the bed and stared at the window and thought about beautiful naked women.

An hour later, freshly showered and wearing a clean polo shirt and cargo shorts, this time with sneakers, I exited room 208 at the Moss Creek Motel. I had already walked back to get my car and brought it to the motel, without seeing the two goddesses. Now I saw that Sarah was in front of the motel office, folding up her ladder. It was nearly seven-o'clock, and the sun was low in the sky. She saw me and smiled. "Going out on the town?" she asked, cheerfully. "There's not much to do here, even on Friday night."

Sarah got to the office with her ladder and stopped in front of the closed door. Just as I rushed over to open it for her, she set the ladder down and opened it herself. I tried to hold it for her, but wasn't much help. "Come on in," she said, and so I followed her.

Andrea was behind the desk. "Are you going out on the town?" Andrea asked. "There isn't much to do here."

Sarah laughed. "We just finished that conversation," she said. "It was a short one."

"Stacy's taking me to dinner," I told them. "At the café. I guess there's just one."

"Yeah, barely," Sarah said. "Whatever you do, don't order the chicken fried steak. It's disgusting."

"You know Stacy thinks you're going to save our town," Andrea said to me. "She has everyone convinced that we have to get you to write that Elephant is a wonderful hidden secret that's just waiting to be discovered."

"Except us," laughed Sarah.

"I don't even know if they'll print my article," I said.

"Really?" said Sarah. "Wouldn't that be funny if they didn't? Well, I guess it wouldn't be for you, would it?"

"The editor doesn't even want to do it. One of the owners told her to. She thinks Elephant is a…" Then I stopped.

"Hell hole?" asked Andrea.

"Shit hole?" asked Sarah.

"Well…actually." Then I smiled. "I was about to say something like that. I don't feel that way myself, of course. And she hasn't been here."

"Oh, we feel that way," exclaimed Andrea, happily.

"This is the armpit of the world," said Sarah, also happily. "But we like it that way."

"You'd better not repeat any of this," said Andrea. "They already don't like us."

"Oh, that's just because we're prettier than they are," said Sarah. "Go ahead and repeat it. They know how we feel."

"My husband says we should advertise Elephant as the 'world's ugliest town'," said Andrea. "He thinks lots of people would come here just to see that."

"Oh, I've seen way uglier towns than this one," I said.

"See? We can't be good at anything," said Sarah, laughing.

"What does your husband do?" I asked Andrea.

"He works in Pendleton, for the County," she answered. "He mostly just sleeps here, and he's gone of the rest of the time."

I had noticed early on that Andrea was wearing a nice diamond wedding ring, but Sarah's ring finger was empty. I asked Sarah what her husband did, hoping for the answer that I got.

"Oh, I'm single, and I'm staying that way," she said with a big smile. "I have one ex-husband and no mother-in-law, and that's the way I like it. Just keep that child support coming."

"That's a job in itself," said Andrea. "When's your next court date, Sarah?"

"I do spend my share of time in court going after that asshole," Sarah said, with an evil smile. "But I enjoy it."

"Sarah's ex is our local law enforcement," said Andrea. "That should make you feel less safe."

"The good thing is that we get to do what we want," said Sarah. "He knows not to mess with us. I'll string him up by his balls if he does!"

Sarah was delighted to describe how much she hated her ex-husband. He was a Sheriff's deputy, and he was the officer assigned to Elephant, even though he had moved 30 miles west to Pendleton two years earlier. I spent another ten minutes listening to the two beautiful ladies talk about their mother and stepfather, and how they had no contact with their biological father. They talked about their kids and how dissatisfied they were with how the schools were run and how their kids deserved to be treated with more respect. All of this conversation was enthusiastic and friendly. And Sarah and Andrea showed no more interest in what I was going to do in Elephant or the article I was writing.

CHAPTER SEVEN

The Elephant Inn was a greasy spoon, and a big one for such a small town. It was the only place to eat, other than Melville's Tavern, which looked like a dive bar. The Inn sat next to the city park, across the highway from the big elephant and a little closer to town. The rectangular one-story building had a giant parking lot surrounding it, with far too much space for the cars it would ever need to hold. Outside it was a dirty brownish white with big windows badly in need of washing.

Inside the aluminum-framed entry door was a large brown free-standing sign with food stains on it that said "Please Seat Yourself." At least thirty tables were spread out in the expanse of the dining room, and many of them were occupied that evening. The room was brown, with dark wood-paneled walls and worn-out brown carpet. It had windows on three sides, but it was still dark inside. A faint odor of cigarettes hung in the air, even though smoking in restaurants was no longer allowed. In the middle of each of the fake-wood Formica tables was a fake candle with a dingy fake-flame bulb in it, flanked by grimy salt and pepper shakers and ketchup bottles in little metal cages.

When I walked into the dining room it became suddenly quiet and at least 30 faces turned to look at me. They were all customers – the wait staff ignored me. I immediately recognized the four historical ladies sitting at a table near the entrance. Gladys was almost shaking with excitement as she stood up and reached both her hands out toward me. "Mr. Smith. Mr. Smith," she said loudly. I told the ladies that I was there to meet Stacy and they all nodded and said they knew that. They simultaneously pointed to Stacy, sitting by herself at a table in the far corner. She was the only customer in the room not looking at me.

I thanked the ladies and turned to walk over to Stacy's table. Just as I did, someone grabbed my arm. It was Helen from the hardware store, although, at that moment I couldn't remember her name. "It's so good to see you Robert," she exclaimed, as if it had been years since the last time she'd seen me, rather than a couple of hours.

"It's great to see you too," I said. And then, after a moment it came to me. "Uh, Helen." She smiled and her eyes followed me as I continued on.

A table of four older men, all wearing plaid shirts and brightly colored baseball caps, stopped eating and stared at me. I smiled back at them and kept walking. I saw the pony-tail guy who I had seen earlier driving the Corvette, now sitting at a table by himself. He was also watching me. As I approached Stacy's table, she looked at me angrily. I greeted her in an overly friendly way as she stared out into the room. "Hi. Sit down," she said coldly.

"Is something wrong?"

"Yes, there's something wrong. These people are all here because of you." She was visibly upset.

"Me? All of them?"

"Yes," she said. "I guess you being here is a big event." I was a bit puzzled, since the motel ladies had told me that Stacy had instructed everyone in town to prepare for my arrival.

"Well hmmm," I said. "How did they find out about me?"

Stacy glared at me but didn't say anything, so I continued. "I heard today that a lot of folks here think I'm going to be the savior of Elephant. You included."

"Who said that? Oh, let me guess. The Hockensmiths."

"The who?"

"The women at the motel. They all have different names, but the mom's name is Hockensmith, so that's what we call them.

"They were very nice. I liked them." Admitting this seemed to make things worse.

"Of course you liked them," Stacy said, "you're a man."

I couldn't help smiling. "Well, yes I am. And I think they're very attractive. I admit it,"

"And they know it, too."

I laughed. "Yes, that did come up." Then I tried to change the subject. "Anyway, everyone I've talked to in Elephant so far seemed to know I was coming, and you say all these folks here did too. The thing is, you're the only person I told that I was coming."

Stacy froze and just stared at me. It hadn't crossed my mind that what I said could make her cry. She suddenly rose from her chair and blurted "excuse me" and rushed to the bathroom. I wasn't sure if she was upset because her excitement about my coming to town had backfired or because I reminded her that the Hockensmith ladies were beautiful. Maybe both.

A young waitress, probably still a teenager and definitely chewing gum, appeared at the table just after Stacy disappeared. She was short, with purplish hair tied in a bun, and she had an acne-pocked face. She would have been thin, except that she was about five months pregnant. She wore a faded gray uniform with a plastic name tag that said "Cybil." "Can I help you?" she snarled. It was a relief to finally meet someone in Elephant who didn't seem to know or care who I was.

"Has my friend ordered?" I asked, in my best big-city voice.

"Nah," she replied. "Stacy won't eat here. What would you like?"

"She won't eat here? Is something wrong with the food?"

Cybil just said, "I don't know", and kept chomping her gum.

"Do you have Pepsi?" I asked. I figured that would be fairly risk-free.

"Coke Okay?"

"Coke's Okay. Let's start with that" Cybil shuffled off without a reply.

I looked around and saw that at least half the people sitting at tables in the Moss Creek Café didn't seem to be eating. It was still quiet in the dining room and most of the customers were trying to glance at me without staring. But not the historical ladies. They were definitely staring. Soon after Cybil wandered off, Ruth got up and came over to my table

"Mr. Smith, you'll have to excuse Stacy," Ruth said. "She gets upset easily, poor thing." Then she sat down in Stacy's chair. "Mr. Smith, our town is dying. We all know that, but we want to try and find a way to turn it around. A lot of people got together and contributed money so we could have a Chamber of Commerce office and an employee to try and help improve business in Elephant. The pay is very low, but Stacy works so hard, and she takes her job so seriously. When she found out you were going to do an article in the, uh… whatever magazine it is, she was so happy and excited. She told us all that your article was the beginning of a… what did she call it?" She paused for a moment. "Ren something. A French word."

"Renaissance?"

"That's it. I'm not sure what that means, but I guess we want one."

"Oh great," I said to myself.

"It would be great, I guess," replied Ruth, thinking I was talking to her.

Just then Stacy returned to the table and glared angrily at the person who had taken her seat. "Ruth! What are you doing?" Then she looked at me. "What is she saying?" She looked like she might explode.

"Relax honey," said Ruth. "It's OK."

"She was saying very nice things about you," I told Stacy.

"You were talking about me?" Stacy was now almost hysterical.

"Oh. Gladys is waving at me," said Ruth suddenly, as she got up to return to her table. "It was nice to talk to you Robert."

Stacy sat back down in the chair Ruth had just vacated. Her face was blotchy red and puffy around her eyes. She stared at me, obviously trying to decide if I had heard anything terrible about her. "Don't worry," I said, "Ruth was just telling me she thinks you're doing a really good job with, you know, with what you have to work with. So what are you eating?"

She ignored my question. "You see, this is the problem," She said in her agitated state. "These people who stand to gain the most from what I'm trying to do are saying bad things about Elephant. They're trashing the town to someone like you who can really help us."

"She wasn't trashing the town," I interrupted her.

"Yes she was. These ladies say they want things to improve, but then they undermine me. I think they do it on purpose. For some reason they want to make me look bad." I could see that Stacy was almost starting to cry again.

I started to tell Stacy I thought Elephant was really a nice town, but I could see it was no use. So I repeated my previous question. "What are you going to eat?"

"Oh, I'm not really hungry," she said. "I haven't been feeling that good. You go ahead and order whatever you want."

"The waitress said …," I started to blurt what Cybil had said about Stacy not ever eating there, but then I thought better of it and stopped.

"The waitress said what?" Stacy said, even more paranoid now.

"Oh, uh, she said, uh," My brain searched for a way out of this dead-end and, unfortunately, Sarah's earlier comment about the Inn was the first thing that popped into it. "She, uh, said the chicken fried steak was really good."

Right at that moment, Cybil walked by and Stacy called out to her. "Cybil, can you get this gentleman an order of chicken fried steak?"

"Yeah," Cybil replied through her gum, without breaking stride.

"Uh, thanks," was all I could say. Somehow, this dinner just wasn't going very well. "So is the food here good?" I asked Stacy, trying to sound hopeful.

Stacy paused to consider possible answers and then went for the outright lie. "Oh, it's pretty good." She almost choked on her words.

"Well, I'm looking forward to it," I lied back.

We sat and silently drank our beverages while Stacy began to compose herself. She had changed clothes and now was wearing black slacks and a tan jacket over a white blouse. She had on a little too much jewelry and makeup for the occasion. She obviously put a lot of effort into her appearance. After a few minutes, she asked the question I knew she was most wanting to know the answer to. "You don't have to put the big elephant at the gas station in your article do you?"

I thought about trying to make a joke, but I could see she was serious and that my answer was going to be important to her. "I really don't know what my angle will be, Stacy. I have to try to make Elephant sound appealing. They won't sell magazines if they write about things that suck. But I have to be honest too."

She just smiled and said, "Well, I guess you'll be a miracle worker if you can do all that."

"Now come on, don't trash your town," I said.

"I just wish there were some way you could leave out the part about the big elephant," she said. "It makes us a laughing stock."

"Well then why don't you just get rid of it? I mean, who owns it?"

"I don't want to talk about the elephant. I hate it."

"Oh come on, we're just talking," I told her. "You have something unique there. It's interesting."

"I was afraid you'd think that. Okay, but I don't know much about it. It's owned by Mr. McCune. Hollister McCune started the gas station a long time ago, with a partner. I don't remember his name. They built the elephant about 50 years ago. In fact, it'll be 50 years old in about a week."

"How do you know that?"

"Because it opened on the Fourth of July in 1960. It will be eligible to become a historic property this year on the Fourth. Then the Historical Preservation Commission can protect it."

"Really? And then no one can tear it down?"

"Not if they make it a historic landmark." Stacy explained that any building or structure that was 50 years could be declared an historic landmark. In order to make any changes to it or tear it down, you had to get the permission of the Historic Preservation Commission.

"So if it were torn down before the Fourth, it would be OK?"

"Well, they wouldn't have to get permission. People here are already fighting about it." Stacy smiled now and seemed to relax. "The historical ladies? You know, the ones sitting over there? They're all on the Historic Preservation Commission and they want to protect the elephant. They want to restore it. There's a meeting on Monday when they'll vote on making the elephant an historic landmark. We already know how they'll vote"

"Well that might be cool."

Stacy got angrier. "As far as I'm concerned, it's just an eyesore, no matter what you do to it."

"Maybe it could be painted like a circus elephant," I said.

That got her to laugh. "Yeah, we could put a hat on it. And a saddle. And people could sit on its back. That would be something for you to write about."

"That might actually fly in the Oasis," I said. "You ought to think about it."

Just then, the ponytail guy got up and walked past us toward the door. "Jonas. Jonas," Stacy called out to him, and he stopped and came toward us. "This is Robert Smith," she said.

Jonas was tall and had a little too much gut. His goatee was gray and his long hair was half gray and half not. He reminded me of Jeff Bridges. "Very pleased to meet you," he said as we shook hands.

"You too," I replied. "How was your dinner?" I thought maybe I'd get a more honest answer.

"Well," he smiled and then rolled his eyes slightly and looked at Stacy knowingly. "It is what it is. This is one of the best places in town." He laughed.

"Jonas is renting the elephant gas station," said Stacy. "He keeps some of his cars there."

"Yup, I'm a car guy. It takes a lot of space though."

Jonas didn't seem like a car guy. He was well-spoken and didn't have a spot of grease on him. And he didn't seem to fit in Elephant at all. "Yeah, I wish I had a place to work on my car," I said.

"I hear you have a Beemer," he replied, smiling. "I'm a Corvette man myself."

I could see Stacy's sudden embarrassment. I looked at her and said, "Everyone here seems really interested in my car. It's just an old beater, you know."

"Well, BMWs are fairly uncommon around here," Jonas said.

I told Jonas that I had seen him driving his Corvette earlier. "That's a really nice car," I said.

"Yeah, I had the '67 out today. Gotta give 'em a little exercise, you know." So obviously Jonas had more than one Corvette. I was intrigued, but I didn't have the nerve to start quizzing him right there.

"Well I gotta run," Jonas said. "Stop by some time, Robert."

I told Jonas that I definitely would. "We'll have to do an interview," I said.

He smiled and said, "I don't do interviews, but you're welcome to come by."

Then, like a good reporter, I tried to interview him. I asked him what he thought about the elephant.

"Oh, I'm non-partisan," he said. "All I can say is that it provides nice shade on a hot day." And then he headed toward the door.

I decided it was time to get Stacy off the subject of the big gray elephant and worrying about what I would write about. I asked her about growing up in Elephant. She said she had graduated from Elephant High School in 2003, and then Oregon State University in 2007. I figured this made her about 25 years old, which made me feel ancient. She moved back to Elephant and married a local guy named Curtis Armbruster, who worked in Pendleton at a paper mill. She said she had studied marketing in college and had turned down a good job at a utility company in Portland, where she had worked as an intern. "I put love ahead of money," she said, but she wasn't smiling when she said it.

Stacy told me she grew up on a farm outside of Elephant, which her parents still ran. She and Curtis now lived in a small house they rented in town, though Curtis often stayed with a friend in Pendleton during the week, to avoid having to commute.

As Stacy began describing her house, Cybil showed up with a plate and dropped it with a clunk in front of me. Half an inch of grease floated over the top of some kind of brown goo that covered the entire plate. I could make out a flat slab of something in the middle of the goo. "Enjoy," said Cybil, as she walked away.

Stacy and I both stared at the plate without saying anything. Finally I said, "OK, now I understand why you don't eat here."

Stacy dropped her chin to her chest and started laughing. She looked up and said, "I'm sorry. Would you like to go?"

"Yes," I said, "let's continue this another time."

CHAPTER EIGHT

An hour after leaving the cafe I enjoyed a quiet dinner by myself in my orange motel room. It consisted of microwave noodles and an apple that I had bought at the Moss Creek Grocery. A small microwave oven in the bathroom next to the tiny coffeemaker allowed me to heat my noodles. Stacy had offered to feed me at her house after we left the Inn, but I declined, and then she told me where the grocery store was. I drove there and bought dinner and breakfast. While I ate, I sat on the bed and watched the Mariners lose another game.

On Saturday morning the motel was quiet. The sun was up early and the air was warm, so I ate my grocery store breakfast while leaning on the railing on the walkway in front of my room. Later, I walked out of the motel and onto Elephant's Main Street. I saw the beautiful Sarah carrying a small ladder, but she was walking the other way and didn't see me, so I continued on. I walked directly downtown to Gladys's hair salon.

The words "Glady's Parlor", complete with misplaced apostrophe, were spelled out on a pink sign above the door of a small Main Street building tucked between two much larger ones. The building to the left was vacant and boarded up, and to the right was a farmers' cooperative office. The front of Gladys's building was a dirty gray color, but inside I could see more pink. The walls and ceiling were painted pink, the chairs were pink, and the sinks and cabinets were pink. The floor was old commercial tile that was white, but it reflected the pink from everything else. It was like walking into a Pepto Bismol bottle. "It's pink in here," I told Gladys, as I shut the door.

"Pink is my favorite color," she replied cheerfully.

"It's a good thing."

Gladys was cleaning the long stretch of mirrors along the left wall of the little room. She was wearing a white sweater and pink slacks. Her unnaturally black hair was coiffed old-lady style and looked like it would protect her in a minor collision. She wore a pink ribbon in it. One chair stood in the middle of the room toward the back. A small pink counter was on the right, with an old-fashioned cash register sitting on it. The cash register was gold – about the only thing the room, besides me, that wasn't pink.

"We'll have a good talk now, Mr. Smith," Gladys said. "And the haircut is no charge."

"I'm happy to pay for it," I told her, but she said she wouldn't think of it.

"You must think this is a pretty ugly old town," said Gladys, "coming from the big city and all."

I started to reply, but she didn't stop. "We like it here though, at least most of us. Now you sit down right here and let me tell you about Elephant."

I sat down in the big old pink salon chair with the plastic bubble hair dryer attached to it. Gladys immediately put her right hand into my unruly hair. "I've cut a lot of men's hair since Jim died," she said. Then she explained: "Jim was the barber here, but he passed away on the Fourth of July – four years ago it was. It was real sudden. He and his wife were sitting on their front porch waiting for the fireworks to start and his wife said she got up to go in the house to the bathroom. When she came back out, Jim was slumped over dead. A lot of people think she poisoned him, but if she did, she got away with it. By Christmas she was living in California with her new boyfriend."

Gladys talked fast and I just listened and tried not to nod. She hadn't asked how I wanted my hair cut, but made the decision herself. "We'll fix you right up Mr. Smith," she said. "You won't recognize yourself." I wasn't encouraged.

"Old Jim's passing left a hole in Elephant," Gladys said. "I declare, the old men here can't stand the thought of a lady cutting their hair, so they all go to barbers in Pendleton now. It don't matter to me – I have plenty of ladies. The younger men like you, though, they come to me."

"Thank you for that, Gladys," I said. "I don't feel all that young anymore."

"If a new barber came in, I'd be just as happy," she said. "I'm getting old and worn out, you know." Gladys talked and talked. She was chopping away at my head with scissors now. Her 84-year-old hands were limber and fast. She worked confidently as she talked.

"Cutting a man's hair is different than a lady's," Gladys said. "The men around here like it short and conservative. None of the permanents and no coloring. I charge 'em less, but I don't tell the ladies that."

I asked Gladys if she grew up in Elephant and what it was like in the old days.

"Oh yes, I was going to tell you all about Elephant," she said. "I was born in my parents' house two blocks over that way." She stopped her cutting and pointing her pink scissors over my head toward the front of the building. "The house is still there, but I don't live in it. Elephant was a lot bigger then," she continued on with hardly a breath. "It's dying now. I went to high school here, class of '44."

"I remember," I said. "That farmer guy in the Chamber office, Gus, he was your boyfriend, right?"

Gladys suddenly stopped cutting and I turned to look at her. Her lips were pursed and she was suddenly speechless. "That man!" she finally said.

"Have you really never spoken to him since you broke up?" I asked.

"It was June 1944," she replied sternly. "Gus joined the navy right out of high school. He said he'd be back for me, and I wrote him letters almost every day. He wasn't much of a writer, but one day I got a letter saying he was breaking up with me. I kept writing but he never wrote me again."

Gladys said that her best friend from high school, a girl named Eunice, had been secretly writing to Gus as well, but she didn't know it then. Gus proposed to Eunice in a letter while he was stationed in Hawaii. They got married in 1946. Gladys never spoke to Eunice again either, even though Gus and Eunice lived on a farm near Elephant from then on. Eunice died in 2004, Gladys told me, and Gus had lived on the farm alone since. Their son, Charlie, was running the farm now.

I asked Gladys about her own marriage. She told me that her husband, Tom, was killed in a car accident in 1974 and she never remarried. They had one daughter, named Jean, who was now living in Portland with her partner, Grace. "Tom was driving to Portland when he was killed," said Gladys. "He found out that Jean liked girls better than boys, and he was going to get her and bring her back home. He never made it. I told him that she was an adult – she was 21 then – and that he should let her live her own life. But he wouldn't listen to me. Jean thinks he deserved what happened, I guess." Gladys said that Jean had moved in with Grace that year and that they had now been together for more than 35 years.

"We're going to put a nice part on the left side," Gladys suddenly told me as she put her scissors away. "We'll put some cream in it first though. You need to give this nice head of hair some discipline."

Gladys showed me my head in the mirror. The sides were cut very short, and the top was greased down. I looked like a TV character from the 1950s.

"That's awesome, Gladys!" I exclaimed, dishonestly. She looked embarrassed. "Are you sure I can't pay you something?" I asked.

I reached for my wallet, but she pushed my hands away and said, "Oh no, Mr. Smith. I wouldn't think of it."

Just then, the door to Gladys's salon swung open and the girl of my dreams walked in with her ladder. "Oh honey," said Gladys. "Thank you so much for coming on Saturday."

"I work Saturdays," chirped Sarah, with a big smile. "I told you." She was wearing a tight V-neck T-shirt. She had small breasts, but they looked perfect to me. She had on a different pair of tight jeans and round-toed cowboy boots.

"Mr. Smith is here," Gladys said in a sing-song voice.

"Oh hi, uh, Rob, is it? You got a haircut I see."

"Yup, it's Rob. And yup, Gladys definitely cut my hair."

Sarah let out a little laugh. "It's, uh, nice," she said, trying not to laugh harder.

"This young man's hair needed a little discipline," said Gladys.

"Well, I'd say you gave it to him, Gladys" Sarah replied. "Those hairs'll be marching in formation for weeks." Sarah set up her stepladder near the back left corner of the room, beneath a burned out florescent tube. "You should get a picture of that haircut Gladys," she said.

"Yes! We need a picture," Gladys said, clapping her hands.

I tried to talk the ladies out of it, but it didn't work. I had laid my phone on the counter before Gladys started in with her pink scissors, so I pointed to it now and told Gladys that my phone had a camera. She took the phone and I showed her the shutter button. She pointed it at me, but before shooting, she said to Sarah, "come on over here, honey, you need to be in the picture too." I held my breath as the beautiful Sarah stood behind me with her hand on my shoulder. She smelled incredible. The flash blinded me, and then Gladys looked at the screen on my phone, laughed and said "Oh, what a cute couple."

Without looking at the photo, Sarah said, "Well, I gotta go out to the truck and get a new tube." And then she left.

"Isn't she gorgeous?" said Gladys as soon as Sarah closed the door. I looked at the photo on the phone and gulped. Sarah looked incredible, and I looked like a dork in a pink apron. I agreed with Gladys's statement, trying to sound indifferent. "When I told her you were coming in this morning, she said she'd be right over to fix the light," Gladys said. "I should have handsome young men in here more often."

I returned the phone to my pocket. "You're way too kind," I said. "And, thanks to you, I'm even handsomer. I'm definitely leaving you a tip."

"She's single, you know," Gladys said then. "Are you married?"

Well, no Gladys, I've never been married."

Before I could say any more, the three other historical ladies appeared on the sidewalk in front of the salon. Gladys rushed out to talk to them, just as Sarah returned with the new tube.

Sarah began talking to me as she went up the ladder. "I hate those bitches, but I guess I told you that already." She kept on talking. She asked me how my room was and I started to answer that it was fine, but she continued before I could finish. It was like having a conversation with a young Gladys. Sarah told me that her 12-year-old daughter had cleaned the room because they were short on housekeeping staff. She said Kenzie was smart enough to run the motel by herself, and sometimes she did. She looked at me with her beautiful smile from the top of the ladder as she reached up to remove the bad tube. My breathing stopped. Sarah told me that she had to go to Pendleton the next week for a court date with her ex-husband's mother. "I'm getting a restraining order," she said, with a laugh. "That bitch ex-mother-in-law of mine won't be able to call me anymore." She was surprisingly cheerful about it. She told me about Carl, her ex-husband who was the Sheriff's Deputy assigned to Elephant. They had met when she was working at a hardware store in Pendleton. Carl came through the checkout line one day and asked her out right on the spot. He was a few years older and had just started his job as a deputy. She thought that was "pretty cool", she said, so she went out with him. She got pregnant and then married him because she thought it was the right thing to do. "I never loved him," she said proudly. Sarah continued talking about her kids and her ex-husband and his mother, until the four ladies entered the shop. Then she stopped. The other ladies looked at her and seemed surprised to see her, but didn't say anything. Sarah stiffened and frowned, and then she turned and went to work silently on the light fixture.

The entire historical committee looked at me for a second and Ruth stepped forward and prepared to speak. "Mr. Smith," she said. "We're very concerned about Elephant's history, as you know. Whenever one of the town's important landmarks is at risk, it's our job to protect it." Ruth went on to explain that very few people appreciated history. "Especially the younger people."

At that point a sharp cough came from the far corner of the room. Sarah froze for a second and seemed surprised at herself. She climbed down the ladder and looked at Gladys, ignoring the others. "Gladys, this light needs a new ballast. I'll be back later. She ignored the other ladies as she quickly went out the door.

"There's a good example of someone who doesn't appreciate history," Bea said, as soon as the door had shut behind Sarah. Beverly and Ruth nodded in agreement, but Gladys tried to defend Sarah.

"Oh, she's a darling girl," Gladys said. "She's had a difficult time, with those kids and that poor excuse for a husband."

"When she's older, she'll thank us for protecting this town," Beverly said. "These young people don't appreciate the past like we do."

"So Mr. Smith," said Ruth. "We're having a public meeting on Monday to discuss the future of the gas station elephant. We want you to come. Then you'll understand the importance of saving this important part of our town's history."

I told the ladies that I was planning to leave Monday morning, and they all spoke up in unison to insist that I stay. I finally agreed, if only to get them to leave me alone. Once they were satisfied, the committee members, except for Gladys, left the salon smiling

Within a minute after they left, Sarah re-entered the salon. "Your ballast is actually fine," she said to Gladys. "I just couldn't listen to any more of that crap."

"Oh, those ladies mean well," said Gladys. "Maybe you should give them a chance. They really do care about Elephant."

Sarah started to argue. "It's the young people who have to live in this town in the future. Maybe they should listen to us . . ." She stopped then and climbed the ladder.

Gladys seemed flustered and I decided it was time to change the subject. I looked at Gladys and asked her "So, Gladys, does Sarah know about your old flame?"

Sarah spun around gracefully on the ladder rung she was standing on and gave Gladys a big smile. "Gladys! Why no, I don't believe I do. Who's the lucky guy?" Gladys looked at me and began to blush.

"There's one big problem," I said. "They haven't spoken in 65 years."

"Holy shit Gladys!" Sarah blurted, before covering her mouth. "Oops, sorry."

Gladys was flustered for a moment, but then relaxed. "Well, I guess the cat's out of the bag," she said. "That's what I get for talking to a reporter."

I asked Sarah if she had any idea who Gladys's old boyfriend might be and she said no. And then I asked "Do you know who Gustav Reimer is?"

Sarah had to steady herself on the ladder as she replied with surprise. "Gus Reimer?! You had a thing with Gus Reimer!?"

Gladys suddenly looked kind of proud. "Why sweetie, he was my high school beau."

"What a hoot!" Sarah said, as she stood on the ladder staring at Gladys. "You haven't talked to Gus since high school? What happened? Did you dump him?" And then she said. "Gladys, Charlie Reimer Jr. was my high school boyfriend. He's Gus's grandson. I wish I didn't have to talk to him now, but he talks to me every time I see him." And then she said, "Hey, if things had worked out differently, we could have been related."

Gladys told Sarah the story of Gus going into the Navy and then marrying her best friend. Sarah stood on her ladder grinning. Then she got a mischievous smile and said, "now that you're both single, maybe you could rekindle the old flame." I expressed my strong agreement with Sarah, and Gladys blushed once again.

"That man," she said. "He won't even talk to me."

"Gladys, men don't talk," replied Sarah. "You have to talk to them."

Gladys didn't say anything more, and Sarah returned to her work. I started to tell the ladies goodbye. Sarah stopped and looked at me and suddenly said, "Rob, I was thinking. If you need someone to do something with in the evening while you're here, let me know."

I was stunned. "Well, I, uh, uh, would you do that?" was all I could say. My stomach began to feel queasy and I thought I might throw up.

Sarah turned her face shyly away from me and smiled, and then she looked back and just said "Yeah. Why not?" Then she reached back up to the light fixture, trying to remove the bulb.

"Well how about that," Gladys said. "You've got date, Mr. Smith." We all stood there silently for a moment as Sarah worked on the light fixture.

When the new tube was installed and shining brightly, the beautiful Sarah descended the ladder, folded it up and gave Gladys a big smile. "There you go, Gladys. You can see again," she said. She packed her tools and began heading for the door. "Well, bye Gladys. See you around, Rob." And then, wearing her tool belt over her beautiful hips, carrying her step ladder, and with a big grin on her face, the beautiful Sarah danced out the door and into my heart.

I know Gladys started talking about something else, but I have no memory of what she said. I felt like the blood vessels in my head might explode and I was having trouble breathing. I think I told Gladys that I needed to go find Stacy, or something. And I then forced a ten dollar bill into her hand and stumbled out the door in a daze.

I walked up and down Main Street a couple of times. People greeted me on the street and everyone was friendly. Except for Billy, who gave me a momentary nod, I don't remember who they were or what they said. I wasn't ready to go back to the motel, because was afraid if I saw Sarah I might vomit right in front of her.

I finally started walking in that direction when I heard a rumble in the distance behind me. It was a car. As it got closer, the ground started to shake. I turned around and saw the front of an old Corvette – one from the '50s. Jonas pulled up beside me and idled the car. "Hey there, Rob. How's it going?" he yelled over the motor. I think I told him Okay, but I'm not sure. "Want to go check out Elephant Gas?" he asked. I nodded, and he told me to hop in. And so I avoided the motel for awhile longer.

CHAPTER NINE

"Nice haircut," Jonas said as I seated myself in the black convertible's red leather bucket seat. "Looks like Gladys got to you."

"Yup," I said. "I think I'll be wearing my hat for awhile."

I hadn't been in a car from the 1950s since I was a kid. Almost everything inside was metal or fabric or leather, with not a speck of plastic in sight. For a sports car, it seemed chunky and heavy. The doors were half a foot thick, and when I swung the long passenger door closed, it felt like I was shutting a vault. The metal dashboard was red with chrome trim and the white round gauges with black numbers looked like antique clock faces. The car had a floor shifter with a chrome shaft and a white ceramic knob. Everything on the interior of Jonas's car looked old, and yet brand new. The car shook when it idled and as soon as Jonas gave it some gas, our conversation stopped. We made a quick U-turn and headed west on Main Street, away from the motel and toward the giant elephant, which loomed over the west end of town. The engine's roar was deafening.

My seat had no belt or headrest, and when Jonas punched the gas, my head snapped back and I felt like I might fly out the back of the car. When he shifted from first to second gear, the rear wheels broke loose and I could feel the car slide slightly sideways, like we were driving on ice – even though it was a hot sunny day. The tires spun and squealed, and we were already going nearly fifty. I could hear the sound of the roaring engine echo off the buildings. I hung on and forgot about the beautiful Sarah, at least for a few minutes. Jonas looked over at me with a dangerous grin and then took his foot off the gas to let the car slow down with the engine's compression. "Of all my 'Vettes, this one's the quickest," he yelled, as we slowed back to the speed limit. "It's pure mayhem." He was laughing now. We cruised, barely above idle, on through town, and pulled into the driveway next to the big gray elephant. When Jonas switched off the engine, my ears rang.

"Fuck," I said as I looked over at him.

"That's how I feel every time I get in this thing," Jonas replied. "This car is so uncivilized I feel like I'm putting my life at risk every time I drive it." Then he smiled and said "I love that feeling!"

"Shit, this is a seriously cool car," was all I could say.

"It's not stock, believe me," he said. "We built the 427 motor from scratch, and put a supercharger on it. It's over 600 horsepower. This car would probably do 175 if I let it."

"Jesus," I said.

"But it's a fifty-year-old car," he continued. "I don't know about you, but I wouldn't want to ride on a fifty-year-old suspension at that speed. I took it to 130 once and nearly shit my pants."

"Fuck," I said again.

"Leaves you speechless, doesn't it?"

I finally got my breath back and felt my heart rate drop a bit. "How many Corvettes do you have, anyway?" I asked.

"Six," Jonas replied. "Two of them are here. Wanna see the shop?"

"What do you think?"

"Okay, but here's the deal," Jonas said. "This isn't a museum, and it's not open to the public. And these cars don't show up in magazines. Get my drift?" Jonas was smiling when he said all of this, but I could tell he was serious.

"My word of honor," I replied, in disappointment.

Jonas reached under his seat for a second and then one of the roll-up doors on the gas station building begin to rise. He restarted the car and we rolled slowly into the building. We were in the left bay of a three-bay garage. The middle bay was empty, and in the far bay sat the car I had seen the previous afternoon: the maroon 1967 Sting Ray coupe.

"I have another building rented on a farm outside of town where I keep most of my cars," Jonas said after he turned off the car we were in. "I don't like to be too showy about these things. This is the shop where we work on them."

"You have someone working with you?" I asked.

"Yeah, his name's Danny," said Jonas "He's just a farm boy from Elephant, but he's an awesome mechanic. And a good body man, too. We should put him to work on your Beemer."

"Oh yeah, you saw the dent?" I said. "It's fresh."

"So what happened? It looks like somebody kicked it."

"Yeah, somebody did. It was a girl."

"Whoa, dude," Jonas said. "You must have really pissed her off. I hope she was worth it."

"I didn't even know her."

"Oh right on. Even better," he said, now laughing.

"It's a long story," I said.

"Well anyway," Jonas said, "we'll have Danny take a look at it and see what he thinks. How about a shop tour?"

I agreed, and we climbed out of the car. Jonas's large frame was imposing as he walked around the low car, his ponytail flopping behind him. He wore an open blue and white Hawaiian shirt with a gray T-shirt under it that had big maroon letters that said "USC." He and I both had on light colored cargo shorts and flip-flops.

Jonas began leading me around the garage, showing me some of the tools and equipment. The shop was spotless and the tools all seemed almost brand new. The maroon car sat between the legs of a large hydraulic lift. Four sets of tool chests, at least six feet high each, were lined up against the far wall of the garage to the right of that car. A large air compressor sat in the corner and I could see a long pneumatic hose emerging from it. A long work bench, with two sinks, ran along the back wall of the garage, with shelves above it. They were as clean and organized as the rest of the shop.

Unlike most "car guy" shops I had seen, this one had no old auto parts signs or advertising posters. And there were no calendars with scantily dressed women. Large framed illustrations of Corvettes and other American cars from the 50s and 60s were hung tastefully in open spots on the walls. "So where are the bikini babe pictures?" I asked Jonas as I looked around. "How can you call yourself a true gear-head?"

"Well," he replied. "I'm not really into that sort of thing. But if I were, it would be Speedo photos of men." He looked at me with a sly grin, to see if I got his point. "I've been in a faithful relationship for thirty years," he said, "and Phil probably wouldn't appreciate that."

"Oh," I said. Jonas grinned at me as he watched the puzzle pieces slowly slide into place. I tried to think of a way to joke about this new discovery, like pointing out how clean and well-organized the shop was, but then decided against it.

"Surprised?" he asked.

"Well yeah," I replied. "I guess I just never met a gay guy who was that into cars."

"Well, in spite of everything you may have heard, Rob, "we're not all alike," he said. "And we don't all know each other either." He was smiling now. "Let me show you the office."

The little room next to the shop fit the stereotype perfectly. The old gas station office looked more like the waiting room of a high-end law firm. A dark leather overstuffed couch and matching chair sat at angles to the walls. An expensive-looking deep pile rug sat on the painted concrete floor. Modern metal lamps and a metal coffee table accented the room, which was painted in two shades of green that a straight guy could never have chosen. The old customer counter had been restored and two bar stools sat next to it. Several pieces of abstract art hung on the walls of the room, and opposite the couch and chair was a tall wood armoire. A large arrangement of tall white flowers sat on the coffee table, along with several magazines that were carefully fanned out like large playing cards.

"Welcome to my man cave," said Jonas, as we walked in. He opened the armoire to show off a large flat-screen TV behind its doors. "We watch the Speed Channel in here," he said, and then smiled. "And yes, I sometimes watch the Home and Garden channel."

"Holy crap Jonas, this is fabulous," I said as I looked around. "I mean it. Can you imagine if the greasy old mechanics who used to work in here saw this?"

"Thanks Rob," replied Jonas. "Sit down, and tell me about the article you're writing. Which magazine is it?"

I sat in the big chair and Jonas leaned his large frame onto the couch. "Western Oasis," I said.

"I like that magazine," he said. "They have great food articles. And the photography is stunning." Then he got a look of concern. "Now wait a minute. They're going to run an article on Elephant in Western Oasis? Is that a good fit?"

"I don't know," I said. "This is my first assignment for them, so I'm not sure how it's going to work."

Jonas started laughing. "No wonder Stacy had herself all fixed up yesterday. She always looks nice, but man, she went the extra mile."

"I know, and I showed up looking like this," I said, pointing to my shorts and flip-flops. "I'm sure I was a huge disappointment."

"You know, I might have one or two copies of Western Oasis here," said Jonas, as he reached into the display of magazines on the coffee table. Out from among the GQs, Architectural Digests and Street Rodder magazines, he produced a copy of Western Oasis from the previous March. On the cover was a photo of the back patio of a luxury home in Big Sur, California. It included a sweeping panorama of the Pacific Ocean. "Not exactly Elephant," said Jonas, as he handed me the copy.

I thumbed through it and saw a lot of articles and recipes about food using odd and unusual ingredients peculiar to California and the northwest. There were some travel articles as well. "Look," I said, "here's an article about another little town. It's in Eastern Washington. It shows pictures of old Victorian homes all fixed up and a beautiful Court House and Train Depot."

Jonas looked at the first page of the article. "Dayton," he said. "I've never heard of it, but it looks like it's not far from here. I might have to check it out. You know, if Elephant looked like that, you might have something. We'd better not show this to Stacy. It'll just piss her off."

While Jonas was talking I heard a vehicle pull into the driveway next to the big elephant. We looked out and saw a patrol car pull around and back up to the building just outside the office. "Shit, it's Carl," said Jonas. Then he smiled. "It's okay, watch this. This'll just take a second."

The door to the office opened and a large doughy man in a sheriff deputy's uniform walked through it slowly. He was well over six feet tall and probably weighed 300 pounds. He looked like he was in his 30s and he also looked nervous. "Jonas, I thought we talked about this. You know I'm always in town on Saturday mornings."

"Oh, right," said Jonas. "Sorry about that, Carl. I was just showing off the '59 to Mr. Smith here. I keep forgetting about your daycare job on Saturdays."

"Very funny," replied Carl. "You know I only get to see my kids for two hours on Saturdays at the motel. And when you go and disturb the peace like that, it eats into my visitation. Like right now." Carl had an unnaturally high squeaky and whiny voice that was very irritating.

"I'm sorry Carl. I really am," said Jonas, with a guilty grin. "I promise it won't happen again. I'll only disturb the peace after two on Saturdays from now on. How are the little darlings, anyway?"

"Oh, they're doing pretty good," Carl replied.

"Are they starting to like you better?"

"That bitch does everything she can to turn them against me," Carl whined at an even higher pitch. "And the judge won't do anything about it."

Jonas looked over at me, and then apologized. He introduced me to Carl, the deputy who was assigned to Elephant. Then he asked, "Rob, did you meet the lovely Hockensmith sisters at the motel?"

"Oh yeah," I said, trying not to sound like I was totally in love with one of them.

"Carl is Sarah's ex," Jonas said. "And she's got his nuts in the vice pretty tightly, doesn't she Carl?" Then Jonas looked back at me. "If you ever get in trouble with the law around here, Rob, just go have a chat with Sarah. She can make things better."

"Dammit Jonas," whined Carl, as he turned to leave. "I gotta go. All I ask is that you keep that car off the road while I'm here."

"You got it Carl," said Jonas.

"Carl's a little behind on his child support," Jonas said, as the deputy eased the patrol car away from the building. "Sarah knows how to use that against him when she needs to. She's learned that she's a lot better off when Carl owes her money. Then she has leverage. She's also got a good lawyer. And the best part is that Carl pays his bill."

"I'm kind of jealous though," I said. "He got to see her naked."

Jonas laughed. "He's paying an awfully high price for that, my friend," he said. "I'm not sure it was worth it. Of course I'm not in that market, so who am I to say?" Then he continued, "Let's go outside. I want to show you something." We walked out onto the cracked asphalt in front of the building and then under the big elephant. "You can go inside the elephant," Jonas said. "Shall we?" I replied that of course we shall.

We walked to the Elephant's right rear leg – the one closest to the entrance to the garage. A gray panel door opened into a small closet-sized room inside the elephant's lower leg. Jonas walked through the door and then pulled a string to his left that turned on a light above it. "Check this out," he said. I followed him into the little room and opposite the door I could see a wooden ladder attached to the wall. The ladder led up into the dark cavern inside the elephant. "There's another light up there," Jonas said, as he began ascending the ladder. He climbed up and turned on the light as I followed him.

The inside of the elephant was lighter in color than the outside, and looked a little oranger. "This is all fiberglass," Jonas said. "It was space-age stuff when this was built. I can't figure out how they molded this thing, but it's pretty fascinating." Jonas explained that the three other legs were solid concrete, which kept the elephant from blowing away in the wind. A huge chain ran down behind the ladder we had just climbed, which anchored that corner of the elephant to the ground. At the top of the ladder was a large plywood platform that stretched to the other three legs, just above the beast's belly. We climbed up onto it and walked around. The single light bulb was mounted inside the elephant's rear, near its tail. From the platform we could see up into the animal's hollow head and the beginning of its trunk. An opening could even be seen into the elephant's ears. An odd framework of trusses stretched in various directions above our heads, supporting the sides of the elephant.

"Hardly anybody knows about this," said Jonas. "It was Holister McCune's secret hideaway. I've been told that he had plans to build an office or apartment or something in here, but then he decided it was too dark and gloomy."

As we looked around, Jonas began telling me about Holister, who had started the gas station in the 1950s with a partner. They built the big fiberglass elephant we were standing in in 1960. "He's in a nursing home in California," said Jonas. I don't know where his partner is. I don't even remember his name, but he's out of it now. The property is held in a trust for McCune that's being handled by Phil's law firm in LA. That's how I found out about it." Jonas explained that living in Los Angeles was slowly driving him insane. Even though Phil was very successful in his law career and their relationship was good, they needed to find Jonas a quiet place where he could take his cars and get away from the city. Jonas had always liked Oregon, and when one of Phil's law partners, who was handling the McCune trust, said he needed to find a tenant for a big garage somewhere in Podunk Oregon, Phil suggested Jonas. That was about two years earlier.

"I think Hollister is in pretty poor health," said Jonas. "He's probably not going to last much longer. I'm not sure what'll happen to the property when he dies."

"Why don't you buy it," I asked him.

"Oh no, I'm trying to leave a light footprint here," Jonas replied. "That means no ownership." Then he quickly changed the subject. He asked me if I'd heard about the "hysterical society" and I told him I'd just gotten their speech a few minutes before. He told me that the ladies were by far in the minority in Elephant, but they usually got their way anyway. "A lot of people would like to see this thing go away before the government gets its hands in there and says they have to preserve it," he said. "Most people around here aren't too keen on outside government interfering with things. And most people aren't too keen on this elephant, either." I told Jonas that I'd agreed to go to the special meeting on Monday night, and he said he'd be there too. "It'll be entertaining, for sure," he said.

"Stacy will probably kill me," I told him. "She's determined that I shouldn't write about the elephant."

"What else is there to write about?" Jonas asked, laughing. "The Elephant Inn? You've got your work cut out for you my friend."

"I guess I've seen all there is to see here," I told Jonas, as we stood in the belly of the elephant. "It's pretty interesting though." We descended the ladder to the bottom of the elephant's leg and I thanked Jonas for the tours. We agreed that I'd bring my car over to the shop the next day so Danny could give his assessment of the big dent in the driver's door.

CHAPTER TEN

I spent the next couple of hours of that sunny Saturday afternoon walking around Elephant's Main Street. The town seemed more worn-out when exposed to the bright overhead sun. The old concrete sidewalk was full of cracks and the cracks were full of weeds. The asphalt street surface was like a moonscape, pocked with bumps and craters. The moonscape was interrupted by newer smooth strips of asphalt covering trenches that had been cut for sewer repairs. It seemed unlikely that speeding cars on Main Street could be a big problem. About half of the downtown buildings were unoccupied, and the sun reflected off plywood sheets that boarded up the windows on a couple of the buildings along the street. A few of those that had life in them were fixed up nicely. As I walked, I passed Billy, who nodded silently and continued on, keys jangling.

One of the nicest storefronts on Main Street was Guns N Things. The small store sat on a corner, on the opposite side of Main Street from "Glady's Parlor" and closer to the elephant. Its front and side, and its flower boxes, were neatly painted in three shades of green. A colorful sandwich board depicting a rifle, a revolver and a gift box tied with a bow had been set neatly on the sidewalk next to the curb. The store was open so I went in. The small room beyond the front door was about the size of Gladys's hair salon, but this room was mostly light green. No customers were in the store, but it was well-stocked with green and bright orange camouflage clothing and hundreds of small gift items. Locked glass cases containing rifles and shotguns lined the left wall behind a counter. On the other walls were framed photos of trophy animals, either lying on the ground with their antlers held up by their smiling assailants, or hanging from trees or stands, with hunters at their sides.

The proprietor greeted me from behind the counter, and she obviously knew who I was. She introduced herself as Eve Breneau, and she was as French as her name. In a lovely accent she told me that all the men and many of the women in Elephant loved to hunt and she was the only licensed gun dealer in the area. She carried a few handguns, but mostly rifles and shotguns, along with shells. And, of course, the gifts. "You Hunt? No?" She asked.

"No, I've never been hunting," I replied. "I'm happy to get meat from the store."

Eve laughed and then said "No hunting in city of Seattle. Like Paris. In France the country people, we love to hunt. But the government makes it much harder than in America." I complimented Eve on her store. "I try to bring woman's touch to the gun store," she said proudly. "We have many gifts for hunters and their lady friends. You will write about us in your article? No?"

"Yes, I might just put you in the article," I said. "We don't have stores like this in Seattle."

"No?"

"No. The gun stores in the city are run by men, and your store is much nicer." She smiled. "And they sell more handguns," I went on. "For hunting people, I guess."

Eve looked at me for a moment to see if I was joking. When I smiled, she laughed out loud. "When is the people-hunting season?" she asked. "All year round, maybe?"

"Yeah, pretty much all year round."

Eve was petite, about five feet tall and maybe 100 pounds. She looked like she was in her fifties. She was fit and had a sophisticated look, like a graying Audrey Hepburn. She wore a long flowing orange sun dress and sandals, and had a green ribbon tying her long graying hair back.

I asked Eve how she ended up owning a gun store in Elephant. "My husband and I have a farm north of Elephant," she replied. "He farms and

I needed something to do. So we started gun store. It was fifteen years ago. We have done nicely." Eve smiled with pride as she told me all of this. Then she said, "You have German car. BMW. They make good cars in Germany. In France too. You know Renault and Peugeot?"

"Yes I know them. They're excellent cars." At this point, the mention of my BMW no longer surprised me. "Do you drive a French car?"

"Oh no," she replied with a smile. "I drive Ford truck. Very good truck."

"Yes, Ford makes good trucks," I said. I told Eve that I was sorry I wasn't in the market for any hunting gifts. I told her I might come back for an interview later.

"I will talk to you about Guns N Things for you to put in the article," she said. I wished Eve a good day and went out onto the hot sidewalk.

As I walked on toward the motel, I felt a vibration against my right leg. I got a queasy feeling at the thought of having to talk to Doris. I slowly extracted the phone and was relieved not to see "DEATH" on the caller ID, but rather an Oregon phone number. I answered and heard Stacy's voice saying my name as a question. I admitted who I was and then looked to my right. I was across the street from her office. Her car was parked in front and I could see her on the phone looking out the window at me. "I'll be right over," I said and pressed "end."

"I'm so sorry about last night," Stacy said, as I opened her office door.

I told her not to worry about it and then I described my evening in my room with the Mariners and the noodles. "The noodles were better than the Mariners," I said. I tried to sound cheerful, and she seemed relieved.

"I see Gladys got hold of you," she said.

"Yup, I'm headed to get my hat right now."

"It's not that bad. Gladys is a little old fashioned, but she does a nice job." Then she started to smirk.

I rubbed my hand in my hair to mess it up. "I look like Wally Cleaver. Or maybe Ward."

Stacy looked puzzled. "Who?"

"Never mind. They're from an old TV show. By the way, I was visiting Jonas this morning. He took me inside the big beast."

"Oh great. There's nothing in there to see, is there? But you're going to write about it, aren't you?"

"I think it's pretty interesting. It's amazing that it's lasted fifty years." I asked Stacy about the upcoming meeting to talk about preserving the elephant as a historic landmark.

"I suppose you want to go to that now," she said in a disappointed voice. "It's just a City Council meeting. They're boring."

"Jonas says there will be a lot of people arguing and yelling. It sounds like fun."

"I wish they'd just blow that thing up. It does nothing but make us look stupid." Stacy was dressed neatly but casually in blue jeans and a sleeveless white top. She looked at me nervously, like she was about to cry again, and changed the subject. "Rob," she said. "I'm so sorry about last night. You must have gotten a terrible impression of Elephant. And of me."

"I told you, it was fine. I know this is a big deal to you, and I know you have a hard job." Stacy started to laugh. "I didn't mean it that way. Although, if you had a decent restaurant here, you might have better luck attracting visitors."

Stacy laughed. "Yeah, that restaurant and the elephant are enough to scare anyone away. I don't know why I don't just quit this job."

"Look," I said. "This isn't such a bad little town. It may not be everyone's cup of tea, but you know what I've learned since I've been here?"

"What?"

I was grasping now, but I gave it a shot. "I've talked to a lot of people and everyone seems pretty happy. People are laid back and relaxed. They're not stressed out like in the city." I mentioned Gladys and Jonas and Eve and the Beautiful Hockensmith Sisters. I talked to them all, I told her, and they all seemed to think Elephant was a really nice place to live. "It's like Mayberry," I said. "That's from another old TV show."

"Yes, I've heard of Mayberry. People are always saying that we're like Mayberry."

"And the setting here is fantastic. Those mountains are beautiful." I was on a roll now and Stacy was smiling. Then I said something stupid. "The only person around here who seems unhappy with the town is you." Her face froze for a second, like an invisible attacker had put a sharp little knife in her back. Then she cut loose. I decided to just let her cry for a few moments, and then I said, "I know you take your job seriously Stacy, and I know all of those people would like to have more visitors come here, because it would help their businesses. But everyone seems to be getting on pretty well the way things are. Maybe you need to just set your sights lower, and understand that you have to work with what you've got. Take baby steps, you know?"

Stacy stopped crying and looked at me and smiled a little. "You're right Rob. I guess maybe it takes someone from out of town to see the situation more clearly."

"That's right," I said. "You can make some improvements, but you don't want to lose the relaxed feeling that makes living here so nice."

Stacy thanked me again and then asked, "Listen, could you do me one favor?"

"You bet." I was feeling proud of myself now, like I'd closed the sale.

"I'd really like to make up for last night," Stacy said. "Wouldn't you let me fix you dinner tonight? After all, there's nowhere good to eat out. You could take it back to your room, if you don't want to eat at my house."

The beautiful Sarah's offer earlier that morning was still fresh in my mind. "You know, I'm sorry. I'm going to have to pass," I said. "I already made plans." It was just a small fib, because I was on my way back to the motel to make those plans.

Stacy looked dejected. "Okay. That's Okay," she said. "So who are you are you having dinner with? Jonas?"

I decided not to lie. "Well no. Actually, uh, Sarah over at the motel said she'd be free, so we made some plans." I grimaced as I watched for her reaction.

"Oh," she said, as her face welled up. "Excuse me a second." Then she rushed back into the hallway to the bathroom. I stood in her office for five minutes, not sure whether to stay or leave. When she returned she apologized one more time and then told me that she needed to go home. "I don't usually work on Saturdays," she said. "I just thought I'd catch up a little. But I've got plenty of catching up to do at home too." She forced a weak smile as she began clearing her desk.

I told Stacy I would probably see her on Monday and then returned to the sidewalk. Farther along the block, I walked past Muriel's Hardware Store. In the window I saw the beautiful Sarah talking to Helen, who had her back to me. Sarah saw me and abruptly stopped her conversation and headed for the door. She was carrying a large brown paper bag.

"Hey Rob," Sarah sang out cheerfully, before she even got through the door.

"Hey there Sarah. Looks like you're ready to go do some more work."

"Yeah, this is for the motel. Is that where you're going? Wanna lift?" Of course I did. "This is my rig," she said. "Hop in." We were standing in front of the tallest pickup I'd ever seen. It was an early '70s Ford that had been lifted more than a foot. It would be a big "hop." The tops of the tires were almost even with Sarah's waist. She had to reach above her head to grab the door handle. She opened it and then boosted her shopping bag up onto the seat. A U-shaped chrome bar hung below the bottom of the door and served as a step to assist her entry into the truck. She reached up and grabbed the right side of the door opening and then expertly bounced her left foot on the step, sliding her beautiful ass onto the seat and into driving position. "You like it?" she asked.

"Uh, you mean the truck?"

"Yeah, silly. It'll go anywhere. It was my ex's, but I got it from him." She grinned with pride.

"How's the view from up there? Can you see the ocean?" Sarah either didn't get the joke or else ignored it. I walked around to the passenger side, dreading how awkward I was going to look trying to hoist myself up into the cab.

Just as I reached up to open the door, Helen came running out of her store. "Oh Mr. Smith. Mr. Smith. I need to talk to you." I was relieved, even though I was looking forward to riding in the same vehicle as the beautiful Sarah for a couple of minutes.

I yelled up into the cab, "You know what? You go ahead. I'll walk on over there in a few minutes."

"Stop in the office and we can visit. My mom's there. You can meet her." Sarah fired up her truck, which roared almost as loudly as Jonas's black Corvette. She backed it slowly away from the curb and eased her way along Main Street toward the motel.

So she wants me to meet her mother. I was pondering the significance of that when Helen accosted me. "Hi Mr. Smith. It's so good to see you! How have you been?" She grabbed my hand and shook it, like she'd been waiting years to do it.

"I've been doing very well since I saw you last night," I said.

"Oh, I'm so glad!" She certainly made me feel special. "I have something very important that I want to talk to you about. Can you come into the store? Just for a moment?"

The hardware store entrance seemed particularly rundown as the afternoon sun shone on it. Paint was peeling around the doors and windows, and one of the big windows had a diagonal crack across it. The door stuck as I pushed the latch to open it. Then it suddenly lurched open and a string of bells hanging above my head nearly deafened me. I held the door for Helen and then followed her into her store. "I want to talk to you about the elephant," said Helen. "It's an important part of our town's history and we need to preserve it. I think I've found just the way to do it."

"I don't see how that involves me," I told her. "That's up to the town to decide. And it's really up to the owner, isn't it?" I had a bad feeling about where this was going.

"Oh, but if you write about how important the elephant is in your article, that will draw attention to it," Helen went on. "It will be very helpful to us in our efforts. The fiftieth anniversary of the elephant is coming up, and I think that would be a great thing for your article."

I started to tell Helen that I was undecided about what I would say about the big elephant, but she cut me off. "Don't you think the elephant could be a big draw for visitors? It could be like our Statue of Liberty." I did my best not to laugh. "You're from the city Mr. Smith. Wouldn't you want to come visit it?"

"I'm probably not a good person to ask that," I said. "I don't travel that much."

Helen looked puzzled. "But you're a travel writer. Surely you must travel a lot for your job." Okay, that was embarrassing. I explained to Helen that I was just a freelance writer, and wasn't actually an employee of the magazine. And I said that this was my first assignment for Western Oasis, and that my previous writing experience had been on other topics, and they were mostly in the city. She was obviously disappointed, and she looked at me as if the wizard behind the curtain had just been exposed. "Well, I know you'll do a fine job with the article, Mr. Smith," she finally said, unconvincingly. Then she went on. "I want you go come up to my office so I can show you something."

I agreed and followed Helen toward the center of the store. A stairway rose between two aisles to a sort of mezzanine level that had been constructed in the back left corner of the store. "This is my office," she said as I followed her up the stairs. We entered a room with a ceiling only a couple of inches above my head. It was like a loft, and it looked out over the store. Helen went to her desk, reached into a drawer and pulled out a pack of cigarettes. "Do you smoke?" she asked cheerfully. When I told her no she pulled a cigarette out of the pack for herself and lit it. She reached into another drawer of her desk and pulled out a pad of large drawing paper. "I want to show you my idea," she said, lowering her gravelly voice almost to a whisper, exhaling smoke. She flipped through the pad until she came to the one she wanted. She drew on her cigarette again and a big grin came over her face as she proudly showed me the drawing on the pad. It was a colorful and elaborate piece of artwork. An elephant. Actually, a circus elephant. "What do you think?" she asked.

"This is beautiful," I said, trying not to inhale. The colorful sketch showed an animated circus elephant in full regalia. It was expertly drawn. It had what looked like a little house sitting on its back with an Arab sheik inside. Its sides were draped with tapestries and it wore some kind of bizarre headdress.

"This is my plan," said Helen. "I want to set up a non-profit organization to create an Elephant Park. And the elephant will only be the beginning. We'll turn the building into a big top tent and we'll have clowns and trapeze artists. And we'll have a real freak show, with real freaks. It'll be a complete circus."

"That's very interesting," I told Helen, trying to sound slightly supportive, but not too much. "Do you have a group working on this?"

"Well, it's just me right now," she said. "But I know some other people that I'm sure will be interested."

I asked Helen if she had talked to Stacy at the Chamber of Commerce about her circus idea. "Well, Stacy's awfully busy," she said, avoiding my question. "She has so many other important things she's doing that I probably shouldn't bother her with this."

"I think your idea could have promise," I told Helen, and I immediately sensed that saying this was a mistake.

"You do?!" she almost shrieked. "Well, I think having a magazine like yours supporting this idea could make a big difference. Will you talk about it in your article? Maybe that could be the main topic."

At that moment I was saved. A young man in his 20s cleared his throat and yelled "hello?" from the store below. He had some fishing lures and a package of fishing line in his hand. "Can someone take my money?" he shouted. "I've been waiting down here for awhile."

"Okay, okay," said Helen, as she and I headed down the stairs. "We'll see you Monday then, Mr. Smith? I think that will be the day of my big unveiling."

"I'm looking forward to it," I told her. I went out the front door and continued down the sidewalk toward the motel. Across the street I saw Billy checking for coins in the change slot of an Oregonian newspaper box.

CHAPTER ELEVEN

Heat rose visibly from the dark roof of the Moss Creek Motel as I walked toward it in the afternoon sun. The air was dry and the temperature was easily in the 90s. I felt like I had traveled from Seattle to another planet. The lush green lawn in front of the motel was a stark contrast to the brown and gold landscape surrounding the town. The motel's parking lot was empty and the whole place was quiet. I saw no sign of any Hockensmiths, or anyone else, around the motel. When I got to my room it was cleaned and made up. And it was still orange. I changed into a clean T-shirt and flip flops and put my baseball cap on over Gladys's haircut. I ate an apple and a small bag of chips left over from the previous night's grocery run and then headed out in search of the beautiful Sarah to ask her for a date.

I pushed open the motel's office door and went into the empty reception area. Almost instantly, 12-year-old Kenzie came from the back. "Mom, Rob's here!" she yelled a little too loudly, as soon as she saw me. In a moment her beautiful mother walked through the door from the back room with her beautiful smile, and at that moment I came closer than I ever have to a heart attack. Sarah was wearing blue denim cut-off shorts that were as short as they could legally be. Except for her skimpy leather sandals, her legs were bare from about four inches below her waist. Otherwise, she had on a pink and white bikini top, and that was it. Her long blonde hair flowed around her shoulders and was slightly curled. She looked like Daisy Duke, only better.

"Hey there Rob, how's it goin'?" she asked in her cheerful voice. I couldn't speak, or even breathe, so I just nodded. "We were just talking about you," she continued. Now I started to feel dizzy. I put my hand out to grab the counter.

"Great," I said, or at least I think I did. "It's, uh, great to, uh, see you." That was an understatement, and she seemed to know it.

"Thanks Rob. You too." She was beaming.

I finally gained a tiny bit of composure and said, "I hope you weren't saying bad things about me."

"No, not at all. Sure is hot, isn't it? At least we're both dressed for the weather. You're probably not used to this, are you?"

I was sweating, but it wasn't from the heat. "Yeah, it's hot. And no, I'm not used to this at all," I tried to concentrate and keep the conversation going as I took in all the bare skin in front of me. "Are you done working for today?"

"Oh no, the work's never done. I'm on duty here now. Mom and Andie and the kids are out back. Wanna come back?" Of course I did. I walked around the counter to the area behind it and then through the door into the private office area. "Excuse the mess," she said casually. She wasn't kidding. Papers and boxes and other random stuff were piled everywhere. The floor, or what I could see of it, was dirty, and kids' and dogs' toys were scattered among a lot of motel stuff. The back room of the motel had originally been a small apartment. A door on the right led to a former bedroom, which was now the office. It contained a desk, a computer and a filing cabinet, all surrounded by more debris. A kitchenette scattered with dishes ran along the far wall on the right side of the former living room. A small bathroom was tucked into the left corner and most of what was originally the living room was now a children's play area. Sarah quickly picked her way through the apartment and out the back door to a small patio, and I carefully followed her. Outside, Andrea and a woman in her fifties were both talking to a little girl of about two, who was obviously being scolded. Taver was in the grass next to the patio with the two rat dogs. Andrea looked up as I followed Sarah onto the patio and said, "Hey Rob. Good to see you."

Sarah then introduced me to her mother, Millie. Millie had black hair and glasses and was nearly as pretty as her daughters, though more stoutly built. She greeted me with a friendly smile. She had on blue jeans and sneakers, and a light blue T-shirt. Andrea wore a short tan skirt and a white sleeveless T-shirt that were much less revealing than what Sarah had on. The patio area was covered and private, and not as cluttered as the apartment. A large white plastic table sat in the middle of it, with several cheap plastic chairs and lounges scatted around. A large lawn stretched out behind the patio and motel buildings to the edge of the property. Beyond that was an unmowed grass field and then the foothills of the mountains.

"So what do you think of Elephant so far?" Andrea asked me. "Not much to write about, huh?"

"I'm still trying to figure out my angle," I said. I was beginning to calm down now.

"Maybe you could call it the world's most boring town," said Sarah enthusiastically. "That might draw visitors."

"Sarah Jean!" exclaimed Millie.

"Actually I've been getting lots of advice," I said. "Mostly about the big elephant."

"Nobody's going to come to visit that ugly thing" Millie said, almost shouting. "You can cross that off the list."

A phone rang inside the apartment. "I'll get it," said Andrea, as she grabbed her daughter and went inside.

"It's my son," Sarah said, leaving no room for doubt.

"Nick wants to know if he can go to Gabriel's house to shoot," yelled Andrea from inside the apartment.

"Whatever," replied Sarah. Then she looked at me. "My 14-year-old son loves his guns," she said. "I hope when he gets married he treats his wife as well as he treats his rifle.

"I never met a man who did that," said Millie, and then she looked at me and said "Sorry Rob."

"That's OK," I said. "I've never had a wife or a gun."

"What about your car?" Andrea shouted from behind the screen door. "Do you love it? Most guys love their cars more than their women."

"Not so much after it got kicked," I said. I started to tell the ladies about the field goal kicking girl, but got interrupted by the screaming two-year-old.

"Baby, what's wrong," said Sarah to the little blonde child who emerged from the apartment with her mother close behind. She ran into Sarah's arms.

The child kept screaming, and Andrea said "Nella shut her finger in the drawer again. I wish you'd keep those locks on them Sarah."

"Yeah yeah," said Sarah. "She'll learn better if she does that a few times." Then she kissed and rubbed Nella's hand.

Taver suddenly jumped up and began running out into the yard and around the building, followed by the two madly barking dogs. "Taver!" yelled Andrea as she ran after him.

"Mom!" It was Kenzie in the apartment.

"Come out here if you want to talk to me, McKenzie Moon," Sarah yelled back.

"I gotta show you in here," Kenzie replied. Sarah then picked up Nella and went into the apartment.

I looked over at Millie and she gave me a big smile. "You're probably wondering if it's always like this," she said. "The answer's yes. But we love it." I asked Millie how long she had owned the Motel. She told me she and her husband had bought the property about five years earlier. It had gotten seedy and rundown by then. They planned to fix it up and sell it for a profit once business picked up. "We were trying to be real estate moguls," Millie said, "not innkeepers. But Sarah changed all that." Millie said that about the time the work on the motel was finished, Sarah's marriage to Carl blew up, and she needed a place to live and something to do. "She was trying to be a housewife and mother," Millie said, "but that doesn't work when you're married to a jerk on a deputy's paycheck. So here we are." She said it with a smile. Millie then told me that her husband, whose name was Bob, was a truck driver and was somewhere in Texas right now. "I drove with him for a few years after the girls moved out," she said, "but I retired when we bought the motel." She told me that Sarah learned her handyman skills when they remodeled the motel and she decided to keep doing it. "Besides helping us with the remodeling, Sarah also became the on-site manager," continued Millie. "We moved that double-wide trailer that's over there onto the property and she and the kids live there now."

Sarah and Nella appeared from the apartment just as Andrea and Taver returned from somewhere beyond the motel yard. "What are you two talking about?" asked Sarah.

"You," replied her mother. "I told Rob that this motel is your fault."

"I guess it is," Sarah replied without a hint of guilt. "But it keeps the family together."

"Yeah," said Andrea. "And it keeps us too busy to fight with each other."

"So Rob, what did you do today?" Sarah asked.

"Well, I went over to Elephant Gas and had a nice visit a guy named Jonas."

"Ah yes, our millionaire gay auto mechanic," said Andrea. "Isn't he great?"

"We love Jonas," said Sarah. "Too bad he's gay. I could fall in love with him."

"You mean his money," said Millie. "He's twice your age, dear."

"Oh, but I like older men," Sarah said, as she turned to look at me with her smile. I tried to swallow, but I couldn't.

After a moment I said, "It sounds like he's very happy with Phil, even though they don't live together."

"That's why they're happy," said Sarah.

"Oh yeah, and I met Carl this morning too," I told her.

"Hah! Isn't he a peach?" Sarah said. "I sent him over there when I heard Jonas's car – just to get him out of the here for a few minutes. He's scared of Jonas."

"I could tell. And Jonas says Carl's scared of you too."

"He'd better be."

"Jonas took me inside the elephant," I said.

"Wow, you can go inside?" asked Andrea.

"Oh yeah, I knew that," Sarah said.

"Oh yeah? How did you know that," Andrea replied mockingly, and the two sisters started to argue. Then Taver started yelling and Andrea grabbed him by the arm and took him into the apartment.

I told Sarah and Millie about our climb up the elephant's leg and walking around on the platform. When I described Hollister McCune's plan to build a little apartment there, Sarah said, "That would be totally cool! I would love to build that." I reminded her that it would be dark, with no windows. "It would have been Hollister's little love shack," she said, "where he could do it with his girlfriends. Inside an elephant, no less."

"Sarah Jean!" exclaimed Millie.

"You know that was his plan," Sarah replied.

Andrea and her kids walked back out onto the patio. "Did you know our grandfather helped build that elephant?" she asked. I told her I didn't.

"That's not something I'd be bragging about," Millie said.

"We haven't seen him since I was two," Andrea told me. "He was our biological father's father."

"Yeah, Jonas told me that Hollister had a partner," I said. "But he didn't know his name."

"Yup, old Peter was a chump," said Millie. "Hollister gave him the heave-ho pretty soon after the elephant was built. And he deserved it."

"Did you know there's a group that wants to preserve the elephant and make it a historic landmark?" I asked. "They cornered me at Gladys's this morning."

"The hysterical society," smiled Sarah. "I told you how I feel about those bitches." Millie and Andrea both nodded.

"According to them, this motel is an historic landmark," said Millie. "Can you believe that?"

"When we bought this place it was a shithole," said Sarah. "We spent a lot of money to fix it up. They still wouldn't let us change the outside."

"We like history too," said Andrea, "But nobody is going to stay in this motel because of its history."

"Unless they were conceived here," said Sarah, with a mischievous smile. "Most of the illegitimate children around here were. That's our claim to fame."

"And there are a lot of them," Andrea added.

Millie and Sarah explained how they had planned to add a covered driveway in front of the office. They were also planning to add a cabana at the end of one of the buildings. "The motel was exactly fifty years old when we bought it in 2005," said Millie. "So we couldn't get a building permit to do anything without approval from the historical Nazis. They turned down our plans because it changed the historical look."

"It's a frickin' motel," said Sarah. "There's a million of them and they all look the same. Nobody cares about the historic look. Those bitches would kill this town if it weren't already dead."

"There's no way we would have bought this place if we'd known there were all those restrictions on making changes," said Millie. "Nobody told us about that." Millie and Sarah described the meeting they attended to present their plan to Elephant's Historical Committee. "Sarah drew up these beautiful plans, showing the entrance, with a nice modern cover over it. She spent hours on it." said Millie. We were going to rebuild the front of the office, with smaller energy efficient windows and a new door. The windows leak like crazy."

"Those bitches should have to pay our power bill," said Sarah.

"Anyway, it ended up in a screaming match," continued Millie, smiling. "Sarah did most of the screaming."

"I told them what I thought of them," Sarah said. "They don't like me now."

All this time, Andrea and I couldn't get a word in. Finally I was able to ask the ladies if they thought the big elephant should be designated as a historic landmark. "There aren't a million of those around," I said.

"It would serve the town right if they were stuck with that thing," said Millie.

"That's our history in a nutshell," said Sarah. "Selling gas to people as they leave town."

At about that time the phone in the office rang and Andrea took both of her kids and went in to answer it. I told Millie and Sarah that Jonas didn't seem to have an opinion on the big Elephant. "He just said it provides good shade for his cars," I said. They both laughed.

"Aren't Jonas's cars cool?" asked Sarah.

"I rode in that loud black Corvette today and it nearly scared me to death," I said.

Kenzie emerged from the office and said "Grandma, Aunt Andrea needs to ask you something." Millie followed her back into the office.

Sarah looked at me with a shy smile but didn't say anything. I swallowed hard and went for it. "So remember when you said if I needed someone to do something with I should ask you?"

"Yeah."

"Well, I need someone to do something with," I said. "You want to go get something to eat tonight?"

Sarah looked hesitant now, but said "Well yeah, OK. Where would we go?"

"I don't know. You're the one who lives here. Is there any place you like?" I felt completely awkward now.

"Not really," she replied. "I don't go out much."

What about Melville's Tavern?" I asked. "We could have a drink. They have food don't they?"

"Well, I don't drink," she said. "But I hear their pizza's good."

It seemed odd that Sarah had no idea of anything to do, when she had lived here all her life, and she was the one who sort of asked me out in the first place. I thought of inviting her to my room to share some of my grocery store dinner, but that might make my motives too obvious. "Pizza it is," I said. "You can have a Coke."

"Well, OK," she replied.

We agreed to meet at 6:00 at the motel office, and I went back to my room and began to plan the rest of my life with the beautiful Sarah.

CHAPTER TWELVE

For some odd reason, a few minutes after I got back to my room I began thinking about Doris's apartments. They were a long way away and seemed less important now. Most of the work there was done and the final inspections were either scheduled or already completed. The buyer was too rich and too busy to give me much trouble. For him, this was a minor piece of his large real estate portfolio. And the seller was an appalling person that I couldn't possibly care about. The whole deal was out of my control now anyway, and that was a good feeling. Even though an entire year's income was on the line, right now I couldn't make myself worry much about it. I had something else to worry about.

I had been away from Seattle for less than two days, but the loss of contact was complete. I had received no phone calls from Doris or text messages from Charles. After meeting the beautiful Sarah, the whole business with Ramona seemed stupid. And I hadn't given two seconds thought to Jennifer at the coffee shop. Meeting all these new people in this weird little town was like being turned on to a new drug. It was exciting, and the old familiar drugs were losing their appeal. I lay on the bed and stared at the ceiling. My mind drifted to the beautiful country girl I had just met. Why was she being so friendly? Did she really like me, or was I just some strange oddity from another universe that she was curious about? Or maybe she just felt sorry for me, being in a new place and not knowing anyone. That was probably it, but what if she did want to get something started? What was I going to do, move here? She had two kids in school here and a family she was really close to, and she was running her mother's business. So it wasn't like I was going to lure her away from Elephant. My brain was out of control now. Once again, I'd met a woman and gotten a thousand miles ahead of myself. But I still couldn't get my mind off that beautiful smile and the cheerful self-confident way she had. And then there was her incredible butt. I've always believed that a well-formed tight ass on a woman is one of the great wonders of nature – right up there with Mount Rainier or the Grand Canyon. Sarah's was as good as they get, and I could stare at it for hours.

The weird thing was that I had become infatuated with the only person in Elephant who didn't seem curious about what I was going to write about in the Oasis. In fact, Sarah didn't seem curious about much of anything. She had her little life here. It was small and contained, but it was full. That is, except that she didn't have a boyfriend. But what chance would any guy have, really? Even if she had a boyfriend, he'd have to compete with the kids and the mom, and even the sister. He'd be an accessory, like a hat that spends most of its time hanging on a hook somewhere, waiting to be brought out for special occasions. So here I was, getting myself tied up in knots over a woman who was completely impractical. Even though this time the woman was more single than Jennifer, and more beautiful, and seemed to be more interested, my crush was probably even more stupid. In a couple of days I'd be back in Seattle and that would be that. But, what the heck, there was still tonight.

I turned on the TV and found a news show that I didn't bother watching. I tried to force myself to think about what I was going to write. This whole thing was pretty farfetched. How could I ever make a town like this look good in a magazine like Western Oasis? I was losing hope. But then, how could a beautiful woman like Sarah want to go out with me? That seemed even more farfetched, and yet I'd heard it with my own ears. While my brain was caught up in that ridiculous trap, I felt my pants vibrate. I pulled my phone out and there it was: "DEATH." Reality was back in a heartbeat. I took a deep breath and answered. "Hello Doris."

"Is this Robert?"

"Yes it is, Doris."

"Robert Smith?"

"Yes Doris, this is Robert Smith."

"Robert, this is Doris Ellington," the voice from hell said, putting special emphasis on its last name.

"So how are you today Doris?" I asked cheerfully, in my new state of only pretending to care.

"Robert, I have a problem," she announced.

No shit, I thought. Then I asked cheerfully, "Is there something I can do?"

"I need you to go to the title company and talk to those people. This paperwork they sent is all wrong."

"I can probably do that later next week."

"Monday morning," she commanded. "This needs to be resolved." I explained to Doris that I was out of town, and that I could go to the title company on Wednesday after I returned to Seattle. I mentioned that I had told her at least twice that I was going to Oregon for a few days. "Well, I'm quite sure you didn't," she insisted. She then explained how completely inconvenient it was of me to leave town and that in the future I needed to make sure she knew I was leaving.

We have no future, I said to her silently. "So what's the problem with the paperwork Doris? Maybe I can shed some light from here."

"This easement. They've got it all wrong. I sent a letter vacating that."

"Doris, the only easement on that property is a power line easement. You can't vacate that. The power company has to have its poles there."

"Well, you need to go talk to them about that."

"It'll have to be Wednesday."

Doris abruptly told me she had to go. "Where did you say you were? Oregon?"

"Yes Doris, I'm in a little town in eastern Oregon."

"Well, I'm sure I've never heard of it." Then she hung up the phone without saying goodbye. It was 4:00 on Saturday afternoon when she got the sudden whim to call and bother me. Now she had another sudden whim to go do something else, and she was done with me.

I tried to put myself back into Elephant mode. I was in a little town where stress should never be an issue, and yet my stress level was off the charts. I was so nervous about my date with the beautiful Sarah that I couldn't keep my mind on anything else. At least I wasn't stressing over Doris or the big commission I was trying to make. Instead, I was stressing over a date with a woman that I had no chance of having a future with. It was completely irrelevant to anything in my life, and yet the real estate deal that meant everything to my future seemed distant and disconnected from where I was.

I finally forced myself to get off the bed. I dug into my bag and began figuring out what to wear for my big date. I felt like a 14-year-old girl. I started straightening up the room, and I didn't even know why. I guess I had a secret fantasy that the beautiful Sarah would agree to come back there. I decided to take a shower.

* * *

When I was clean and dressed, I still had an hour to kill, so I went for a drive to try to clear my head. I drove along Main Street and then turned left onto one of the residential areas on the south side of town. In Elephant, neighborhoods weren't defined by wealth or the sizes of houses. Everything was intermixed, and the ages of the homes varied as well. I saw a couple of large Victorian homes that were perfectly restored and looked like the painted ladies of San Francisco. Others were in various states of disrepair. Small plain houses from a later era had been built between them. On one corner I saw a huge stately Victorian home that would have been one of the nicest in Seattle. Next to it was a small shack: a one-story rectangle with a slightly pitched roof and most of its paint peeled off. Its roof was multicolored and in disrepair, and its eaves were lined with white ice cycle Christmas lights. Four 1980s-era cars were parked in the front yard. None appeared to be in running condition. Several lawn mowers and other yard implements were scattered around. Just like the cars, they were neglected and inoperable, and since the lawn and shrub beds were all dead, this made perfect sense. And this house was hardly unique.

I wondered again how a real estate broker could survive in a town like

Elephant. Who would want to move here and buy most of these houses? Even the nice ones? If I ended up living here with Sarah, I thought, I might have to find out. I couldn't think of anything else I could do for a job here. Unless this writing gig took off. Or maybe I could become a handyman's assistant.

I saw a for sale sign in front of a neat little one-story bungalow. The house had obviously been fixed up to sell – it was in better condition than any of the houses around it. The sign said the real estate broker was in Pendleton. A little plastic box under the sign held some flyers, so I got out and took one. The price was $65,000. Even a house this small would probably be worth over $200,000 in a nice Seattle neighborhood. I did some math in my head and determined that there was no way I could live on real estate commissions here. I'd better get going on my writing career then, or else buy some tools.

I drove around for the rest of the hour, mostly thinking of things to talk to Sarah about during our date. I could ask her about the remodeling projects she was doing. And of course about her kids. I would interview her, like a writer would for an article. In my three-day-old writing career, I had been surprised by how much people love to talk about themselves. Even the shy ones just need a little encouragement. Sarah was hardly shy, and she definitely liked to talk about herself. I wondered what she would wear. Something tight, I hoped. And just a little bit revealing. And how would she wear her hair? Would it be all out, flowing over those beautiful sexy shoulders? I almost ran off the road thinking about it.

At about 5:30, I headed back to the motel. As I pulled into the parking lot, I saw Sarah, with her back to me, walking along the sidewalk carrying Taver. She was still wearing her short shorts, but now she had on a plaid shirt. Her hair was now in a pony tail. You'd better start getting ready, dammit, I said to the steering wheel. At five-fifty-five I was ready to go. I had shaved and put on my cleanest polo shirt and Levis, along with my Nike running shoes. I left my room and walked over to the office. When I got there, Andrea was behind the counter. "Hey Rob," she said with a friendly smile. "How's it going?" My throat tightened as I returned her greeting. I asked her if Sarah was around. "Oh, she's around here somewhere. She's watching my kids." She made no move to go find her.

"I was supposed to meet her," I said. "At six."

Andrea looked surprised. "Oh," she said. "Hang on." Then she walked back to the office door, pushed it open a foot and loudly yelled Sarah's name.

After about a minute, Sarah stuck her head through the door. She looked just the same as she had half an hour earlier. "Oh. Hi Rob," she said when she saw me. "Uh, how's it going?"

"I just came by," I said. "I thought we were going to go do something." In my mind I sounded like a pathetic wimp. I had this sudden fear that I had just dreamed this whole thing up. But then, by her face, I could tell that she remembered.

"Oh, yeah. You know what? I'm going to have to cancel on ya." I could see wheels spinning inside that pretty little head. "We're kinda busy here, and I need to stay and watch the kids."

"Oh, Okay. Well, that's alright." Now I needed to find a rock to climb under.

"Sorry, I'm just a 'seat-of-the-pants' sort of gal," she said."You can hang out here and visit if you want." She forced a big smile, and her cheery sing-song voice didn't change.

I begged off. "Well, I need to go get something to eat," I said. "Thanks though." And then I got out of there as quickly as I could.

Back in my orange motel room, I lay face down on the bed and didn't move for half an hour. I'd done it again. I'd let a woman completely emasculate me. I finally got up and went into the bathroom and soaked my face in cold water. I was actually feeling hungry, and I remembered Stacy's invitation. What the hell. I might as well have some kind of company.

CHAPTER THIRTEEN

S pending the evening with Stacy was a big step down from Sarah in my mind. Stacy was cute, but she was a little chunky and a little young, and I had no fantasy about spending the rest of my life with her. I found her number in my cell phone and pushed "send." She answered almost immediately. Hearing that Sarah had stood me up obviously cheered her up. "Curtis is here," she said. "He's sleeping, so we should go somewhere else."

"Let's go try the tavern. I could use a drink"

"Oh, I don't know. They have a pretty rough crowd in there."

"I'm from the big city," I said. "I think I can handle myself. Do they have fights there?"

"There was a gunfight about five years ago. No one was killed though."

"That's comforting. Meet you there in ten minutes?"

Stacy reluctantly agreed. I was ready to go, so I snuck past the motel office, hoping no one would see me, and then headed downtown on foot.

Melville's Tavern was on a side street, two doors down from Guns N Things. It was obviously a biker bar. Two Harley Davidson Road Kings were parked directly in front of the entrance, with an old Chevy pickup next to them. Two more V-twin motorcycles were parked across the street. Several other cars and trucks filled the rest of the parking spaces. I had told Stacy I would meet her in front so she didn't have to go in alone. As I walked past Melville's on the sidewalk, the door opened and a drunken couple staggered out with their arms around each other. The guy was a big farm boy, about 25, wearing cowboy boots and hat and a red plaid shirt. His blonde girlfriend had on a frilly sleeveless top and baggy blue jeans. She was kind of ugly. They ignored me as they passed by. Stacy came walking past the couple, looking the other way and shielding her eyes as they walked down the sidewalk toward Main Street. She had a disgusted look when she walked up to me. She said, "Ryan Jones was in Melville's? That's about right."

"You know them?"

"I went out with that jerk in high school. What a pig!"

"That's a good Chamber of Commerce attitude. Let's go in. I'm thirsty."

I held the door for Stacy and we walked into the almost full and very noisy bar. A country music song was playing that I didn't recognize. It had something to do with fast women and loose cars. Stacy looked mortified. "I can't believe I'm in here," she yelled over the noise. "Let's go to the back." Most of the tables, booths and barstools in the main room of Melville's were occupied, and many more people were standing. The room had a nautical theme, with white life rings and long oars hanging on the wall. Large fishing nets hung from the ceiling. A long wooden bar stretched along one wall of the main room, and a large ship's wheel dominated the wall beyond it. A doorway behind the bar led to a kitchen, which appeared to be in the adjacent building, behind a common wall. Near the back of the room was a split stairway, with a short flight leading down and another next to it leading up. Downstairs were two pool tables, with chairs and tables lining the walls. The pool tables were busy. The upstairs room had more tables and chairs. This room was about half full, and much quieter. We went up and took a table in the far corner where we could hold a conversation.

"Here's a business in Elephant that seems to be prospering," I told Stacy as we sat down. "The Chamber of Commerce should be proud."

"I've never been in here before," she said. "Honestly."

"It's not so bad. Everyone's having fun."

Sitting at the table, I faced the back wall and Stacy sat across from me, looking toward the front of the bar. Suddenly she froze and then screamed "Oh my God! Lindsay!" She jumped up and ran over to the cocktail waitress who had just walked up the stairs with a tray full of beer mugs. Lindsay also screamed when she saw Stacy and quickly set her tray down in front of two startled motorcyclists. Both girls jumped up and down and embraced, talking so fast they couldn't possibly have heard what each other said. Lindsay was thin and had short, straight Joan Jett black hair with a hint of purple in it. She was wearing a tight black tank top, black jeans and black velvet boots, along with heavy black eye makeup. She had tattoos on both arms and was wearing a lot of silver costume jewelry. Finally the girls released their embrace and Stacy came over to the table with an excited grin. "That's my best friend from high school," she said. "I haven't talked to her in two years. She went to college in Virginia and we kind of had a falling out. I didn't know she was back in town." Stacy was talking fast and actually shaking. "She's getting off in a few minutes and she'll come and visit. Oh Rob, this is unbelievable!"

"So it's a good thing we came then?" I asked.

"Oh my God! Oh my God!" Stacy started breathing deeply and tried to calm down.

"For someone who runs the Chamber of Commerce, there seems to be a lot going on around here that you don't know about," I said. Stacy gave me an angry look. "I'm just saying."

"I can't believe it," Stacy said then, shaking her head. "Lindsay was this sweet innocent virgin. And now look at her."

"I'm guessing she's not a virgin anymore."

"Very funny. In high school, I was the wild one. Lindsay was always trying to straighten me out. I guess maybe it worked too well."

We talked for a few minutes more about Lindsay and her and their fights over boyfriends. Then Lindsay came over to the table with her handbag. Stacy introduced us.

"So what are you guys eating," Lindsay said. "The pizza here's to die for."

"Pizza? That sounds awesome," I looked at Stacy and said "You didn't tell me they had pizza here." She ignored me.

"I'll get you guys a Moby," Lindsay said. "It's got everything. You'll love it."

"You like beer?" I asked Stacy.

"I did in college. A lot." She had a sly grin. "I haven't had a beer in months."

"Well you're having one tonight. I'm buying." I looked at Lindsay and she nodded, and then she disappeared to the kitchen. A card with Melleville's food menu was sitting on the table and I picked it up. The pizza list included various selections with different combinations of toppings. Each had a unique name, such as the Ahab, the Queequeg, the Ishmael, the Starbuck and the Pequod. The most expensive choice was the Moby Dick.

"Have you ever read Moby Dick?" I asked Stacy?

"Well, yeah, I read about half of it in college." She gave me a puzzled look. "It was kind of a guys' book."

"Look at this pizza list," I told her, handing her the menu. "Do you recognize those names?"

"Yeah, I guess."

"Melville's Tavern. Get it? Herman Melville wrote Moby Dick. All those pizza names are characters from the book. Except the Pequod. That was the ship."

"That's weird," said Stacy. "This tavern's owned by a guy named Rick Melville. He used to be a motorcycle gang member. And he went to jail for beating his wife. He's a total jerk."

"Hmmm. Well anyway, Moby Dick is my favorite book," I said. "And there's nothing better than good pizza and good beer. I think I'm going to like this place."

"Well, we'll see if the pizza's any good."

Lindsay returned to our table carrying three pints of ale. "This is a microbrew from up in Washington," she said. "It's really good. We just got it in."

Lindsay was right. "This is delicious," I said, after tasting the beer. "I hope the pizza's this good."

"It's better," said Lindsay. "Rick makes them all from scratch. Himself."

"I can't believe you're working for Rick Melville," Stacy told Lindsay. "Were you desperate for a job or what? You should have come and talked to me first."

"Stacy, didn't you know? I'm living with Rick."

Stacy was stunned and didn't say anything for a few seconds. She took a huge gulp of beer and then said, "Jesus fucking Christ, Lindsay. That guy abuses women."

Lindsay rolled her eyes. "Well, he's had anger issues, but we're working on that."

"Anger issues?"

"Stacy, he's really smart. And really sweet."

"And he's twice your age," Stacy said. "Isn't he 50?"

"Forty-nine," Lindsay said with a big smile. "But he's got the energy of a 48-year-old."

"You've really changed," said Stacy.

"Yeah, so have you," replied Lindsay, showing a bit of anger now herself.

They stared at each other and I said, "Well, college changes people. And that's a good thing. Right?"

"Yeah, I guess," said Stacy.

"All right then," I said. "So what did you girls do for fun in high school? I mean when you weren't fighting over boys?"

Both of them sat silently for a moment, and then Stacy said "Remember when we used to listen to Pink Floyd?"

"Yeah, Dark Side of the Moon," said Lindsay, "and you smoked all that dope."

I had to chime in. "Wait a minute. Pink Floyd?! How old are you two?"

"Twenty four," they replied, simultaneously.

I did some math in my head. "You weren't even born when that album came out," I said. "I was just a little kid, and I'm 20 years older than you."

"Well, it stood the test of time," said Lindsay.

I looked at Stacy. "You smoked pot in high school? In Elephant?"

"Man, you should have seen her," said Lindsay.

"Lindsay!"

"And we listened to the Beach Boys too," said Lindsay. "California Girls. Oldies were in then."

Stacy and Lindsay began talking about the parties they went to in high school and how Lindsay had to drive Stacy home when she got so drunk she couldn't walk. I listened for awhile. Then I asked both girls about their college. Stacy said she studied economics at Oregon. I told her I had gotten an economics degree at Washington. "I was a Husky. And you were a Beaver, right?" I asked her, knowing that that was the wrong mascot.

Stacy grinned at me "Nooo, I was a Duck."

Lindsay laughed out loud. Then she told us that she left the small private college she had gone to in Virginia and moved to New York. After taking a couple of years off, she enrolled at New York University in Manhattan. "I studied fine art," she said. "I wanted to run a gallery. I came home to visit my folks last Christmas. That's when I met Rick. At the bar down there."

"So you abandoned your art career?" I asked.

"I finished my degree and then came back. We'll see what happens. Rick says I should open an art gallery in Elephant."

"Oh yeah, right," Stacy replied sarcastically. "That would never work. You couldn't sell art in Elephant."

"Oh come on, Miss Chamber of Commerce," I said.

Just then a loud male voice yelled Lindsay's name from the kitchen. "That's Rick. Gotta go." Lindsay got up and said she'd come to Stacy's office sometime, and then walked off.

Stacy made a joke to me about how her secret former life had come out to a reporter. "So there's the headline for your article," she said. "How about 'Former Bad Girl Runs Chamber of Commerce'"

"I was thinking more like 'Former straight-A student and virgin runs off with motorcycle gang member'," I said.

"I like it!"

"So were you smoking pot when you read the first half of Moby Dick?" I asked.

"Very funny. No. But I smoked pot and read Tom Sawyer and Huckleberry Finn. Mark Twain's hilarious when you're stoned."

"He's pretty hilarious when you're not stoned, too."

"And there was this children's book called 'The Wind in the Willows'? With characters like Ratty and The Mole, and Toad of Toad Hall?"

"I've heard of it," I said.

"That was incredible. I read it over and over." Then she asked, "So you never smoked pot?"

"Oh, I didn't say that. I smoked pot like a fiend for about four years. But I was more into Steely Dan and The Cars. And Ken Kesey."

"One Flew Over the Cuckoo's Nest!" declared Stacy.

"Very good. Try reading that when you're stoned. Your brain will explode."

Stacy laughed. "You're funny." Then she got a dangerous look in her eye. "Are you married? I don't see a ring."

"Never been. Women scare me too much."

"Do you think you'll ever get married?"

"Well, I had a fantasy this afternoon about marrying Sarah. Before she flaked out on me."

"You men. No, seriously. I mean to a woman with some intelligence, and some common interests. Not just for her looks."

"Oh . . . right."

"Wouldn't you like to have kids sometime?"

"Maybe, but I'm getting a little old for that. What about you?"

"I did want kids," she said, "until Curtis started his little disappearing act. I never know if he's coming home or not. He won't tell me. Sometimes he just shows up, but most weeknights he doesn't. When he does, I can tell he's trying to sneak in and see if I'm cheating on him. He's totally jealous, but I'm sure he's sleeping with someone in Pendleton. I can just tell."

Stacy looked like she was going to cry now. "I don't know what I'm going to do, Rob," she said.

Right at that moment another waitress delivered the largest pizza I'd ever seen. It was mountainous. It was definitely the whale of pizzas. It was nearly two feet in diameter, and in the middle it was more than two inches thick. "Good God," I said. "We can't even eat a quarter of that." Then I ordered another round of beers. Stacy looked shell-shocked. "This is incredible," I said. "You should be promoting this at the Chamber of Commerce,"

She sat silently for a moment and drank more beer. Then she said, "You're right, there's a lot going on around here that I don't know about."

We each grabbed a giant slab of the Moby. Between bites, Stacy started asking me about Sarah. "So is it just her looks? Do guys really not care about anything else?"

I tried to be bluntly honest. "Well yeah, a lot of it's about her looks. OK, most of it. But it's not that simple," I said. "It's the whole presentation. It's like this pizza." Stacy scrunched up her face with skepticism, but I went on. "This pizza is good, but it reminds me of a woman who wears too much makeup and jewelry, and her boobs are too big. She's attractive, but everything's just a little out of proportion and overdone. This is sort of like a 'floozy' pizza."

Stacy laughed. "So what's Sarah?"

I smiled. "OK, here goes. Sarah is like one of those expensive gourmet pizzas. Just the right amount of toppings and sauce. And the crust is perfect. Everything's subtle, but the flavors are combined to perfection."

"Oh please!"

I went on. "With Sarah, there's no jewelry or make-up. And she's very self-confident and not self-conscious or trying too hard. The parts fit together perfectly."

"So then what about our brains?" Stacy asked. "What are they? Like anchovies? 'I'll take the works, but hold the brains, please'."

"That's very good," I said. "But that's not it. Sarah's got brains. She's not stupid. She knows how to fix stuff. And she can run the motel. And she seems to be a good mom."

"Maybe it's just that she's not educated."

"That's part of it," I said. "But I think it's more that she's not very worldly. She hasn't been to college or lived anywhere else. And she's not curious about the world; or about much of anything. She just has her little life here in Elephant."

Stacy looked even more skeptical, but I kept going. "Do you know that Sarah's the only person that I've talked to in Elephant that's never asked me about my article, or what I was going to write about? Everyone else is dying to know. The whole time I talked to her, I don't think she asked me any questions at all. She just talked about herself and her family."

"So that's why you want to marry her?"

"Ha ha. Good one. No," I said. "On those rare occasions when I'm thinking with my brain, I know that she's not wife material. But she's really sweet. And she's fun to talk to. Or should I say, listen to. And most importantly, I really think she likes me, even though she stood me up. You have to understand that, for a guy, being liked by a woman who's really beautiful is better than any drug that's ever been invented."

All the time I was talking, Stacy stared at me as if she thought I was nuts. I knew I might be digging myself a hole that would be hard to climb out of, and sure enough: "So what kind of pizza am I?" she asked.

"Hoo boy! I knew that was coming." I thought for a moment. "Would you be insulted if I told you that you're not fully cooked yet, so it's a little hard to tell?"

I might have avoided stepping in the hole, because Stacy laughed out loud. "That's hilarious," she said. "Do I really seem that young to you?"

"You don't seem young for 24. But you're 24."

She wasn't going to let it go. "But still, the toppings and crust and stuff are all there. Right? What kind do you think I'll be?"

She may not have been fully cooked, but I was starting to feel like I was. "Oh, I'm sure you'll be plenty tasty when you're done," I told her.

With her next statement, I knew Stacy was getting drunk. She looked at me with a big grin and said, "Really Rob? Do you think you'd want to eat me?"

"OK, what I think is, that it's time for us to change the subject," I said. "And you've had enough beer."

"Okay. I want to talk to you some more about your article," she said, drunkenly. Then she took another gulp of beer and gazed into my eyes.

"How about this," I said. "How about if I fix you breakfast in the morning and we can talk about the article then."

She got a big smile. "Does that mean I'm sleeping over?"

"No Stacy, I'm taking you home. You can come over in the morning. I have plenty of coffee too. You'll need it" She looked disappointed, but didn't say anything more. I asked the waitress for a box for the rest of our pizza, which was most of it. I helped Stacy down the stairs and then paid the bill at the bar. Stacy lived about five blocks west of Melville's, which was in the opposite direction from the motel, so I did a lot of walking that evening. When we got to her house, Stacy grabbed my arm and leaned in close, looking up at me with her lips ready for a kiss. I planted a light one on her forehead and pushed her toward the door. "See you in the a.m.," I said. She frowned and then turned and walked toward her front door, without saying anything more.

The next morning, Stacy didn't show up for breakfast and I was just as glad.

CHAPTER FOURTEEN

My plan on that beautiful Sunday morning was to avoid the motel office. My room was situated so that the window looked out in the opposite direction and I couldn't see the office entrance, but the fence along the side of the property made it so that if I wanted to walk downtown, I had to pass near the office. Therefore, that day I drove to the easily walkable downtown of Elephant, simply to avoid having a chance encounter with the beautiful woman who had stood me up the night before.

At the Elephant Grocery Store, I bought a package of frozen waffles and a bottle of syrup, along with more apples. Then I drove back to the motel to make more coffee and eat my breakfast. As I entered the parking lot, I saw Sarah out in front of the office, wearing conservative slacks and a blouse. Even in her church clothes she looked hot. This morning her long, slightly wavy hair was untied and flowed over her back and shoulders. I swallowed hard as she smiled and waved. I waved back but kept driving around the side of the motel to my room. And then I hurried inside. I turned on the lights and closed the curtains and tried not to think about Sarah naked. While the waffles were in the toaster, I flipped on the TV. I found a Mets-Phillies game and tried to shift my brain to baseball. The season wasn't even half over, but the Seattle Mariners were already out of the race. The Mets were pretty much out of it too, but the Phillies were a hot team, so I rooted for the Mets. When I turned on the game, the Mets were ahead three-nothing in the second inning.

I heated some syrup in the microwave and then realized I had no dishes to eat the waffles on. A sheet of paper on the table said that dishes were available from the office. That was out of the question. I looked around the room and found nothing suitable to serve waffles on other than a clean hand towel. So I folded the towel neatly and set it on the sheet of paper on the table. Then I placed the two hot waffles on the towel. I carefully poured the syrup so it filled the little waffle holes without spilling onto the towel. The waffles were still too dry, so I poured more on, drenching the waffles in syrup, along with the towel, the table and the sheet of paper that described how to get dishes. As I began eating the syrupy waffles with my fingers, I cursed all women for all the ridiculous things they cause me to do.

I had told Jonas I would meet him at Elephant Gas at 1:00. I thought about calling Stacy to check on her, but she probably already had an angry husband on her hands, so I decided to let it go. Getting a phone call from the guy she was with the evening before couldn't possibly make things better. And so, on this beautiful sunny perfect day, I sat in my orange room with the curtains drawn and watched TV. The Phillies tied the score in the bottom of the third inning on a three-run homer. The Mets' pitching coach come to the mound and yelled at the pitcher who had just given up the mammoth hit. The next two innings were scoreless.

Cabin fever overcame me at about noon. With the game still tied, I hustled out to the car and drove to Main Street. This time I saw no sign of Sarah or anyone else around the motel office. Back at the grocery store I bought a pre-prepared turkey sandwich that looked marginally edible. It came with separate packages of mayonnaise and mustard, which I applied liberally. I sat in my car in the parking lot and ate it and drank a Pepsi. Then I drove to the little gas station a block away and filled the Beemer.

For more than half an hour I drove around Elephant and out into the countryside with the warm air rushing through the open windows. Only a few people were walking on the street, and they all stared at me. I wasn't sure if it was the car or the dent, or just me.

At a few minutes before one-o'clock I drove into the Elephant gas parking lot. The left roll-up door on the shop building was open. In the morning sun, the giant elephant cast a perfect shadow on the front of the shop. Jonas was standing in the shade next to the maroon '67 Corvette. He was talking to another man who was at least six inches shorter and 30 years younger than he was. It was obviously Danny, the mechanic. Even though the temperature was well above 80 by now – and Jonas and I were both wearing shorts and flip-flops – Danny had on blue coveralls with long sleeves, and heavy black boots. He had black hair and olive skin and a very serious face. Jonas had on a blue Hawaiian shirt open halfway down his chest and Rayban sunglasses. He looked even more like a ponytailed Jeff Bridges than he did before.

The car's hood was up and Danny was describing something to Jonas with exuberance and a lot of hand motion. He seemed concerned, but Jonas didn't. Jonas gave me a friendly wave when I drove up and walked over to my car. He looked at the driver's door and then motioned Danny over. I introduced myself to Danny and he nodded and mumbled, "Hows't goin'?"

"Danny's going to give us an estimate on this," said Jonas. "It doesn't look like so much trouble to me. What do you think , Danny?"

Danny shook his head as if he thought the job were impossible. "German panels are expensive, man. I don't know."

"But it's doable if you've got the panel?" asked Jonas.

Danny motioned with his hands and declared "Oh, it's a piece a cake. Two-hour job. We can even re-use the trim. Just gotta get the panel." Then he looked at me. "So what was it that hit you?"

Jonas laughed out loud. "It was a girl," he said. "She kicked it with her foot."

"No shit? A girl did that? With her foot?" Danny looked at the dent and then looked at me with a big smile. "Dude, you musta pissed her off good."

"That's what I told him," said Jonas, "but he didn't even know her."

"Bummer," said Danny. "At least you shoulda got a good piece of ass for something like that, dude. A girl, huh?"

"A girl," I repeated. "She had legs like that elephant. I think she might have been one of those girls who kick footballs for the boy's team."

Jonas and Danny both laughed out loud. "You gotta stay away from that kind," Danny said.

OK, Danny boy," said Jonas. "You go check on that door, and write something up." Jonas started looking around at the rest of the car. "Put a total respray in there too. I'd say she's ready."

I protested and told Jonas I wasn't in a financial position to have my car painted. Probably not even to have the door fixed. I was just planning to drive it the way it was until my big apartment sale went through. Then I would probably just get another car. But Jonas said we should at least put numbers to it.

"Now, Mr. Smith," said Jonas, "you and me and Mister Sting Ray are going for a little ride. Danny gave the timing a tweak, so we need to try her out."

* * *

The maroon 1967 Corvette Sting Ray looked like it was brand new. The paint shined and the chrome was unblemished. I climbed into the black vinyl passenger seat, which was also perfect.

In the enclosed cabin of the Sting Ray, turning the ignition key caused only a mild rumble. It was nothing like the deafening roar of the black convertible I'd ridden in the day before. The car vibrated slightly. "This car has a completely stock 327," Jonas said, without having to raise his voice. "This whole car is box-stock." And then he said "The black '64 is kind of like a punk band, but this car's more like a symphony orchestra." Then Jonas reached for the dashboard and turned on the music. "The stereo's not stock though," he said. "This is my music car."

The clear full voice of Willie Nelson filled the interior of the car like we were in a concert hall. "Nice," I said.

"I'll bet you were expecting show tunes or Barbara Streisand or something, weren't you?" Jonas said with a smile. "I don't know how those queers can listen to that shit. I'd rather listen to some real men, like Willie or Merle Haggard." He grinned at me and backed the car very gently out of the shop, while Willie Nelson sang "Pancho and Lefty." We both rolled our windows down. Unlike the day before, Jonas raised the clutch slowly and we eased through town, past Billy on the sidewalk, and past the motel, and then out onto an empty country road. Jonas slowly increased our speed as we began climbing into some trees and the road began to curve.

"How's the timing feel?" I asked.

"There's just a bit of lag when I punch it," he said, as he punched it. My head snapped back as we went from 45 to 65 in about three seconds. "Well, not much," he said then, with a smile. "Even a stock Corvette can make your heart jump."

We drove for another few minutes without talking while Lefty left Mexico for a cheap hotel in Cleveland. The car glided effortlessly through the winding country road, and Jonas didn't push it. We cruised seamlessly and quickly, and the car seemed to be barely above idle. This was the kind of road this car was made for. Willie moved on to "Blue Skies", and we came to a stop sign and turned left. After about half a mile, an old barn and a large modern shop building that looked more like a warehouse appeared on the right. A moment later I could see a large white farmhouse further off the road on a little rise above the other buildings. Jonas eased off the gas and shifted down and we turned into the gravel driveway and drove toward the big shop building.

"An old farmer lives up there," he said, pointing to the house. "His name's Gus. He's a widower, and I rent this shop from him. It's where I keep most of the cars. It's a nice secluded spot where nobody bothers them."

"I think I met him," I said. "Is it Reemer?"

"Yeah, Reimer," he replied. "It rhymes with 'rhymer'."

In front of the house I saw the big Chevy pickup that Gus had driven when I met him at Stacy's office. Jonas turned off Willie and then reached under the seat. The giant roll-up door on the end of the big white shop building began to open. He looked over at me and smiled. "This is my toy box," he said. As the door rose, the lights in the big building automatically came on. Inside was what could only be called an automobile museum. The building was huge and held at least 20 cars. Several of them were Corvettes, but there were others as well. I saw a couple of old 1950s Chevys and an old Ford woody wagon. Most of the cars were American, but I also saw a Jaguar and a Volkswagen Bus. Jonas pulled the maroon Corvette up in front of the entrance and shut off the motor. "I have an obscenely expensive hobby," he said, smiling, "but it sure is fun." As we walked into the building I asked Jonas how many cars he had, and he said he wasn't sure, but there were about 30 total, and 22 or 23 were in this building. He told me he started buying cars in the '70s and some of the cars here he'd had over 30 years. Others he had purchased within the past year or two.

In this building, the lights were bright. There was no art on the wall and I didn't see any tools around. On the far wall, another door led out of the building. To the right of it was a refrigerator and a long table below some cabinets. "There must be over a million dollars worth of cars in here," I said.

Jonas nodded, and then said, "You know, that's true. But when Gus was running his farm, I guarantee you the equipment he kept in here – the combines and tractors – those were worth at least as much as these cars." Then Jonas started talking about Gus. "When Gus's son Charlie took over the farm after his mother died, he already had his own shop, so all the stuff got moved out of this one. No other farmer has a shop as big or as nice as this, so I told Gus it would be perfect for me, and he rented it to me."

I told Jonas about meeting Gus at the Chamber of Commerce office, and how it came out that Gus and Gladys the hairdresser had been high school sweethearts, and then hadn't talked since the 1940s. Jonas shook his head and smiled. "You know, there are all kinds of stories like that around here," he said. "There are so many grudges and feuds you couldn't even count 'em. Most of them are between relatives – fighting over land, or family estates or whatever. Either that or somebody got caught sleeping with somebody else's wife over at the no-tell motel, where you're staying. You know, those Hockensmith's would probably be broke if it weren't for all the affairs that go on around here. They even have a special hidden parking spot for, you know, special guests."

I started looking at the Jaguar that was parked in the right front corner of the shop. It was a dark green E-Type convertible that looked perfect. "That's a '63," said Jonas. "A lot of people consider this the most beautiful car ever made. I bought it in '70 and it was my main car for five years. I paid 2,500 bucks for it. It was in L.A. until three years ago. I had it restored there and then drove it up here." He smiled. "That was fun."

Jonas told me that Danny was excellent with restorations on American cars, but he had his foreign cars that needed major restoration done in California. "But don't worry," he said, "he can handle the door on your car."

As we walked out toward the middle of the shop, Jonas said "Check this one out." He pointed to a beautiful red Camaro convertible. "I just got this '69 last year. Danny painted it a couple of weeks ago. It's the first car I've bought in Elephant. Some old guy from town had parked it in a farmer's barn and just left it. He kept saying he'd get it out of there, but he never did. When he died, I got hold of his daughter and she offered it to me too cheap. I insisted that she take more than she was asking, but it was still a steal."

Just then a door in the back of the shop opened and Gus Reimer walked in. "Hello Jonas," he said. "Showing off the museum, I see." Gus seemed more relaxed now than he had been in Stacy's office.

"We have a celebrity in town," Jonas said. "Did you meet Mr. Smith?"

Gus smiled and admitted that he had met me. Then he reached out and squeezed my right hand like he was cutting barbed wire with a pair of dikes. "Good to see you again, Gus," I said, as my eyes began to water.

"Let me show you Gus's car," said Jonas. "We're doing a little trade." We walked to the back left corner of the building, near the door Gus had just come through.

"It's a Plymouth," said Gus. "Bought it new in Pendleton in '51, after Eunice and I got married." The car's color was a combination of light green and the copper color of surface rust. It had an odd shape, with two doors and a short roof ahead of a trunk that was too long.

"It's a 'business coupe'," said Jonas. "There's no back seat. This was a sporty unit back in the day, huh Gus?"

"I wanted to have the sharpest car in town," Gus replied. "And I did, until Merle Smock got his Lincoln two months later." He was laughing now. "I didn't speak to him for two years after that," he said. "I sold this car in '55 to Eunice's cousin Roy right after our son was born. It changed hands a couple more times. Sometime in the late '60s, the kid who owned it got killed in Viet Nam. Real sad. His mother put it in their barn and it sat there until last year, when Jonas heard about it. When he found out I was the original owner, he told me about it and I figured I'd better buy it back. I had no idea it was still in town."

"What a story," I said. "So you're going to restore it?"

"It's Danny's next project," said Jonas.

Just then, the faint sound of thunder began to build outside the building. The roar became louder, but it wasn't a storm rolling in. "I think Danny's come to join us," Jonas said. He told us that he had asked Danny to bring the black convertible out to the farm and take the newer yellow car in to get it ready for a road trip.

The black '59 roadster rolled up to the shop and shook the ground. Danny had a big smile on his face and let the car idle for a moment, revving it gently. Then he shut it off. "Is it tea time?" he yelled from the driver's seat. "And I don't mean golf."

Jonas looked at Gus. "Spot of tea, Gus?" he asked.

"Don't mind if I do," Gus replied.

Then Jonas smiled at me. "Smith, we have a little tradition around here," he said. "It's called the men's tea party. It was Danny's idea, since he doesn't drink coffee."

"I like tea," I said.

CHAPTER FIFTEEN

"**G**us, I think it's your turn to be hostess," Jonas said. Gus nodded and walked toward the back of the building to start heating water. Gus was wearing a light blue short-sleeve oxford shirt and dark blue slacks that rode a little too high. And he had on red and white running shoes that squeaked on the concrete floor. "Come on, let's get the table up," said Jonas. The rest of us followed Gus to the back corner near the refrigerator. Jonas pulled out a dark brown folding table with a fake wood grain plastic top and a stack of four white plastic patio chairs, and set them out in the corner. We were next to the Volkswagen Bus and a 1950s Ford pickup that was unrestored. The bright florescent tubes gave everything in the big room a harsh glare. The electric kettle soon whistled and Gus poured the boiling water into a large ceramic teapot containing several tea bags. Jonas set out four cups and saucers and brought over a small pitcher, a sugar bowl and a jar of honey. Then he opened a cabinet and brought out a white bud vase with a single red plastic rose in it, set it in the middle of the table and said, "This is our phallic rose."

Gus picked up the pitcher and offered it to me. "Cream?" he asked.

"Got any milk? I normally use skim milk."

Jonas stared at me with an exasperated look. "No, we ain't got no skim milk. Be a man, Smith. Put cream in your tea."

I gave in and Danny and Gus both laughed as they waited for the pitcher. All four of us were soon slouched comfortably back in our plastic chairs, holding our cups and saucers. "Now this is a proper tea party," Jonas said as he adjusted the rose so it was exactly in the center of the table. "So ladies," he said, "what shall we talk about?"

I looked at Gus. "Gladys told me she knew you a long time ago Gus," I said.

Jonas smiled and looked at him. "That's right, Gus. Speaking of people who refuse to speak to each other, was Gladys really your high school sweetheart?"

"Well, that cat's out of the bag," Gus said with a smile. He was clearly embarrassed.

"You mean you've lived in the same town all these years and never spoken to each other?" asked Danny.

"Gladys and my wife were sworn enemies," Gus said. "Eunice was sure Gladys would never forgive her for stealing me away like she did." Gus went on to explain how he had changed his mind about which girl he wanted to marry after he had left for the war. "After Eunice and I got married, the only way to keep the peace at home was to stay the hell away from Gladys," Gus said. "It just got to be a habit, I guess. Still is."

"But you and Gladys are bachelor and bachelorette now," said Jonas. "Don't you ever think about calling her up to talk about old times?"

"You could have her cut your hair," I said, looking at Gus's full head of gray hair. "She cut mine yesterday."

"I can tell," said Gus. "I recognize the haircut." Then Gus got a look in his eyes that told us the conversation on that topic was nearing its conclusion. "No gentlemen, I appreciate your concern," he said. "But I'm a little too old to start worrying about that sort of thing. I've often thought I made the wrong choice back then, when I was overseas. Goodness knows Eunice could be a difficult woman. But you can't un-ring a bell. Besides, Charlie'd kill me if I started something like that."

So that was that. I looked around at the Corvettes and the other cars in Jonas's museum. I asked him what model years his Corvettes were. He said that they ranged from 1954, the second year Corvettes were made, up to 2001.

"That one's a Z06," Danny said enthusiastically of Jonas's newest

Corvette. "It's basically a racecar. A car almost identical to that one won its class at Le Mans that year."

As I admired the cars, Jonas asked me what I thought of Elephant so far. I told him I thought it was a very comfortable place, but I wasn't sure it was magazine-worthy. "I bet you never thought you'd find babes like those Hockensmith sisters in a place like this," he said.

"No shit," I said. "That Sarah's already turned my brain to mush. We were supposed to have a date last night, but she stood me up."

"I went out with her sister in high school a few times," said Danny. "But then she hooked up with some football player, and that was the last anyone saw of me – with her, at least." He smiled

"Women who look like those two don't understand the effect they have on men," said Jonas. "They're living on a different planet." Then he smiled. "Of course I mean straight men. But the same goes for queers." He smiled toward Gus. "The really hot ones are mostly jerks."

"When Sarah told me she couldn't go out last night, she said she was a 'seat of the pants kind of gal', whatever the hell that means," I said.

"That's just a nice way of saying she's a flake," Jonas said. "Anyway, you're better off. I mean, look at Carl. You want to end up like him?"

"Boy, what a chump that guy is," said Danny. "But what the hell. He got to see her naked."

"You boys," said Jonas. "Smith here said the same thing yesterday. How much misery are you guys prepared to put yourselves through to see a woman like her naked? It's pretty pathetic, when you think about it."

"Oh, I could be pretty miserable," I said with a big smile.

"No shit," said Danny. "Your pecker can ruin your life if you're not careful. Look at Carl. He's a perfect example."

Then Gus spoke up for the first time in several minutes. "I'll tell you guys a secret I've never told anyone. If you want to hear it," he said.

We all wanted to hear it and we leaned forward in our chairs as Gus spoke.

"All the time we were sweethearts in high school, Gladys and I never slept together. Things were different then," he said with a grin. "The night before I shipped out to Hawaii in '44, I tried to get Gladys to sleep with me and she wouldn't. She told me she was still a good girl. I guess she said something about it to her best friend, because a few hours later got a phone call from Eunice. Let's just say I was a happy camper on the flight out." He had a huge schoolboy smile now. "But that changed everything, and not necessarily for the better."

The three of us sat there silently, looking at Gus. Then Jonas said, "Holy shit, Gus!"

Gus continued. "All the time I was in the Navy, all I could think about was Eunice and how good she made me feel that night. I was so lonely. Gladys kept writing me letters, and I don't think she ever knew what happened with Eunice and me. But I just wasn't interested in her after that. So I ignored her, and I proposed to Eunice in a letter. That's my penis story, boys."

We all sat silently for a moment more. Then I said, "Yup, those little fellas are nothing but trouble."

"I jumped out of an airplane once to get laid," said Jonas. "He was beautiful, and it was worth it. But I don't think I'd do it again." We all laughed.

I decided it was time to change the subject. "So do you guys think the Mariners are out of it for the year? I watched them stink up Safeco Field Friday night."

"Are they losing now?" Jonas asked. "I don't follow baseball much."

Gus spoke up. "I quit following baseball about the time they got the designated hitter," he said. "I guess I'm a purist. I think pitchers should hit."

"They didn't always have designated hitters?" Danny asked.

"They started that in the American League in '69," said Gus. "I still remember what a controversy it was."

"I wasn't even born then," Danny said, looking slightly embarrassed. We all looked at him like we were very annoyed, but didn't say anything. "Most of these cars in here are older than me," he said.

"OK, time to change the subject again," Jonas said, with a laugh. "So what did you end up doing last night, Smith?"

"I went to Melville's. With Stacy."

"Melville's," said Danny. "Man, did you have a Moby?"

"Yeah, between us we ate less than half of it. I think I'll be having it for dinner tonight. And maybe again for breakfast."

"That Stacy's a cutie, huh Smith?" Jonas said.

"She might be single soon, when she dumps that loser she's married to," said Danny."

"She's a little young," I said. "But she's definitely lonely." I explained how Stacy got drunk and needed an escort home.

"A guy like you looks good to a young girl like her, you know," Jonas said. "Women are like high performance sports cars, Smith. You know, like Corvettes. They're beautiful and sexy and fun when they're new. But they require a lot of maintenance. And after they've got some mileage on them, they really need somebody who can take care of them properly. You know, like a mechanic. Otherwise they fall apart. I think that's about where Stacy's at now."

"That's really profound Jonas," said Danny. "For a gay guy, you seem to have a real feel for women."

"Hey, relationships are relationships," Jonas said. "I've played the mechanic a few times."

"So what about Sarah?" I said. "She doesn't seem to need taking care of at all."

"I don't know Smith. I sort of just made all that up on the spot," laughed Jonas.

"I know," said Danny. "It's that family. Her mom and her sister are like her mechanics. She doesn't need a guy. And besides that, she knows how to fix stuff herself."

Then Gus spoke up. "When they were in high school, Sarah Ellington was Charlie Junior's girlfriend. She was a looker, even back then."

"No Gus, we're talking about Sarah Cline," said Danny. "Carl's ex. You know, Carl Cline, the cop?"

"One and the same," said Gus. "Her name was Ellington before she married Carl." Then Gus thought for a minute. "You know, old Peter Ellington was her grandfather. He and Hollister McCune built the big elephant."

"You mean my elephant?" asked Jonas.

"Who's Peter Ellington?" Danny asked.

"He was Hollister McCune's partner in the gas station," Gus said. "They put up the big elephant in 1960. Then they got into a big fight and Hollister kicked him out of the partnership. I guess old Peter got almost nothing. Hollister was not a likeable man."

"People sure do fight around here," said Danny. "So does that Hollister guy still own Elephant Gas? Is he still alive?"

"Yeah, he has it in a trust," said Jonas. "My partner Phil's law firm is the trustee. That's how I ended up renting it."

"So where's Hollister?" Danny asked.

"He's in a nursing home in L.A. from what I hear," said Gus. "He hasn't been to Elephant in many years; since the station closed back in the eighties."

"And Old Peter's dead, right?" Jonas said.

"Nobody knows," said Gus. "His son Johnny, Sarah's real father, he was a big problem. When those girls were little, he ran off with some motorcycle babe and left Millie high and dry. She made Peter's life so difficult that he took off soon after that, and nobody's seen hide nor hair of either one of them in 25 years."

"So Millie remarried then I guess," I said, after being silent and just listening for several minutes.

"Yeah, old Bob Hockensmith has been a rock for her and those girls," Gus said.

"So what did you say Sarah's name was before she got married?" I asked Gus.

"Ellington. Like Duke, the jazz player."

"That's really weird," I said. "I have a client named Doris Ellington. That's kind of an unusual name. She's the bitch of the century. I hope she's not related to Sarah." That seemed to put a damper on the conversation.

The other three men sat silently for a minute. Then Danny spoke. "I'll tell you one thing. That Stacy was a wild child in high school," he said. "My little brother was in her class. I think she screwed him and most his friends. She was like their sex education teacher."

"She's obviously changed," I said. I told them about Stacy's friend Lindsay and Rick Melville. We decided Lindsay was a perfect example of the "girl needing a mechanic" syndrome.

Finally Jonas said. "Smith, I need to tell you about our plan for your car. We're going to need to keep it here for a few days."

"What do you mean?"

"Danny's got the door panel ordered, and he's ordered the paint in the original BMW color. And don't argue with me."

"But I can't afford that."

"It's on the house," he said. "But there's something you have to do for me in return."

"No sexual favors," I said.

Jonas shook his head and didn't laugh. "Here's the deal," he told me. "Old Jonas and his cars get left out of your little magazine story. And there's no need to mention our ladies' gabfest here either. Everything that was said here stays here. Capiche?"

"I don't know what to say, Jonas," I said. Then I smiled. "I'll make that deal, but I don't know what the hell I'm going to write about. And what am I supposed to do without a car. I have to go back to Seattle in a couple of days."

"I can't help you with the first problem," said Jonas. "But I can with the second. You ever drive a race car cross country?"

"Just my Beemer. They used to race those."

"I'm talking about the oh-one Corvette," he said. "You think you could handle that for a week?" I sat stunned for a moment, and then told Jonas that I would do my best not to kill myself. "Can you come back next weekend?" he asked. "It's Fourth of July. There's some big doin's here."

"Yeah," said Danny. "There's a big picnic. And fireworks. The whole town turns out. You should come back for it."

"Compared to Seattle, it's probably not very impressive," said Jonas. "But we all have fun."

I thought about the fact that I would probably end up spending the Fourth with Charles and his annoying wife. Coming back to Elephant would mean another weekend of avoiding Sarah, but I agreed.

The men's tea party went on for another ten minutes or so, mostly covering topics relating to cars and farm equipment and cleanliness. I listened as Danny explained what one speck of dust can do to fresh paint on a car and Gus explained how important it is to keep hydraulic lines on a tractor clean. "So it's sort of like having sex on the beach then?" asked Danny. "Getting sand in there can cause a lot of, uh, difficulties?"

"Yes, something like that," said Gus, with an annoyed look on his face.

Then we all put our dishes away, along with the chairs and the table. We said goodbye to Gus, and Jonas and I got back in the Sting Ray. Danny stayed to swap the black Corvette for the newer yellow one. As we headed back toward town, Willie Nelson resumed singing. Jonas tried to explain to me how a Corvette, with a light fiberglass body and a big heavy engine in front can be prone to under steer. I thought maybe he was having second thoughts about letting me take his car to Seattle, but he didn't change his mind. Back at Elephant Gas, Jonas told me to check with him the next morning and he'd have Danny's information about repairing the Beemer's door. I spent the rest of that Sunday avoiding the beautiful Sarah.

CHAPTER SIXTEEN

"It seems like I keep having to apologize to you," Stacy said, as I sat in her office at 9:05 on Monday morning. "I was so excited that you were coming to Elephant to write about us, and I've done nothing but make a fool of myself since you got here." Her face was pale and seemed weighed down by the puffiness around her eyes.

"So I have an idea," I said, ignoring her comment. "You know that horrible restaurant down the road?" Stacy laughed and nodded. "I'll bet they have pancakes for breakfast. We haven't done our interview for the article yet. How about we do it over breakfast?"

Stacy started to object, but then she dropped her shoulders and smiled and said, "What the heck. Maybe our third time out will be the charm."

"How bad can they screw up pancakes? I mean really?"

Cybil was standing near the entrance of the Moss Creek Inn giving her gum a workout when we walked in. She ignored us as she grabbed a coffee pot and headed to the only occupied table in the place. "We can just sit," Stacy said, walking toward a booth by the window. "And I'm actually going to eat here for once. I'm starved. I haven't eaten since Melville's."

"Yeah, that gut bomb pizza held me for awhile too," I said.

"Well it didn't hold me. Or I guess I should say, I didn't hold it. It ended up in the toilet right after you took me home."

The cigarette odor in the Moss Creek Inn's dining room was a bit less oppressive, and the mixed aromas of bacon grease and coffee smells livened the place up. I told Stacy I wanted as many pancakes as I could get, so she walked over to the kitchen door where Cybil was standing and ordered our breakfast. After she sat down again, we started out talking – mostly about Curtis. Stacy told me she had slept on the couch the night after Melville's and that he confronted her at 6:00 Sunday morning and tried to start a fight. She ignored him and pretended she was sleeping. When he didn't give up, she suddenly exploded in a rage and told him she knew about his girlfriend in Pendleton. She was bluffing, she said, because she didn't really know for sure he had one, even though she suspected it. But he fell for it. After a few more accusations between them, he left, slamming the door and breaking a window. That was the last she had heard from him. "I called Sarah this morning and she's over there right now fixing the window," said Stacy. "You can go over there if you want to talk to her."

"No, I'm avoiding her," I said.

"Good idea," she said. "And I'm done with Curtis. I'm changing the locks. From now on I'm just going to be a single working girl and forget about men." I told her that that was a drastic move and she seemed pretty calm about it. "Don't worry, I'll totally fall apart later. But it's Okay." She said it with a smile. "I've got that routine down."

I asked Stacy about the City Council meeting that evening where the public could comment on whether the big elephant should be a historic landmark. I told her I had planned to drive back to Seattle that day, but then decided I couldn't miss that meeting. This time, she didn't try to argue with me.

"The whole town's going to be there," she said. "I think only about five people around here care about that elephant and want to save it. But they're a very influential group and they're making a lot of noise. Nobody else cares that much either way. Personally, I don't either anymore."

Just then, Cybil brought my stack of pancakes and Stacy's toast and honey. She had earlier poured us each a cup of thin black coffee that had almost no flavor. Next to my pancakes she set down a stained plastic squeeze bottle that contained some sort of brown liquid that looked like used motor oil.

"I came prepared," I said. After Cybil disappeared into the kitchen, I reached into the right cargo pocket of my shorts and pulled out a small bottle of real maple syrup that I had bought earlier for my waffles. Stacy's left hand, holding her toast, froze in front of her mouth as she watched me drench my pancakes with the good syrup. "I hate dry pancakes," I said. "And I also hate bad syrup." I did an exaggerated "look-both-ways" with my head and then recapped the bottle and returned it to my pocket. "There now."

Stacy put her toast down and laughed out loud. "I don't know why I'm so worried about embarrassing myself," she said. "You're a goofball."

"You know," I told her between bites, "After many years, I finally figured out that about ninety-five percent of what I do looks really stupid to other people. But that's true for everybody. Once you get that worked out in your head, everything's easier. You just quit worrying about it."

"It's really sad, but that might be the most profound thing I've learned in my life up to now," she said, smiling.

"Seriously Stacy, start watching other people. If you really pay attention to them, you'll see that most of what they do is pretty dumb. And yet they're happy to keep doing it. I mean look at Gladys. All that pink shit she's got. It's awful, and yet she's just as happy as she can be to show it off. You gotta hand it to her."

"And that Sarah," said Stacy, "Strutting around telling everyone how pretty she is. She makes me sick."

"Careful," I said. "You're talking about the woman I love."

"Sorry, she's just been getting on my nerves lately."

Stacy and I never did our interview, but she was in a much better mood when she told me she needed to get back to the office, and left me with half my pancakes. I stayed and finished them, and then I left the restaurant and drove the Beemer across the street and around the elephant's legs and parked in front of Jonas's shop. Jonas was gone, but Danny had the yellow 2001 Corvette ready for me. It was parked, freshly washed, in front of the shop door, facing the road. I handed him the Beemer key and he said he should have it all ready to go by the following Saturday. Then he handed me the key to the race car. "You'd better go out and practice a bit this afternoon. This is a death machine. It'll kill you if you let it. Of course Jonas has insurance, so don't worry about that," he said with a grin.

"Thanks a lot," I said. "I'll go out for a little ride this afternoon. If I survive that, I should be good to go."

I asked Danny if he was going to the meeting that night and, to my surprise, he said yes. "I want to see what happens. I'll miss the old girl if they take her down," he said, looking up at the giant fiberglass elephant. "I've decided she's a girl. No pee-pee, you know?" I walked over to the yellow car. "Have fun," Danny said, as he walked toward the BMW.

This newer Corvette was much more civilized than the 1950s and 60s versions I'd ridden in earlier. The driver's door was thinner and lighter, and everything in the interior was plastic and modern. This was an exotic modern car. It felt like going from Detroit to Disneyland. But when I turned the key, I was back in the Motor City. The monster race engine exploded to life, more like the black convertible did. The car shook, but the interior was more insulated than the older cars had been. This car had an automatic transmission, which slid easily into drive. I let up on the brake and the car rolled easily out of the driveway and past the elephant.

Danny had already filled the tank, and for the next two hours I went sightseeing. The farm roads around elephant were nearly empty on this Monday morning. The wheat fields were golden, and the farmers hadn't yet begun to harvest their crops. A couple of times I stopped on a long straight section and then punched the gas. The wide rear tires barely spun, but my head snapped back like I was in a rocket ship. Danny told me later that the car was equipped with something called "launch control", which is like the opposite of anti-lock braking. "A car can actually accelerate much faster when the wheels aren't allowed to spin," he had said. As I settled in behind the wheel of my new toy, I felt like I had finally found my calling. I had had more fun in my three days as a writer than in three years selling real estate. At noon I went back to the motel to try and actually write something.

* * *

Four hours and two discarded rough drafts later, I eased the yellow Corvette into the parking lot at the Elephant School District Gymnasium. It was about five minutes until seven and at least 40 cars were already there.

Several more were approaching as I arrived. The gymnasium building looked like a big brick barn with an arched roof. People were talking and laughing as they walked toward it. Inside, dozens of people milled around and visited in the hallway next to the big gym. This could have been a basketball championship game rather than a small town government meeting. Inside the gym, the collapsible bleachers were pulled out and spectators were already spread across them. A few tables were set out on the gym floor. Everyone in the gym appeared to know that they needed to remove their shoes, so I followed suit. The entire meeting took place with all participants and spectators in their stocking feet.

On the wall at the end of the basketball court was a sheet of rolled out butcher paper with lettering crudely scrolled on it. It read: "Save the Elephant!" I could hear the clicks and squeaks of a PA system being set up.

Near the end of the row of bleachers, I saw Eve Breneau, the proprietor of Guns-N-Things, sitting on the lowest bench with her farmer husband. Gladys, Ruth, Bea and Beverly sat together in the exact middle of the gym on the lowest bench. A lot of activity was taking place at the far end of the gym near the top of the bleachers. Children of varying ages were talking and yelling and climbing on the bleachers. The two beautiful mothers, Sarah and Andrea were trying to keep the children calm, including several who weren't theirs. Gus and some other older men stood in the doorway to the gym, removing their shoes. I saw Billy sitting alone at the top of the bleachers above me. I didn't know most of the people in the gym, but almost everyone stared at me as I walked in. The squeaky microphone became even squeakier as an older gray-haired gentleman stepped up and began fiddling with it. He put his lips against it and the words "testing, testing" exploded out of the speakers on the wall above the bleachers. Kids and adults alike put their hands over their ears. "Oh, excuse me" came out equally loud and squeakily.

A younger woman, probably in her 30s, came up to the microphone and said "Mr. Mayor, let me help you." The mayor looked befuddled as he stepped aside while the woman made a quick adjustment. The squeaks stopped immediately and the words "here you go, Mr. Mayor," came out at a perfect volume. "Just speak into it normally," she told him.

"Thank you Marla," said the mayor. He leaned into the microphone and still spoke too loudly. "Let's all rise and say the Pledge of Allegiance."

A large American flag hung on the wall at the end of the gymnasium opposite the "Save the Elephant" sign, above the basketball hoop. The crowd on the floor and in the bleachers rose to its feet with the muffled sound of socks shuffling. People who were still entering the gym stopped and collected around the door. Hats came off and hands went to chests. The words of the pledge were mumbled almost incoherently. The shuffling was repeated as everyone sat and new participants entered the room. "Let's everyone get seated now. We need to begin," the Mayor said impatiently. He was short, with a light blue and maroon plaid shirt stretched over his large belly. His face had a permanent red cast, and he had gray hair greased back and silver-rimmed glasses that were too large for his face. Many people in the room ignored the Mayor and he began to look annoyed. The bleachers were filling up, and people greeted each other. Some shook hands or hugged. The slam of one of the doors could be heard, and then it immediately opened up again. "Everyone please be seated," the mayor shouted into the microphone now. Once more he was mostly ignored.

On the gym floor, the City Council members were lined up along one side of two long metal tables. Each had a name plate in front of him or her. Seven council members were present. "I now call this meeting of the Elephant City Council to order," the Mayor declared over the din of the crowd.

CHAPTER SEVENTEEN

The bleachers in the Elephant School District Gymnasium were half full when the Elephant City Council meeting was called to order. Many people sat with their shoes in their laps, while others left theirs in the large group that filled a corner of the gym. The mayor stood at the podium in his socks and began with some small talk about how rare it was for all seven members of the City Council to be in attendance at once. He thanked everyone for coming to the school gym, rather than the City Council meeting room at City Hall. The meeting had been moved to the gym because a large crowd was expected. The minutes of the previous council meeting were approved along with several expense vouchers. A rumbling of complaints rolled through the crowd as the Mayor announced that committee reports would be heard before the public hearing for the Historic Preservation Commission.

As the meeting began, I sat by myself on the bottom bench of the bleachers at the opposite end from the Hockensmith sisters. People continued to arrive at the gym by ones and twos. At about ten after seven, Jonas walked in. He removed his flip-flops and left them near the door. He saw me and walked over in his bare feet and sat to my left. Several people acknowledged him and waved, and he did the same. "No fireworks yet?" he asked in a whisper after he sat down. I shook my head and then he added, "They're coming. Trust me."

Less than a minute later, Stacy entered the same door and slipped off her pumps. She carried them in her hand as she walked over to the bleachers. She wore the same light green suit and nylons she had had on at breakfast. She greeted Jonas and me and then sat to my right. "Everyone seems calm," she said.

"Just wait," said Jonas.

The chairman of the Public Works Committee, a short wiry man with a crew cut and the nickname "Buzz" on his nameplate, reported that the city had been turned down by the state of Oregon for a grant to resurface Elephant's Main Street. This was the third year in a row that the grant had been declined, he said. A few boos came from the crowd. "The state doesn't give a rip about little towns in eastern Oregon," said Buzz excitedly. "They'd just as soon we died off. But we're not going to, are we folks?!" Buzz got a few no's, but otherwise the crowd seemed to get quieter.

Reports from the Parks and Recreation Committee, the Finance Committee and the Cemetery committee followed. It was reported that sales of plots at the city cemetery were 50% below the first half of the previous year, and that the demise of a few more of Elephant's citizens in the near future would be a big help to the city's finances. This was said as a joke by the only woman on the council, but it got only a few chuckles. The mayor then asked if any members of the public wished to make a comment. He stressed that these should be unrelated to the upcoming public hearing on the big elephant, since comments on that topic would be taken separately later.

Helen, from Muriel's Hardware raised her hand. Before the Mayor could even call on her, she said, "Mister Mayor, I'd like to present my idea for the restoration and development of Elephant Gas."

The Mayor interrupted her. "Helen, I just said that we will address the issue of historic preservation of the elephant during the hearing later."

"Oh, I'm sorry mister Mayor." Helen continued to stand for a few seconds and then sat down.

A thin gentleman in his thirties with a beard and long dark brown hair stood and raised his hand. He was wearing a blue plaid flannel shirt, even though the temperature outside was still in the eighties and the air conditioner in the gym was losing its battle.

"Yes Woodrow," said the Mayor, with an exasperated expression.

"What is it now?"

Woodrow spoke in a demanding tone. "Mayor, the police are spying on the people of Elephant and I want something done. Yesterday I saw an officer peering into my bedroom while I was sleeping."

"Woodrow, we've been over this before. If you have a concern about local law enforcement, you need to…"

Before the Mayor could finish his sentence, someone from the crowd yelled "I have a concern about local law enforcement. We don't have any!" A number of people in the crowd cheered at that. I looked up in the corner of the bleachers where the beautiful Sarah was sitting and saw that she was clapping and cheering now. Her ex-husband, Carl, was sitting in uniform in the front row of the bleachers staring straight ahead with a frown.

"Let me remind members of the audience," said the Mayor, "that we must respect the institutions of our government. Outbursts like this are uncalled for." This caused a number of other outbursts from the stocking-footed bleachers. The Mayor waited silently for the crowd to quiet and then continued. "As I was saying, Woodrow, You need to take up your concerns with the County Sheriff's office in Pendleton. This is not a city government issue."

As the mayor spoke to Woodrow, Jonas leaned over to me and whispered. "Woodrow's our local nut job. He forgets to take his medication and then he imagines a lot of bad things. He thinks Carl's trying to take over the world."

"Are there any more comments?" asked the Mayor, ignoring Woodrow as he continued to stand in the bleachers with his hand raised."

An older woman raised her hand and began asking questions about the government grant to repave Main Street. "Let's get on with it!" yelled someone else in the crowd. Several others agreed and a loud commotion began. The Mayor had a gavel on the table and he grabbed it now and began banging it, which only made the crowd louder. He said something into the microphone, but it was drowned out by the crowd. Then he pointed toward the ladies in the center of the front row of the bleachers. From that group, Bea rose and walked purposefully to the podium where the Mayor was standing, still banging his gavel. She stood there silently, staring up at the crowd. The Mayor shook his head angrily and walked back to his seat. The crowd began to quiet. After another minute, the gym became almost completely silent. Bea stepped forward and leaned into the podium. She was barely five feet tall and she had to reach up to bend the microphone toward her face. She began to speak, but no sound came from the speakers. "We can't heeeear yooooou," came a shout from the audience. Then laughter.

"Ladies and gentleman, can you hear me now?" Bea's squeaky voice was barely audible.

"Yes," came a few voices. "Yell louder," came the original heckler's voice.

"Ladies and gentlemen," Bea said again, a little more clearly now. "Oh. Wait just a moment." She then reached into a pocket in her blue and white dress and pulled out a single folded up piece of paper. She opened it and reached out just below her chin to spread it out on the top of the podium.

"Ladies and Gentlemen," Bea said yet a third time. "As Chairwoman of the Elephant Historic Preservation Commission, I want to thank you all for coming out tonight to discuss the preservation of Elephant's most important and cherished landmark."

"It's an eyesore. Tear it down!" came another yell from the audience. It was the same heckler again.

Bea looked annoyed, but continued after a pause. She read the words in a monotone voice directly from the piece of paper in front of her. "Fifty years ago next month, Hollister McCune and Peter Ellington, two of Elephant's most important businessmen, made an investment in the future of Elephant. They had a vision for a landmark that would bring pride and recognition to the fine people of this town." Bea went on reading her glowing description of the big gray elephant and its creators, and the selfless sacrifice they supposedly made for the town by building it.

Soon the heckler chimed in again: "Bullcrap, they were businessmen. They just wanted to sell more gas than Joe Mark. They didn't do it for the town."

"Hector, the public will have its opportunity to speak tonight," Bea said calmly. "Please hold your comments until the designated time for public comments."

"He's right," yelled a female voice from near where Hector spoke. "They were capitalists. They weren't thinking about the town." A combination of cheers and boos came from the crowd.

Bea looked up to where Hector and his lady-friend were sitting, but didn't respond. She continued reading from the paper in front of her. After describing in great detail the importance of the big elephant and how it was the heart and soul of the town, she began reading from the city's ordinance for historic preservation. It described the procedure for designating a structure more than 50 years old as a historic landmark. "The Historic Preservation Commission of Elephant will vote tonight on whether or not to designate this important part of Elephant's history as an official historic landmark. But before we do that, we will take public comments."

Bea looked up into the crowd as at least fifteen hands shot into the air. Bea called on Ruth, whose hand was not raised. Ruth started to rise from her seat on the bottom bench next to where Bea had been sitting.

Hector yelled first. "Hey, she's on the Hysterical Committee. This is for the public." The crowd erupted. Ruth looked around at the angry people behind her. She started to sit down again, but Gladys pushed her toward the podium. As Ruth began to move forward, the yelling got even louder. She froze.

Then the mayor rushed over to the podium and spoke into Bea's ear. "Hey, this is a public meeting," yelled Hector. "No secret communiqués." The crowd laughed.

Bea spoke into the microphone. "Okay. Members of the Historic Preservation Commission will have an opportunity to speak after the public comment period." She then paused for a moment, looking first at Hector, who was sitting in the upper bleachers to her left. Then she looked far over to her right and called on a young man who looked like he was high school age. "Stuart, would you like to comment?"

Stuart stood up and yelled: "I yield the floor to Hector Martin." He grinned and sat down as the crowd gave out a big cheer. Bea was now visibly annoyed for the first time. She looked over at Hector and he was already halfway down to the gym floor. He had on a black T-shirt with a white gothic image on the front, and black jeans and socks. His hair was jet black hair and he wore a black Fu Manchu mustache. Both of his arms were muscular and covered with tattoos. He was beaming with pride as he stepped onto the gym floor.

"I haven't called on you yet Hector," Bea said into the microphone as she stared up at him. Hector was more than a foot taller than Bea.

"Let him speak," came a voice from the bleachers. Hector grimaced at Bea and she stepped away from the microphone silently.

Hector stepped up to the podium and bent down, placing his mouth almost against the microphone. He cleared his throat. Marla jumped up and showed Hector how to raise the mic so he could stand upright. He cleared his throat again. "People of Elephant," he began. "Last I heard, this was America. The greatest country in the world!" he yelled the last sentence out and pumped his fist in the air. A chorus of "yea!" emerged from the crowd. "Last I heard, America was a democracy. Am I right?!" More cheering came from the crowd. "Am I right people?!" Hector yelled it much more loudly, pumping his fist again. "Last I heard," yelled Hector, "in a democracy, the people get to decide, and the people have decided we don't want that fucking elephant." A loud chorus of cheers and boos came from the crowd. Hector grinned sheepishly and looked back at the table behind him. "Oh, sorry mister Mayor." The Mayor sat with his arms folded and frowned. "Last I heard, we don't want that elephant. Right people?!" Hector pumped his fist again, and mostly cheers rang from the crowd. "Last I heard it was 2010, so it's time Elephant moved into the twentieth century."

A few people in the crowd began to laugh and Jonas yelled out "it's the twenty-first century, Hector."

Hector looked puzzled and then grinned sheepishly again. "Oh yeah. I never got that," he said. I looked over at Jonas and he shook his head and rolled his eyes. Stacy did the same.

As Hector walked back to the Bleachers, a lot more hands went up. Bea called on a woman who appeared to be in her fifties, sitting in the second row of the bleachers below where Hector was sitting. She walked nervously to the podium. "Can you state your name please?" Bea asked her.

The woman spoke softly and said "Mary Abernathy." She looked over to Bea for approval and got it. She pulled the microphone down and seemed very nervous as she spoke into it. "My family has lived in Elephant for three generations," Mary said. The crowd was quiet and attentive. "My father worked at Elephant Gas when he was in high school. It was his first job, and he had fond memories of it." The crowd was totally engrossed in what Mary was saying. "That being said however," Mary continued, "my late father would not be in favor of trying to freeze Elephant in the past." This brought a few cheers. "He used to say 'the future is for the young, and they should be free to create it.'" This brought more cheers. "I say the young people should be the ones to decide the fate of the elephant, not a committee of old people, who are out of touch and won't be around to live with the results of the decisions that are made." This brought a much greater cheer from the crowd, and Mary had a big smile as she walked back to the bleachers and took her seat. Bea's face was bright red now.

Helen had been raising her hand from the beginning and Bea finally called on her. She proudly got up and walked to the podium carrying an armful of materials. Next to it she set up a tripod with a large whiteboard attached. She placed an eraser and several markers in a tray at the bottom of the whiteboard. Then she set the pad with the colorful drawing of the circus elephant she had shown me in her store on the whiteboard tray. As soon as Helen put the drawing up, Hector yelled, "what the hell is that?!" A number of other hecklers chimed in.

Helen looked annoyed, but continued to set up her props. When she finished she said: "I think you're all going to love this idea. With this idea, Elephant Gas can become a first-class tourist attraction. It will have a circus theme, and the rest of the property can be developed as a sort of 'mini-circus'." Helen started to describe the trapeze artists and clowns and ponies that would be included in her circus. A couple of boos arose from the crowd now. Helen held her hand up. "Wait a minute, wait a minute," she urged them. "I want you to know that I gave a preview of this idea to our visitor, the writer from that magazine. He loved it and said it would be perfect for our town."

Many in the crowd looked over at me. Helen was beaming at me. Stacy glared at me and yelled "Excuse me?!" over the boos. I looked down and put my head in my hands. At that point, a loud chorus of boos came pouring from the crowd. Jonas started laughing.

"She misunderstood," I told Stacy and Jonas. "I was just trying to be nice."

"Well it worked," said Stacy.

"Go sit down!" yelled Hector. Helen looked mortified, but walked slowly back to her seat, her face red with embarrassment.

To my right, Stacy now stood up, raised her hand and walked purposefully toward the podium without being called on. Bea looked at her with a startled expression, but then stepped back as Stacy grabbed the microphone to adjust it and looked up into the crowd. "Ladies and gentlemen, the business owners of Elephant have given me the great honor of representing them as the Executive Director of the Greater Elephant Chamber of Commerce. They've also asked me to use my professional judgment in how we promote our business community." It was obvious that Stacy had spent a lot of time rehearsing this speech. She continued confidently: "A run-down fiberglass structure at an abandoned gas station is not a tourist attraction. In my professional opinion, it is not something that will draw business to our town. The history of our town is important, but a marketing gimmick built for a private business is not the part of our history that is important. Therefore, I urge the Historic Preservation Commission to vote no on the question of making the elephant a historic landmark." A few people began clapping as Stacy walked back toward Jonas and me. The clapping grew louder and soon the people in the bleachers were giving Stacy a standing ovation. Her face turned red and she was clearly embarrassed, but pleased.

At least ten more speakers came to the podium and spoke out against the elephant. Almost all of them echoed the opinions of Hector and Mary and Stacy. Platitudes rang out, like "last I heard, the future belongs to the young," and "this is America," and "a small group of old rich people doesn't get to decide." I heard a few snickers behind me after that comment.

Only one person spoke out in favor of saving the elephant. It was a gentleman who appeared to be in his eighties. He was thin and short and wore a red plaid shirt and red baseball cap. He talked about the importance of respecting the history of the town and that young people should be thankful that such a nice town had been left to them by their ancestors. "It's a hell hole!" came a voice from the bleachers. The gentleman ignored the comment, and as he walked back toward the bleachers, Beverly got up from her seat next to Ruth and gave him a hug and peck on the cheek. A few people started booing.

"That's Beverly's husband," Jonas whispered into my ear.

After the boos subsided, Gus got up from his spot at the end of the bleachers and walked over to the podium. I looked over at Gladys and her face was bright red. The crowd quickly quieted as Gus stepped to the microphone. "History is important," he said softly. "I'm a veteran, and I know as well as anyone that we must never forget our history. But we can't live in the past, either. As Stacy said, marketing gimmicks to sell more gasoline are not what this town is about. It's about the people who live here, especially the young people, and making their lives and their futures as successful as possible. America is a free country, and the owners of that elephant should be able to do what they want with it without the government's interference." At that point, cheers rang out from the crowd and Gus was also given a standing ovation. It was clear that he had intended to say more, but he just smiled then and walked back to his seat. I looked over at Gladys and she had a startled look on her face, but she was clapping until the ladies next to her made her stop.

The last person to speak was the woman sitting next to Hector. She rushed to the podium and gave a speech that was almost a word-for-word repeat of Hector's. After a rousing "it's the twenty-first century!" she pumped her fist above her head and yelled "yeah!" to which the crowd responded vigorously.

The ladies in the center front of the bleachers sat silently and looked straight ahead as the crowd continued its commotion. The Mayor walked up to the podium and stood silently. After nearly five minutes, the crowd began to quiet and the Mayor banged his gavel. "Would the ladies of the Historic Preservation Commission like to come forward?" Ruth, Beverly and Gladys looked at each other and then got up and walked silently toward the podium, joining Bea. "Oh, and the gentleman too," the Mayor said then. At that point, a young man sitting directly above me got up and began walking down the bleachers. He walked toward the podium and stood at the end of the line of older ladies, keeping his distance from Ruth.

"Would any of the members of the commission like to make a comment before the vote?" asked the Mayor. The ladies all looked at each other and then shook their heads. The young man looked at them and then stepped up to the podium.

"My name is Jason Herndon," he said. "I have been on this commission only three months, but it has been a pleasure." By the look on his face I could tell he was lying. "I agree with almost all of the speakers tonight," he said in a voice that was much more mature than he looked. "The future of Elephant belongs to us young people. It should be our decision. The elephant is a symbol of the past and not the future. I think you can tell how I will vote." Many in the crowd cheered.

After Jason stepped back from the podium, Bea stepped up and pulled the microphone down to her mouth. "As Chair of the Elephant Historic Preservation Commission, I will entertain a motion."

Ruth immediately raised her hand. "Madame Chairwoman," she said. "I move that the historic elephant sculpture at 551 West Main Street be declared a historic landmark on its 50th anniversary, July 4th, 2010."

A chorus of boos rang out from the bleachers as the Mayor ran up and began pounding on the podium with his gavel. "Order, order," he yelled, in vain. After a couple of minutes the commotion began to die down. "Do I have a second?" Bea asked, as if nothing had happened. Beverly sheepishly raised her hand, and a few more boos rang out. "Any discussion," Bea asked then. All of the members shook their heads.

"All those in favor, raise their hands," Bea commanded. The four ladies looked at each other and ignored Jason. All four then slowly raised up their hands. The crowd immediately exploded.

Everyone on the gym floor looked stunned as the crowd, now all standing, began moving toward the floor. A young man of high school age ran over to the white board that Helen had set up and grabbed the eraser. He flung it like a relief pitcher toward the center of the gym floor. It barely missed the Mayor's head and then harmlessly slid across the floor. Suddenly a white sneaker flew out of the crowd from the center of the bleachers. It too missed its mark and slid along the floor to the back of the gym. Then came the onslaught. Shoes of all shapes and sizes were launched from the crowd. City Council members climbed under their table. Jason and the ladies standing near the podium all tried to crouch down behind it. A group of young men rushed toward the pile of shoes in the corner. Soon they were launching them back into the crowd on the bleachers. Women and children started screaming.

Then the lights went out. Or at least they did for me. I remember opening my eyes and seeing Stacy's face a few inches away. She was holding my head and had a look of great concern. At first I thought I had lost my hearing, but the room was actually almost completely silent. "He's alive," I heard someone yell from above me.

CHAPTER EIGHTEEN

The parking spot nearest the front door of Ugly Al's Coffee Emporium was empty, so I gently eased the shiny yellow Corvette into it. I had washed the car right before I went for coffee. It was mid-morning Wednesday and the street was mostly quiet. Seattle was enjoying an unseasonable hot spell, and it was nearly ninety degrees already. Jennifer had no customers when I opened the wooden screen door and walked into her shop. The door slammed behind me and my dull headache suddenly got a little worse. Jennifer gave me the wide grin and quizzical look I was hoping for. Then she came out from behind the counter, gave me a hug and asked, "What the fuck is that, Robert Smith?"

"Like my new car?"

"Yeah, right. Rookie magazine writers don't get paid that well. Who'd you steal it from?"

"You mean borrow. It was loaned to me by a really rich gay guy."

"Oh, no. Don't tell me you've stooped to that?" Then she grinned. "Yes, pun intended."

I laughed and shook my head. "Very funny." I assured her that no, I hadn't stooped to that. It was a trade, but not that kind. Then I rubbed the welt on the back of my head and asked her if she had any Advil. She pulled a bottle out of the cash register and gave me four, and then began creating my vente iced mocha while I told her the story of taking the heel of a size 13 cowboy boot on the back of my head.

"I gotta say Rob, you have the best stories lately," she said. "First a girl kicks your car and then you go to a strange town and a hillbilly whacks you in the head with his boot. And on top of that you show up at my shop in a new Corvette. You should write a book."

"Yeah, right. I'll be lucky to get this article written." I told Jennifer about the historic preservation meeting that turned into a riot, and about Stacy taking me home to put ice on my head. And I told her about Jonas and how his mechanic was fixing the door on my car and he had let me borrow the Corvette, and that I was going back to Elephant for the Fourth of July weekend.

"You're going right back?" she asked. "Are you sure nothing's going on between you two?"

"He's fixing it because I promised not to include him in my article. That's it. And it's a bummer, because he's definitely the most interesting person there."

"So how's your article coming along, anyway?"

"It's not," I said. Then I told Jennifer about the beautiful Sarah. I described how she had flirted and basically asked me out, and then she backed out when I showed up for the date. So now I had to avoid her, which was going to be hard, since she ran the only motel in town. Jennifer gave me an unsympathetic smile.

I had started my Advil regimen right after the Monday night meeting and left Elephant early Tuesday morning for the uneventful drive home. The car was fun to drive, but the rumbling engine and the stiff suspension made my headache worse. It got worse yet when I received a call from Doris just as I pulled into a rest area near Yakima. She wanted to know if I had checked on the easement issue yet, even though I had told her I would do that on Wednesday. "That's where I'm headed next," I told Jennifer. "Then I get to call her back and give her the bad news. That old witch is driving me insane. I don't suppose you have any Vicodin." Jennifer shook her head. When Doris had called, I thought about asking her if she was related to the beautiful Sarah, but I didn't. I couldn't bear the thought that it might be true.

"Do you think you're in love with this girl?" Jennifer asked, staring directly into my eyes.

"Well, I admit I'm in love with her looks. But I don't know her that well."

"You men. Since when did that matter?" Then she gave me a big grin. "Hey, how about a ride?"

"Huh?"

"A ride. In your new 'Vette. I love Corvettes. It's dead here this morning. I'll put a sign on the door saying I went to the Post Office."

"Uh, Okay." I looked at my fresh mocha. "I can't take this. I don't consume food or beverage in that car." Jennifer put it in her freezer.

We drove out of Fremont, past the Lenin statue – which seemed small compared to the big elephant – and then through Seattle's University District and out across Lake Washington on the floating bridge. Just before we got to the end of the bridge, Jennifer asked me something that stunned me more than the cowboy boot had. "Do you think you and I would be going out if I were single?" she asked.

I choked. "Excuse me?"

She looked over at me with a big grin, and then looked out the windshield. "I was just wondering. This is fun."

"You're killing me, man." We were east of the lake now, heading for the exits into Bellevue. "Are you asking that because of the car?"

"Well, it's not the car exactly," she replied. "It's just that you seem different now. A lot more confident. I like that."

"I think it's time to go back," I said. We drove in silence as I steered onto an exit in Bellevue and then back on the freeway heading west toward Seattle.

After awhile I said, "Jen, I've had a giant crush on you for, like, years."

She smiled and looked at me. "I know. I could tell. I don't get 50% tips from guys who don't have crushes on me. Especially when they're broke. It's just that …"

"Of course we'd be going out. If you wanted to."

"I just think it's so cool. You're out doing really interesting things. Writing articles for a cool magazine and driving a rich gay guy's car." She had a big grin now. "And I'm sure it's perfectly innocent. Chris just works all the time, and he doesn't ever want to do anything anymore. With you, if you feel like going out and doing something fun and interesting, you just go do it."

We were right in the middle of the floating bridge in the beautiful sunshine, looking out at water skiers on the lake. I looked over at her. "Holy shit, Jennifer, I can't believe we're having this conversation."

She gave me a pout. "I'm sorry Rob. I guess that was out of line."

"Are you kidding? I'm totally thrilled that you'd even consider going out with me. Even if it's just hypothetical."

The second that sentence was out of my mouth, my pants rang. I'd been wrong before, so this time I assumed it wasn't Doris. I had just talked to her the day before and she knew it would be later in the day before I had an answer about the easement. I was probably Charles. Or maybe it was the beautiful Sarah, calling from Elephant to apologize for being a giant flake. Yeah, and maybe a blizzard was about to hit Seattle in July. "Aren't you going to answer that?" Jennifer asked.

"It's probably nothing," I said, as I reached into my pocket to silence the ring. "I'm sure it's not the client from hell." Then I slid the phone out of my pocket and looked down at the screen. "DEATH," it said. I grunted audibly as Jennifer looked at me with a puzzled expression. "Shit. I can't believe it. That ..." I stopped myself before I called Doris a really bad name.

"Cunt?" Jennifer offered with a big smile. Then she added, "You should never, ever call anyone that. It's a terrible word."

"I didn't. You're the one who said it. But I love your dirty mouth. And you know what else?"

"What?"

"I'm dumping her."

"Who?"

"Doris. I've had enough."

"What?! You can't. You really need the money Rob."

I didn't respond. I just got pissed and we drove the rest of the way to Freemont in silence.

Back at Ugly Al's, Jennifer retrieved my mocha from her fridge and poured it down the drain. "You deserve a fresh one, big guy," she said.

"And no tip. I mean it." She gave me a big smile and I didn't argue. I pulled the phone out again and listened to Doris's message.

"Robert, this is Doris Ellington. I'm at your office. Why aren't you here? I need to talk to you. Right away." That was it.

"Fuck. She's at my office."

"You'd better get over there. You can't afford to lose that deal, Rob."

"I've got an idea. I'll tell her to come here. I'll buy her a coffee before I shit-can her. At least you'll get some money out of her. I'm sure I won't."

Jennifer shook her head and rolled her eyes. "Whatever. But I think you're making a really big mistake."

"Remember when you said you admire me because when I get an idea in my head I just go for it?"

"That's not exactly what I meant, Rob."

I made the call and I must have sounded threatening, because Doris was surprisingly agreeable on the phone. She said she'd to come to Ugly Al's, but I had to explain in detail how to get there. Doris lived in the suburbs and rarely came into the city. Within five minutes, a large maroon Cadillac rolled up and parked behind the Corvette. The door opened and a thin, well-dressed woman in her seventies emerged. Her hair was gray and perfectly set. She wore an expensive looking suit that approximately matched the color of her car. I stepped out the screen door to greet her and she stretched her hand out and said, "Hello Robert, Doris Ellington."

"Yes, I know who you are, Doris."

"I need to talk to you," she said

"Let's go in and I'll buy you a coffee." I introduced Doris to Jennifer and told her I'd buy her whatever she wanted. Doris glanced at me with a smile and then ordered a cup of hot tea with two tea bags.

"This is just a lovely shop you have here, dear," Doris said to Jennifer. She sounded almost genuine.

Jennifer thanked her and then said, "Rob here's my best customer."

Doris actually made small talk with me as we sat down at the table by the window. "You're in a good neighborhood," she said. "Are you finding your business successful?" This was an amazing breakthrough. Doris had never shown any interest in me or my business. Something was definitely up. I gave her an ambiguous answer that led her to believe that I meant yes. Then she said, "Robert, I know I've been difficult. You've been a good agent for me, and I just want you to know that." I thanked her, trying not to seem stunned. "And I have something else to tell you. My son-in-law works for Puget Sound Energy. I had dinner with him and Suzy the other night, and I asked Robert – his name is also Robert; very nice young man – I told Robert about our easement issue at the apartments with the power poles. He explained to me how they work and why they have to be there. And he said I have nothing to worry about."

I looked over at Jennifer and she was watching and listening with a huge grin. She pointed toward Doris and silently mouthed the words "fire her." I told Doris that I appreciated her making the effort to come to my office to let me know that that issue had been resolved for her, and again I thanked her for her compliments. She was the most relaxed I had ever seen her, and for the first time she actually asked my opinion about the deal with the Los Angeles Attorney and whether I felt we were close to getting it closed. I told her yes and she looked kind of surprised, but didn't say anything. We made more small talk for a few minutes. She talked about her daughter and son-in-law, and then asked me about my family. I explained my lack of a family situation as vaguely as I could. Then she started to get up to leave.

I stopped her. "Wait a minute Doris. I need to ask you something." She sat back down and looked at me. "I was in eastern Oregon over the weekend. I think I told you. I was in a little town called Elephant." Doris's Eyes got suddenly bigger and she had a strange look on her face. "I take it you've heard of it?"

"Well, yes," she replied, obviously having an unpleasant recollection. "My late husband's brother lived there at one time. He was a fool. Actually, he probably still is. He's among the living."

"Would his name be Peter, by any chance?"

"My goodness. Are they still talking about him there?" Doris asked back. "He practically got run out of town twenty-five years ago. It was Pete Junior's fault, of course."

A cold shiver came over me and I felt sick to my stomach as I came to the sudden realization that my hated client, my sworn enemy, was actually related to the beautiful Sarah, even if only by marriage. Pete Junior had to be Sarah's biological father.

I'm sure I looked as surprised as Doris did when I asked her, "He's still alive?"

"Pete Junior?"

"Well, both."

"Yes they're both still alive. Peter senior lives just a few miles from here, I believe. At a place called Tall Pines or something like that. He's not in good health, from what I hear. I haven't seen him since Roy's funeral."

"And what about his son?"

"Oh, he flew the coop. He was in Nevada, and then Florida. Who knows? He was in jail for awhile. Probably still is. He broke his father's heart, I'll tell you that."

Then I asked Doris the million-dollar question. "Was Pete Junior ever married to a woman named Millie?"

"You certainly got to know the town, young man. My goodness, I haven't thought of her in years. Is she still there? She and Pete Junior had two lovely daughters." Doris was being nostalgic now. "And he just up and left them. It was such a shame. Those little girls were just darling."

"Doris, Millie's still there. She owns the motel in Elephant. I stayed there. Her daughters both work there, and they're beautiful." I was blurting now.

Doris and I visited for several more minutes. I told her about Sarah's and Andrea's children and about the gas station with the big gray elephant. "Yes, I believe Peter sold gasoline for awhile," she said. "He tried many different things to get rich. He failed at all of them."

"Did you know his business partner? His name was Hollister."

"Oh, I didn't pay any attention to what Peter was doing out there in the boondocks," she replied. And that was that. Doris told me that she was ready to get the sale of her apartments done and that I should make a final settlement with the buyer in Los Angeles to cover the problems he found in his inspections. Then she left. As soon as Doris was out the door, I told Jennifer that she must have been on drugs, or at least some new form of medication. She had never been this reasonable in all the time I had known her.

"She seemed really sweet, Rob. I can't believe you call her the client from hell." I just shrugged. I visited with Jennifer for a few more minutes before going back out into the hot Seattle sun. It was barely afternoon and easily in the nineties now.

* * *

Since my planned trip to the title company had been made unnecessary by Doris's sudden lurch back to being human, I decided to show off my borrowed car to Charles. I drove to his house unannounced and gave the engine one loud rev. He came out onto the front porch immediately. The sight of the yellow race car brought out his inner 16-year-old. "Dude, this car is righteous!" Charles loved Corvettes, though he admitted he had never ridden in one. He had, however, used them for his room-surround car racing video game. As I had with Jennifer, I made the mistake of informing Charles that the car had been loaned to me by a wealthy gay man. He made the same lame joke she did, telling me he couldn't believe I would stoop to that level. I assured him that nothing could be further from the truth – this was just one of the perks of being an important writer. "Besides, being heterosexual is nothing to be ashamed of," I told him. "And I'm not going to apologize for it." Then he made me take him driving.

"Let's cruise Alki," he said. I protested, since it would take half an hour to get to Alki Beach in West Seattle from Charles's North Seattle home. But we did it. On that rare beautiful hot sunny day in Seattle, even at mid-week, the beach was packed with people. For about 20 days a year, Alki Beach is like Seattle's version of Venice Beach. The rest of the year, it's just another gray, rainy spot in a gray, rainy city.

The yellow Corvette had its desired effect, and Charles basked in its glow. Young women stared at us and Charles smiled and waved. "You know what we look like, don't you Charles?" I said. He didn't respond. "We look like a couple of insecure middle-aged men who are using a phallic car to make up for our other deficiencies. You realize that, don't you Charles?" He ignored me and kept smiling out the window. "I recall a couple of weeks ago you told me I needed to keep my pecker in my pants. Now look at you. You're pathetic." He continued to ignore me, and then I took him home.

CHAPTER NINETEEN

Aurora Avenue stretches vertically like a spine through North Seattle for many miles. It's lined with strip malls, used car lots and big box stores. Stop lights interrupt traffic at frequent intervals and six lanes barely contain it. Scattered in the background behind the retail establishments are an assortment of large apartment buildings, condominium complexes and retirement homes. This being Seattle, many of these residential behemoths sit in the shade of stands of much taller fir trees. The incongruity of concrete sprawl spidering out through the forest is a feature of much of the Seattle area, and nowhere more than here.

I sat in the yellow Corvette, crawling slowly northward in Aurora's thick traffic. The car's power and nimbleness were completely neutered. It was like Tiger Woods playing miniature golf. As I inched along, people stared from neighboring cars. Most of the women smiled and most of the men frowned. I decided they were jealous, and left it at that. I was on my way to Kmart, the source of just about everything I owned. My toothpaste and my couch were both purchased there, along with most of my clothes. Today I was nearly out of Advil and I needed a new pair of flip-flops for my return visit to Elephant. Other than that, I planned to just look around.

About five miles north of Freemont, and less than a mile from my destination, I noticed a sign on the right that I hadn't remembered ever seeing. It was a large painted arrow – in shades of green – pointing down a side street. The words "Tall Pines Senior Living" were spelled out inside the arrow, and below in smaller letters it said, "Your new home in the pines!"

Almost all the trees around there were Douglas fir, not pine, but that's not what caught my attention. I was sure that was the name Doris had given for the nursing home where her brother-in-law Peter supposedly lived. I had probably driven up Aurora Avenue a thousand times without noticing that sign before. Of course, it was one of hundreds.

So this was the home of Peter Ellington, I thought; biological grandfather of the beautiful Sarah. It was a strange feeling just being in the neighborhood of one of her relatives. I quickly sped up and moved into the left lane, passing a Volvo box truck that said "Aurora Rents" on the side. I put Jonas's car at risk as I slalomed my way through traffic and then back over to the right just in time to turn into the Kmart parking lot. I parked in a far corner, away from other cars. Then I shopped quickly and left, without looking around.

* * *

Back at the condo that evening, I watched the Mariners lose an away game to the pathetic Baltimore Orioles. It was still early when the game ended, and the evening was warm, so I went to the deck with a notebook to take another stab drafting my article; or at least to think about taking another stab. I sat down and put the pencil in my hand, and my mind was blank. I started thinking about the beautiful Sarah, and her grandfather, Peter. He must have been in his twenties or thirties when he and Hollister McCune built that big strange elephant. I pictured a couple of young ambitious businessmen, hoping to turn Elephant into a boom town and dreaming of riches. John F. Kennedy was running for president then, and Seattle was preparing to host a world's fair with the theme "Century 21." It was the dawn of the "Space Age" in America, and it was the dawn of the "gas station age" in Elephant. It seemed like somehow this ought to be the angle for my article, but I didn't see how it would work. Most of that optimism was gone now. In Elephant, the nostalgia for those days among a few of the old-timers was all that was left. The town was dying and the younger people didn't care about all that. I doubted this was a direction that Agnes at the Oasis would want me to go.

At about ten o'clock, with no progress made, I suddenly remembered that I needed to send the LA attorney an email telling him what Doris had said about getting the deal done on her building. And it occurred to me that sending it at that hour of the evening would look impressive. I sat down at the computer and explained to him that we were ready to agree to his offer to reduce the price of the apartments slightly if he would take the property as-is and close the deal quickly. Then I slept. At least for a couple of hours.

Most of the night I lay awake. I couldn't get my mind off that sign I saw along Aurora Avenue. Somewhere back in the woods was the beautiful Sarah's biological grandfather. I pictured him as a vegetable, being fed through a tube. Even if he were mentally coherent, he was probably so bitter and angry about what happened in Elephant that he'd throw me out of his room if I showed up there. But I was getting desperate for something for my article, and my curiosity about the man who shared DNA with the beautiful woman I was so infatuated with was killing me. I decided to go see him.

* * *

Just inside the entrance into Tall Pines Senior Living, to the right of the lobby behind a glass wall, was a large workout room filled with elliptical machines, stair-climbers and stationary bikes. Two state-of-the-art universal gyms sat in opposite corners and free weights lined the walls. At least half-a-dozen people were in the room using the equipment. They were all obviously over sixty, and they were working up a good sweat. The lobby was as plush as Jonas's office at Elephant Gas. The carpet and the furnishings were expensive-looking and spotless. A friendly woman in her twenties sat at a reception desk and greeted me warmly. I asked her if Peter Ellington lived here, and she immediately gave me a big smile. "Oh yes, that's him on the bicycle." She pointed into the workout room, where only one of the stationary bikes was being used. "He's a bike addict, that one."

Peter Ellington was definitely not a vegetable. He was at least six feet tall and muscular and spinning his pedals at a high cadence. He looked about 65 to me, but he had to be older – his elephant was just turning fifty. The receptionist paged him, but got no response. Then she smiled and said "just a moment" and went into the gym and tapped Peter on the shoulder. He stopped peddling and looked up, then wiped his forehead with a towel. He pulled the white iPod earphones out of his ears, and looked out at me with a squint and a frown.

After a little more explanation from the receptionist, Peter came out of the gym and greeted me with a strong handshake and a puzzled look. I introduced myself as a writer for Western Oasis Magazine, and said that his sister-in-law, Doris, had told me where he lived. He looked even more puzzled until I brought up the name Elephant. Then he laughed out loud. In a booming voice he exclaimed, "You're doing an article on that place? My goodness, are you magazine people running out of things to write about?" I explained to him that this weekend was the fiftieth anniversary of the big elephant he had helped build. He looked surprised and thought for a moment. "Oh my gosh, I guess that's right. Fourth of July, 1960. Hard to believe." He laughed and shook his head. "You say you know Doris? How did you get so lucky?" I explained about my other job in real estate, and that Doris was my client. Peter said his late brother, Roy, had built the apartment building I was selling in the early 1970s. "That woman drove Roy to his grave," he said.

"She told me you were in a nursing home," I said.

He laughed again and looked around and said, "This is my kind of nursing home." Then he added, "I'm surprised Doris knows I'm alive." Peter had a full head of white hair and a white goatee. His green eyes sparkled and reminded me of Sarah's. He wore a gray sweat suit and white sneakers. "Let's go to the mess hall and talk," he said. He wiped his face with his towel again as we walked briskly down a corridor to what looked like an upscale restaurant. "Order whatever," Peter told me. "We get ten guest meals a month, and I'm not even close to my quota." We sat at a table next to a large window looking out on an immaculate yard and garden. It felt like we were a thousand miles from Aurora Avenue. A young waitress suggested a chicken panini sandwich, and I accepted. Several other people, all around Peter's age and most looking as healthy as he did, were sitting at tables visiting. An Elton John song from the '70s played overhead. I asked

Peter to tell me the story of how the big elephant was built. He was eating a salad and drinking Gatorade. "Isn't this a great place? If I'd had any idea what these places were like, I'd have moved into one a lot sooner. Anyway…" Then he began his story:

"Elephant had a lot more people back then. It was an optimistic time. There were lots of young farmers and they hired lots of workers. High school kids – even girls. They knew they could stay in town and get work. It's not like that now. With the equipment they have now, one old farmer can farm a thousand acres all by himself. Maybe hire a truck driver for harvest, but that's just for a couple of weeks.

"Anyway, Hollister McCune and I were school chums. Here in Seattle. We grew up together. Holly went off to Washington State University out in eastern Washington. I went in the Army for two years and then came back to Seattle and went to work as a mechanic in a gas station. School wasn't my thing, but I loved cars. I started working on cars when I was twelve, and I'm still doing it. Anyway, in college Holly met a gal from Elephant, Oregon, and he went out with her for awhile. Her dad owned that gas station. He owned a lot of other businesses in Elephant too, mostly supplying farmers with fuel and supplies. Holly hit it off with the gal's dad a lot better than he did with her. Long story short, the girl took off and went to Montana and Holly moved to Elephant to become a farm supply tycoon. That was a great business, by the way. The girl's father owned an airstrip and two airplanes for spraying fields. That was a new thing then. Holly even learned to fly.

"This all happened in the '50s," Peter continued. "Everybody was into cars. Elephant even had a couple of car dealerships then. Can you believe that? Holly was smart; he knew that gas was going to be a booming business. Casper Farrell, his boss, who was the girl's dad, had a couple of pumps at the west end of town, alongside a big fuel storage area. That's where the big elephant is now. People could buy gas for their cars, but that was just a sideline for Casper, since he had the gas anyway. He was focused on his farm customers. He wasn't interested in the highway trade. So Holly, being the dreamer that he was, talked Casper into selling the gas station to him. He was 24-years-old then, and Casper thought he was a real up-and-comer."

I asked Peter if Hollister was still alive. "Oh yes, we'll get to that," he replied. "Anyway, in '56, Holly was a business owner and he needed a mechanic. He knew I worked in a gas station over here in Seattle, so he made me an offer I couldn't refuse. I had a new wife and a couple of kids – just toddlers. Pete Junior was four, I think. So off we went to the middle of nowhere to manage Elephant Gas. That's what Holly called it after he bought it. Elephant Gas."

Peter kept working on his big salad while he talked. He was as energetic an eater as he was a talker. "Things went well at first," he said, "and by '58, Holly offered me a partnership in the gas station. It was doing well, but he had his eyes on a bigger prize. He wanted to buy Casper out and build a business empire in Elephant. That's called being a big fish in a tiny pond. More like a mud puddle. But Holly, he had an ego. He was still in his twenties, and he was a big shot in that little town. And he liked it. "Me, I just enjoyed running the little station and working on the cars. It served me well. The people there were nice and friendly. But that wasn't enough for Holly. A gentleman named Joe Mark owned another station at the other end of town, and Holly was determined that Elephant Gas would be the number one station, even though Joe had a 20-year head start. Holly was competitive as hell. So he dreamed up the idea for that big fiberglass elephant. I thought he was crazy, but he was sort of a genius, in a way. Fiberglass was a brand new material then, and it was cheap. Holly had read about a big fiberglass statue of Paul Bunyon, the logger, somewhere in Minnesota, and it gave him the idea. His father had a friend in Seattle who built fiberglass boat hulls. He talked the guy into making this elephant, telling him he could get great publicity from it. He was right, because there was a front page story in the Seattle Times when the damn thing was first molded. After the epoxy all cured, they cut the elephant into pieces and trucked it out there to Elephant. Then they glued it back together somehow. It was the damnedest thing. And it worked. We had a big advantage over Joe Mark, because we were at the end of town where travelers arrived and left. We already had more of the visitor business, then that damn elephant started drawing locals. Our business increased a ton.

"But I was a naïve fool," Peter said. "That elephant cost over $20,000. In 1960! Can you imagine? I just assumed that Holly and Casper were paying for it out of the farm supply business, but there was no agreement. After all was said and done, Holly informed me that the cost had to come out of the gas station profits. That was a big problem, because the gas station profits were what I lived on. That was our agreement. He owned half the business, but he didn't have to do anything there. I did all the work and kept the net profit. As the business grew, his ownership stake was worth more. But in 1960, the station showed a loss because of building that damn elephant, so I had no income. And that was that. It was pretty obvious that Holly had changed his mind about having me as a partner in the gas station, and this was his way of getting me out. He tricked me, and I didn't forgive him for a long time."

Peter told me that he handed his share in the gas station back over to Hollister and took a job as a mechanic at a tractor repair business. He stayed in Elephant for another 20 years, working on farm equipment. "Pete Junior got into a lot of trouble," he said. "He was doing drugs when he met Millie. She was a bit of a rough customer back then herself, but she thought she could save him. The day his second daughter was born, Pete was off at a bar drinking. Millie gave him the boot after that, and he went downhill from there. That was 1982. I had tried to help him, but I gave up after that. Somehow, Millie decided I was part of the problem, and she made my life hell after Pete Junior left. She's one headstrong woman. We decided it was time to come back to Seattle. Best move we ever made. I got a job in a Ford dealership here. On Aurora Avenue, actually. I worked my way up to service manager after a few years, and made us a nice living. But I'm sorry I didn't get to see those girls grow up.

"My wife, her name was Ida, she died three years ago. I always thought she'd outlive me. We have a daughter, Lisa. She's a nurse here in Seattle. She's the one who found this place for us, when Ida got sick. We sold our house at the top of the market in Seattle, so we could afford this. Lisa takes good care of me now, that's for sure. She's divorced but she has two kids at the University. They're doing great. I haven't heard from Pete Junior in three years. Last I heard he was in jail again."

I told Peter that Sarah and Andrea looked like fashion models now, and he beamed with pride. "And they each have two kids now too," I said. "You're a great-grandfather."

Then I remembered the picture of Sarah and me that Gladys had taken in her shop, and I pulled my phone out and showed it to him. There I was, sitting in a salon chair with my goofy haircut and pink apron, while Sarah stood behind me looking perfect. Peter's eyes teared up. "She kind of looks like me," he said. "So what's she like?"

"I think she takes after you, too," I said. "Not only is she gorgeous, but she's really good with tools. She has a handyman business."

"Is that right?" Peter was suddenly speechless as he stared into my phone with a smile. Then he asked, "Can I have that picture? You can Bluetooth it to me."

"I can what?"

Peter reached into his pocket and pulled out an Apple iPhone. "You don't know how to do that, do you?" I told him no, and he took my phone and started tapping away. "Isn't technology great? There." He looked up with a grin and then took his phone and pressed a couple of keys, and said, "Voila!" The photo of Sarah and me was now on his iPhone screen. "Let's go to my apartment. We'll blow this up."

We walked down a wide corridor lined with artwork. Peter gave a warm greeting to everyone we saw. I asked Peter if he could crop out the pink apron and he said he'd try. A small man who looked younger than Peter came toward us in an electric wheelchair. "Hey Parnelli," Peter said with a warm smile. "I want you to meet someone." I was introduced to Owen Stringfellow. "Owen owned half of Seattle at one time," Peter said.

Owen chuckled and denied it. "I've done alright," he said.

"Mr. Smith here's a 'real tore'," Peter said, pronouncing my line of work as if it contained two words. "He's selling my sister-in-law's place. He's either a saint or an idiot if he's working with her."

"That right?" said Owen. "You and I should talk. Got a business card? I'm in liquidation mode myself, since none of my kids wants to be in the apartment business." I had one card left in my wallet and half the ink was worn off it, and I gave it to Owen apologetically. "No worries. It's a good sign that you're out of cards. I'll be in touch," he told me. I told Owen I'd be very happy to discuss my services with him, and we continued on.

Peter's apartment was a computer nerd's dream. "I love the internet," he said, as he showed me his den. Two large computer monitors sat on a spotless desk that filled nearly half the room. A side table held several tiny gadgets, along with their charging cords. "I'm 78 years old," he said. "I was born 50 years too early."

Peter grabbed his phone and punched the keyboard a few times, then set it on the desk. "Watch this." He opened up a window on the left monitor and the photo of Sarah and me filled the screen. "My God, she's beautiful," he said. "You say she's a contractor?"

"People hire her to fix stuff," I told him. "And she does all the maintenance at the motel. She has the tallest truck I've ever seen." We talked about Sarah for a few more minutes, and I told Peter about her kids and her ex-husband, the cop. He asked me about Elephant, and I described the downtown and some of the stores and buildings.

"It sounds like it hasn't changed all that much," he said. "Just slowly dying. Like all of us." Then he said, "Let me show you something. I'll see if I can find it." After a few moments of tapping on his keyboard and searching through files on his computer, a black-and-white photo appeared on the screen of a young man sitting in a hot rod. In the passenger seat was a boy of less than ten. The car was parked next to a set of gas pumps which were directly under the giant elephant. In the background the working gas station building was clearly visible, with new tires displayed in front and a couple of 1950s cars parked nearby. "I built that car at Elephant Gas," Peter said, pointing to the hot rod. "It's a '32 Ford; a deuce roadster. That was the car to have when I was a young buck. That or a Corvette, if you had more money, which I didn't. Back then '32 Fords were cheap. Dime a dozen. That's Pete Junior there. We had fun in those days." Peter stared at the screen for at least a minute, and I thought maybe he forgot I was there. "I haven't looked at this for a long time," he said. He was a handsome young man in the photo.

"I can see where Sarah got her looks," I told him. Then he switched to the other photo, but didn't say anything. I told Peter that Sarah had been hired to work on the Elephant Gas building.

"Isn't that ironic. Who'd have ever thought?"

Then I mentioned that I'd been told that Hollister still owned the building and the big elephant. "Oh yes," he said. "He thinks it's not worth enough to go to the trouble of selling it. I guess he's got a good tenant that covers the taxes and keeps it maintained. Some old ladies contacted him about restoring the elephant and he told them to go fly a kite. He wasn't putting a dime into it." Peter laughed.

I told Peter I knew which old ladies he was talking about. Then I told him about Jonas and his Corvettes. "He's got money," I said.

"I should say."

When I told him the story of the Beemer and that I was now driving Jonas's new Corvette, his eyes lit up. "How about a ride? I haven't been in a 'Vette in 20 years."

Peter guided me quickly away from Aurora Avenue and toward Puget Sound. "We'll go up to Edmonds. You can't do this car justice around here, but that's a beautiful drive." Over the rumble of the engine, I asked Peter what Hollister planned to do with his property in Elephant. He told me that the gas station was all Hollister still owned there. He had overextended himself and then gone bankrupt after fuel prices went through the roof. The rest of his property had been sold to partially settle the debt he owed. "Nobody wanted an abandoned gas station in a podunk town after the energy crisis hit, so he kept it." We were driving along a narrow winding road now, on a hillside above Puget Sound. The road was lined with expensive homes with views of the water and the Olympic Mountains beyond. But Peter didn't seem interested in the view. "I've got an idea. I'll text Holly." As he typed into his iPhone, Peter told me that he and Hollister had reconnected after thirty years of not speaking. He said Hollister had moved to Los Angeles after the collapse of his businesses in Elephant. "I was diagnosed with cancer in '92," he said. "I was barely sixty, and I figured that was it. My daughter contacted Holly, without telling me, and told him about my cancer. After she bugged him three times, I got a lame get-well card in the mail. I was shocked."

Peter told me he beat the cancer, and after getting his "second life", as he called it, he flew to Southern California and had lunch with Hollister. "He was working as a sales rep for an import company," Peter said. "He was definitely humbled, and he'd given up his entrepreneurial dreams long before." Since their visit, Peter said they had kept in touch regularly. "I talked him into getting a computer, which helped him a lot in his job. I've kind of been his consultant. We've stayed in touch by email, and I finally got him to text on his cell phone last year."

As he talked and I drove, Peter kept tapping away at his iPhone. "I told him I'm with a reporter who's doing a magazine story on Elephant, and he just wrote back. It just says 'LOL', with three exclamation points. Then I texted him the photo of you and Sarah. He says she's beautiful and she looks like me. How do you like that? I told him she's going to be sprucing up the station."

We were back on Aurora Avenue now, approaching Peter's apartment from the north. I said I'd be in touch after my trip back to elephant. I dropped him off at the front door and shook his hand. Then I sat in a traffic jam and spent the next hour trying to get home.

CHAPTER TWENTY

A real estate broker working on commission becomes well-acquainted with the terms "wasted time" and "wasted effort." For every person he spends three hours convincing to become his customer, ten don't. For every client's property he puts on the market that sells, one doesn't. About 90% of what he does amounts to nothing. The worst hitters in baseball have a better rate of success than most real estate brokers.

The economics of real estate sales works because commissions are high enough on successful sales to cover all the time and effort wasted on everything else. But the psychological toll on the broker can be brutal. After awhile, he begins second-guessing himself. He tries to improve his odds by predicting which properties or potential clients will be failures, and then avoiding them. But this is an impossible task. One day he'll be driving around town and see a "sold" sign in front of a house he had given up on. Or, on a Sunday morning, he'll be relaxing drinking coffee and reading the real estate classifieds in the newspaper – which he must do – when a listing shows up in one of his competitor's ads for a property owner he was sure was shining him on. Before long he's looking for a high bridge or a ledge on a tall building. Or at least for another line of work.

At the time I agreed to go to Elephant and write the Oasis article, I had predicted certain failure for the apartment building in Bothell owned by Doris Ellington. She was a mean-spirited, emotionally unstable person who was completely unrealistic about what it would take to sell her property.

Even after her more human side had come out in Jennifer's shop that week, I was still sure she would ultimately tank the deal. I was sick to death of her and ready to move on. I didn't know how I was going to pay my bills in the future, but I was certain it wouldn't be from a commission on the sale of Doris's apartments.

When I checked my email early Friday morning, as I prepared to return to Elephant in the yellow Corvette, it appeared that I had once again misread the situation completely. A scanned letter had arrived, signed by the L.A. Attorney, waiving all contingencies and committing to close on the sale of Doris's apartments the following week. So maybe it was going to happen. Maybe I would get my "home run" commission after all. Just maybe, in less than ten days, I would be out of debt. I stared at the letter on the screen for awhile, trying to decide whether or not to believe it.

* * *

Eight hours later, after a relaxing drive through the Cascade Mountains and across Eastern Washington and Oregon in the air conditioned yellow 2001 Corvette, I laid eyes on a pristine maroon 1990 BMW. It was mine. The driver's door was perfect, the paint sparkled and the car looked like it belonged on a showroom floor. Jonas handed me the keys, like a proud father to his teenage son. "Welcome back to Elephant. How's your head?" I told him the painkillers were doing their job. Danny wiped his hands on a blue rag and then stuck it in a pocket in his blue overalls. He came over and shook my hand with a smile and told me I was the talk of the town after taking the boot on my noggin. Then he pointed to the BMW with a big grin. The tan leather seats of my car were spotless and supple and three shades lighter than when I had last seen them, covered with many years of grime.

"We detailed it," said Jonas. "Open the hood." The German six-cylinder engine looked like a sculpture. Every nook and cranny in the engine compartment was spotless. "Danny tuned it up, too."

"This is a damn nice car, you know," Danny said. "You should hang on to it. It's almost a classic."

I walked around the car and said "Holy shit!" about five times. And then I added, "I don't know what to say, boys."

"Our pleasure," said Jonas. "Danny's never worked on a Beemer before, and he's impressed. I might have to get one now."

Just as I finished walking around the car in shock, I heard a rumble and saw the tall red Ford pickup rolling up Main Street toward Elephant Gas. It pulled up under the elephant and stopped. "Here comes Miss Hotsie-Totsie," Danny announced.

The beautiful Sarah emerged from the driver's door of her truck and made a graceful three foot drop onto the asphalt. She ran over to me with her arms out for a hug. "It's really great to see you, Rob," she said. "How's that bump on your head?" She smiled into my eyes and reached up and rubbed the back of my head." Before I could answer she pouted and said, "I missed you when you left." I tried to swallow, but couldn't. She released her grip and asked me if I missed Elephant. Then, before I could answer that she said: "I'll bet you didn't miss this hell-hole at all, did you? I know I wouldn't." I asked Sarah if she was starting to paint the elephant. "I'm not painting the elephant silly," she said in a girly voice, "I'm painting the building. Tangerine. Right, Jonas? They'll be gay colors, for sure."

Jonas laughed. "They'll be extremely tasteful," he assured us.

"I'm scraping the back," said Sarah. "Wanna come see?" I definitely wanted to come see. Sarah was practically hopping up and down with enthusiasm, and she looked even more beautiful than I remembered. She was wearing her Daisy Duke outfit again, but with a different top – blue plaid this time. Her legs were breathtaking. I took a deep breath and followed her around the building. She looked back at me and said "I had to get more sandpaper from Muriel's." A 12- foot stepladder stood sideways next to the back wall of the garage building. The wide trim board across the top of the building was peeling badly, and Sarah had scraped half of it to bare wood.

"You're room's all ready for you," Sarah told me, as she climbed the ladder. Andie's got the key. I think you'll like it." She had a funny smile when she said that. "Well, gotta go scrape." It was late afternoon and the sun was at a three-quarter angle in the sky. I watched that perfect ass and those flawless legs go up the ladder and the beautiful blonde hair emerge from the shade into the sun. I decided I'd better leave and told Sarah I'd see her later.

"You've got yourself a friend there, Mr. Smith," Jonas said laughing when I walked back to the front of the garage. "She asked me three times when you were coming back. If I were straight and a little younger, I'd be all over that." I told Jonas that I didn't make a habit of giving women a second chance to stand me up.

"I can't believe you took no for an answer," said Danny.

"What was I supposed to do, put a gun to her head?"

Jonas shook his head. Then he gave me a lecture about how the most important element of success in any endeavor is perseverance. "Never give up, cowboy. You gotta get back on that horse." Right at that moment a loud explosion pierced the air and we all jumped. "The fireworks have begun," said Jonas. Then he pointed to my car. "Fire 'er up. She purrs like a kitten. Danny says you needed a tune-up bad." I admitted as much and turned the key. It sounded like a different car. The idle was smooth as glass, and there was no lag when I touched the gas pedal.

"The Germans make almost perfect engines, but you gotta maintain 'em," Danny scolded me. "You're going to be quicker now, and use less gas." I sat in the driver's seat and didn't say anything, recalling the lack of power a few days earlier while climbing toward Snoqualmie Pass.

Then Sarah came around from the back of the building. "That sure is a nice car," she said with her trademark smile. Jonas and Danny both grinned.

"Thanks everyone," I said. "Time to go clean up."

I pulled out onto Main Street in my like-new BMW, while my three new friends smiled and waved. I almost hit Billy, who didn't flinch and just nodded at me as he walked by, keys still jangling. Everything seemed better in Elephant this time. The buildings looked nicer and the street seemed cleaner. The afternoon sun left shadows on the sidewalks and gave the whole town more definition. As I approached the Elephant Chamber of Commerce office I saw Stacy's car, so I stopped. My encounter with the beautiful Sarah had made me a bit dizzy, and I wasn't quite ready to face her family. As I walked toward Stacy's office, I heard the whistle and pop of more fireworks in the distance. When she saw me, she got up from her desk and almost ran around it. She gave me a hug as soon as I had closed the door behind me. I was starting to like Elephant a lot more. "How's your head, Mr. Rob?" was the first thing she asked me. She reached around and gave the bump on the back of my head a rub. "You certainly gave everyone a scare at that meeting. I can't believe you came back after that." I told Stacy there was the small matter of my car being here, but that I really was looking forward to coming back to Elephant anyway. "Hard to believe," was her reply. I asked her if the town was still up in arms over the big elephant. She said she hadn't heard anything more about it and that everyone just gets back to normal around here. "A lot of people told me they felt bad that you got conked though. Do you still have a bruise?"

"It's going away," I told her. "I'm down to twenty Advil a day."

After an awkward silence, Stacy said, "Well, we're gearing up for the Fourth of July over at the park. Are you looking forward to it? It'll be pretty lame compared to Seattle, I'm sure. There's no Space Needle here."

"There's an elephant. That's sort of like your Space Needle."

"Very funny."

"They shoot fireworks out of the top of the Space Needle you know," I said. "Maybe you could shoot fireworks out of the Elephant's trunk. You have fireworks, right?" I asked.

"A few. Mostly, everyone does their own. It's like a war zone around here on the Fourth."

"No kidding. It's already started."

"The fireworks stand is the biggest fundraiser of the year for the Chamber." Stacy said that she didn't like it that so much of her paycheck came from money people spent so they could risk blowing their fingers off. "A gal's gotta pay the bills though."

Then Stacy got serious. "Listen. We really need to try this dinner thing one more time. You haven't made plans, have you?" I told her I had a date with the produce section at the grocery store. "No, you have a date with me, and I'm not taking no for an answer. You'll eat at my house and it'll be a lot less healthy than that. But I won't have a drop to drink," she said. "I'll be a lady and you'll be the gentleman you always are, and we'll shake hands good night when you leave." I asked her if she would hold a gun to my head if she had to, and she said yes.

Stacy looked out the window of her office and said, "There's a committee out there staring at your car." She meant it literally. The four female members of the Elephant Historic Preservation Commission were standing next to the driver's door of the shiny BMW in front of Stacy's office. One of them was wearing a solid pink dress and had unnaturally black hair. Gladys could see us through the window and she waved vigorously in our direction. Stacy and I set the time for our dinner date, and then I stepped out the door to face my next assailants.

I saw no moving cars or other pedestrians anywhere on Main Street, other than Billy a block away. As soon as I stepped out the door, Gladys held her arms out in the Elephant hugging posture that I was getting used to. "How's your head, you poor thing?" she said, reaching behind me and rubbing it. "I can't believe you came back after what they did to you." I hugged Gladys gently while the other ladies smiled silently.

I told Gladys I'd forgotten all about the knock on the head, but I thought Elephant would have erupted in civil war by now. "Everyone seems perfectly friendly."

"We all have to get along in this little town," she said. "Your car is all fixed. It looks very nice."

"All thanks to Jonas."

Then Ruth eased in and said, "I deserve a hug too." So I gave the entire hysterical committee a group hug.

"What's going on out there," A voice from across the street shouted. It was Eve from Guns-N-Things. She walked over to my car. "Is head OK?" she asked as she reached out to give me a hug of her own. "We all worried sick. Thought you write bad things." Eve told me that the Mayor signed the proclamation that would place the big gray elephant on the Historic Register. The formal ceremony would be the next day, July fourth, after the fireworks. "There's nothing anyone can do," she said, glaring at Beverly.

"They'll be glad some day," said Ruth, with complete certainty.

"Just so everybody keeps their shoes on," I said. "That's all I ask."

The front door on Muriel's hardware store swung open and out flew

Helen like she was being evicted from a bar. She smothered me, right there on the sidewalk, as if I'd just returned from being kidnapped by aliens. "I was sure you'd never come back," said Helen. She then apologized for the town, and Gladys and Eve joined in. "I guess we won't have our little circus," Helen said, "but we've still got our little elephant."

"You mean big elephant," said Eve. "It is very big."

I told the group of ladies hovered around my car that I needed to go get a clean room and a shower, but that I was looking forward to the Fourth of July festivities the next day. As I stepped toward the driver's door, a man and a woman I didn't recognize walked up to the car. "He's back, I see," said the man.

Then the woman looked at me with a smile. "I never doubted you'd be back," she said. "Oh, I'm Nancy. I work for the Farmer's Co-op, just down the street." I held out my hand, and she put both of her arms out. So we hugged. "This is our manager, Jack."

I looked at Jack apprehensively, and he shook his head. "Hand shake'll do," he said.

"Well, gotta go," I said to the growing crowd after shaking Jack's hand. "It's been nice." Helen forced another hug on me, and then I opened the undented car door, looking around to make sure there were no random huggers hiding in the shadows. I made it safely to the East end of town and into the Motel Parking lot. Billy had just turned around and headed the other direction when I pulled in.

Sarah's sister Andrea must have seen me drive up, because she was around the counter with her arms out by the time I opened the front door of the motel office. "Welcome back to Elephant," she said with a hug and a smile as beautiful as her sister's. She asked me about my head, and then reached behind and rubbed it. "We have your room all ready. Or rooms, I should say. Hope you can handle the Bridal Suite." I told Andrea that I had no plans to be a bride. She laughed and then said, "Well, maybe you'll be a groom soon," and gave me a little wink. I wasn't sure what that meant. Then she said, "My, your car looks all shiny." I told her that Advil and fresh paint both worked wonders. "Kenzie, Rob's here," Andrea yelled into the back room.

Sarah's daughter emerged from the back room with a serious expression. She already knew that her job was to take me to the bridal suite of the Moss Creek Motel. "C'mon," she ordered, and marched out the front door before I could pick up my bag. The bridal suite consisted of two motel rooms with part of the wall opened up between them. Unlike my room the previous week, the suite was painted in inoffensive beige colors. One of the rooms was now a living room and Kitchen, with furniture from the eighties, rather than the seventies. The other room had a king-sized bed with a white comforter. Kenzie said "here ya go," handed me the key, and marched out of the room as quickly as she had marched in. She must have suddenly remembered her customer service training because, two seconds later, she stuck her head back through the door and said "Let us know if you need anything. Have a nice stay." And then off she went.

The Mariners were starting a series in Kansas City that evening against the equally futile Royals. So I flipped on the TV to see which team would suck worse. I had three hours before I was to arrive at Stacy's house. In spite of the warm greeting I had received from Sarah, I intended to continue avoiding her. The game was tied 8-8 in the third inning and I watched the for another two hours until the game went into extra innings – now tied at 12 apiece. Then I turned off the TV and took a shower.

CHAPTER TWENTY-ONE

When I arrived at Stacy's house in my newly restored BMW, I was surprised to see the freshly-washed yellow Corvette – the same one I had been driving for the past week – parked in the driveway behind Stacy's car. I had to park in the street. Stacy opened the front door and greeted me as I walked up, and in the living room I saw Jonas standing next to a short, thin gay man wearing a blue blazer, khaki slacks and an open necked blue dress shirt. He was clean-shaven with closely cropped hair and he spoke in a high-pitched, whiney voice with a trace of lisp when he introduced himself as Phil. Jonas had on a different Hawaiian shirt, along with his tan cargo shorts and flip-flops. "Phil hates the Fourth of July," Jonas said. "So he thought he'd come spend it with me. Of course he hates all holidays, because they keep him from working." Phil looked annoyed, but kept silent while Jonas spoke.

"I invited Jonas and Phil to join us for dinner," said Stacy. "They'll be our chaperones, so you know I'll be on my best behavior."

"You and Phil haven't had Stacy's cooking," Jonas said to me. "She has a hidden talent." Stacy denied it, but the aroma of basil and oregano now caught my attention. Stacy's house smelled like a restaurant should, unlike the two restaurants in town that smelled more like beer, cigarettes and lard.

"It smells fabulous," I told Stacy. That sounded obligatory, but it was true. She thanked me from the kitchen. Stacy's furnishings were inexpensive, but the house was neat and spotlessly clean. She kept house like she dressed, trying to appear older than she was.

Phil sat silently on the couch while Jonas and I discussed Corvettes and BMWs. "Phil drives a Lexus," Jonas said after a few minutes. "It's a very boring car."

"Washing machines are boring too," said Phil in his extremely gay voice, "but they serve an important purpose, just like cars." Then he looked at me. "I've encouraged Jonas to start collecting large household appliances, but he can't seem to develop the interest."

Jonas changed to subject. "Phil and I are going to Walla Walla next week to go wine tasting. Do you know that here in Elephant, we're just two hours away from where they make some of the best wine in the world?"

"In fact, Jonas and I are talking about starting a winery right here in Elephant," said Phil, with a broad smile. "We're going to call it Chateau Corvette."

"Yes," said Jonas. "It'll have hints of motor oil and notes of exhaust." Stacy laughed from the kitchen.

Stacy came to the kitchen door and announced that dinner would be ready in about 20 minutes. We could hear her working in her kitchen as we discussed a variety of topics, including traffic on L.A. freeways ("Cars are actually a blight," Jonas admitted), whether or not Bruce Springsteen was as important as Bob Dylan ("what about Eddie Vedder?" Stacy yelled from the kitchen, which brought only silence) and why, in the 21st century, men wearing cowboy hats looked ridiculous. (No one present disagreed with that, though many men in Elephant wore them.) Then Phil said, "I dated a guy who wore a cowboy hat once. He was totally hot." Jonas rolled his eyes.

Stacy began placing food on her old wooden dining table which she had covered with a spotless white table cloth. "I just threw a little something together," she lied. All of this was clearly meant to impress, and it did. A bowl of pasta sprinkled with basil sat next to a plate of Chicken in a cream sauce with mushrooms and tomatoes that could have sold for $25 a plate. A wine glass was placed next to each plate, except Stacy's.

"Where in the world did you learn to cook like this?" Phil asked Stacy enthusiastically, as he examined the pasta. "This is fantastic, Jonas. No wonder you don't miss dining in LA. You've got a world-class chef right here."

Stacy was embarrassed. "One of my college boyfriends was a chef in Portland," she said. "It's amazing what you can learn." Then she looked at me. "Yes Rob, one of my many boyfriends."

We sat down at the table and began dishing up our food. A separate plate with green salad, perfectly garnished, sat next to each dinner plate. Stacy poured red wine for the three of us. "It's a Merlot, from Walla Walla." A large candle and an arrangement of wildflowers sat in the middle of the table. The conversation continued, and Stacy had no trouble keeping up with the topics covered by three college-educated men over forty. About ten minutes into the meal she turned to Jonas and asked him where he lived. "It's weird. I've never known that," she said.

"Oh, it's a little place out of town that I rent," he replied.

"It's a hovel, trust me," Phil said. I was pretty sure Phil was being sarcastic, but he had a voice that made everything he said sound like he was being sarcastic.

"My my, you're such a man of mystery," Stacy said to Jonas.

"Let's change the subject," Jonas said. "Say Rob, I had a very interesting conversation with your hot girlfriend today. You know, 'Miss Hotsy-Totsy', as Danny calls her. It was right after you left the garage."

Stacy stopped eating and frowned. "Yes, he knows. He's totally in love with her. And she thinks she's so pretty."

Phil perked up. "Well well. Tell us more Jonas."

"It seems that Sarah was very disappointed that our friend Rob here left town without saying goodbye the other day. She thinks he's avoiding her."

"We had a date and she stood me up," I said. "And she was the one who suggested it in the first place. But it obviously wasn't that big a deal to her."

"She asked you out?" asked Phil.

"She's a real hottie," said Jonas. Then he smiled at Phil. "If anyone could make me go straight, it would be Sarah."

Now Phil was rolling his eyes. "You're probably old enough to be her grandfather. I'll have to meet this girl."

"Okay, I admit it," I said. "I'm totally in love with Sarah." Stacy frowned at me.

"So here's the deal, Smith" said Jonas. "Sarah said she really was too busy last weekend. But she wants to do something with you this weekend. She told me to tell you that."

"She did?"

"In fact, you know what she said?" Jonas was grinning broadly now. I shook my head and Stacy scowled. "She said you need to put on your big-boy panties and get over there and ask her out."

"My what?"

"That's what she said; your 'big-boy panties'. That's a good one, huh? I guess that's how moms talk." Jonas and Phil were laughing out loud, but Stacy wasn't. I was stunned.

"He's speechless," said Phil. "This woman must be something."

"Oh, she's something alright," Stacy snarked. "Those Hockensmith bitches are so full of themselves."

"Sounds like somebody's jealous," said Phil.

Stacy stared at me while my brain turned to mush. Was Jonas joking? I couldn't breathe.

"So you're back in the saddle now, dude." Jonas said. "Like it or not."

"Panties and all, I guess," I said.

The conversation moved on to famous Hollywood men while I began feeling ill. Jonas, Phil and Stacy all gave their opinions about whether or not Arnold Schwarzenegger is sexy. Only Phil gave him more than a 2.5. Johnny Depp got all fives, but Russell Crowe rated lower. Stacy brought up Eddie Vedder again. Jonas didn't know what he looked like and Phil said, "he's kind of scruffy."

Then Stacy said, "I'm not into country music much, but that Kenny Chesney is to die for; even though he wears a cowboy hat." Jonas and Phil both said they couldn't disagree.

"You look kind of pale, Rob" Jonas said to me suddenly. "All this talk of sexy men isn't turning you on, is it? Don't tell me ..."

"No." I said. "Were you talking about sexy men? I wasn't even listening."

"Oh, I know," Jonas said then. "Getting back on that horse is making you nervous, isn't it?" Then he decided to give me some fatherly advice while Stacy and Phil listened intently. "So here's the deal, Smith," his speech began. "Sarah's a beautiful girl, but she's a little shallow and her world is pretty small. She hasn't seen a whole lot. You're just the guy to help her see the bigger world out there. You're a writer. You're a student of the world. You can open her eyes to the wonderful things out there. She senses that, and that's what she finds attractive."

Phil started getting agitated and interrupted Jonas. "That is such bullshit, Jonas. Don't listen to him, Rob."

"I don't know," said Stacy, gazing at me with a smile. "That might work for me."

Phil shook his head. "No, girls like that are looking for guys with money. How much money do you have, Rob?"

"Yeah, money works for me, too," Stacy said.

"It worked for Phil," Jonas said with a grin.

"Ha ha."

"I'm in debt, but I might have a big commission coming," I said, taking Phil's question seriously. "But if she's looking for a rich guy. I ain't it."

"You're wrong," Phil insisted. "It's not the reality, it's the perception. With that fancy European car and that big commission, you smell like money. It's the smell that's important."

"You smell pretty good to me, Rob," said Stacy, smiling.

"Let's change the subject," I said. "You know what? My client on that apartment sale is sort of related to Sarah." That brought complete silence. "They have the same last name and I found out that her brother-in-law is Sarah's biological grandfather. I met him yesterday; in Seattle."

After a few seconds Jonas said, "Well that's weird."

"He and his partner built the big elephant," I said. "He told me all about it."

"That is weird," Stacy said. "He must be really old. Does he still own it?"

I told the group at the table about Peter and Hollister and how Peter had been forced out of the business. "Hollister McCune. That's our client at the law firm," said Phil. "That's how Jonas ended up in Elephant. I have Hollister to thank."

"What a great place to disappear to," said Jonas. "You should think about moving here, Smith. You can leave all your troubles far away."

Stacy laughed then. "Yeah, you can get into a whole new set of troubles here, Rob."

"It's funny though," I said. "Peter and Hollister both did a pretty good job of disappearing when they left Elephant."

"L.A. is an excellent place to disappear to," Phil said, looking at Jonas with a frown. Jonas frowned back, and then asked Stacy what she had studied in college besides boys and cooking.

"Business and economics," she said. She told us she had also studied French, which was her favorite subject. She said she spent a semester in Paris and almost moved there to become a business consultant. At this point Phil said something to Stacy in French, to which she immediately replied, and then gave a little laugh. They conversed in French for several more sentences, while Jonas got annoyed.

"Par-doe-nay-mwa," Jonas finally said. "Voulez-vous coucher avec moi ce soir?"

"Not with your attitude," said Phil. Stacy laughed and then looked at me and raised her eyebrows a couple of times. "That's the only thing you know in French, isn't it?" Phil said to Jonas. "A randy song title."

"Yup. That and bouillabaisse," Jonas replied.

Jonas, Phil and I finished a bottle and a half of wine while Stacy drank her mineral water. We talked about the economy, which Stacy knew more about than the rest of us, and we talked about how the farmers around Elephant needed one more good rain before harvest – another subject that favored Stacy. Soon Phil cleared his throat and Jonas announced it was time for them to go. Both of them heaped praise on Stacy's food and conversation and helped carry dishes to the kitchen. Jonas told me to stop by the next day to let him and Danny know how the car was running. "Let's go, Rockefeller," said Phil. Jonas suddenly got an angry look and glanced back at us, but said nothing. Then they left.

"Stacy immediately looked at me with a big smile. "You don't think?"

"Nah, he couldn't be. Could he?"

"That would explain the money," she said.

"And the secrecy."

"Maybe I'll get him drunk and force it out of him one of these days," Stacy said.

I stayed at the table with Stacy. A half-bottle of wine remained and I told her she had been so well-behaved that I thought she should have one glass. "There's no way I can finish that myself," I told her, "and it's too good to waste." At first she refused, but I talked her into it. We each looked around the room in silence for awhile, and Stacy took two very small sips from her glass. I looked at her left hand. "The ring is off, I see. Is it really over with Curtis?"

"Oh yes. He's already moved in with Gwenn in Pendleton. What a dumb name. Gwenn, I mean."

"Curtis is a pretty dumb name too," I said, and she laughed.

I asked Stacy if she had talked to Lindsay since we saw her at Melville's. She said she hadn't. "She probably told Rick what a bad influence I was. A reputation's a tough thing to shake."

"You should call her. Invite her to lunch."

"Yeah, I should I guess."

Stacy asked me about Seattle, and I told her about Freemont and the crappy real estate market and how it is very beautiful in Seattle in the summer. "They have a weird statue there too," I said, "of Vladimir Lenin." She told me she had been all over the world, but she'd never been to Seattle. "You should invite me," she said, but I didn't respond. We finished our wine and I was just getting ready to make a graceful exit when the doorbell rang.

"It's probably Jonas," said Stacy. "He must have forgotten something." She started toward the door, but it burst open before she got there.

An angry overweight man in his late twenties who appeared to have been drinking stormed in and confronted her. "Boy, you're not wasting any time, are you," the man said, looking past her at me.

"Curtis, what the fuck are you doing here?!"

"Checking up on you. You're right back to your slutty ways, aren't you, you bitch!"

"You need to leave. Now!"

Curtis didn't leave. He walked toward me, as I sat frozen at the dining table. "Let me introduce myself," he said gruffly and stuck out his hand. Curtis was easily fifty pounds heavier than me and at least fifteen years younger. And he had definitely been drinking.

I stood up nervously and reached out my hand. "Curtis, right?"

"I'm sure she's told you all about me," he said, pulling his hand back without shaking mine. He then lifted his chin up and looked down his nose at me, as threateningly as he could. "Don't believe any of it. She's full of shit."

Stacy rushed over and shoved herself in front of Curtis. "Leave him alone. It's not what you think." She tried to push Curtis toward the door. He grabbed her left shoulder and easily shoved her to the side.

He looked at me again and then said, "Fine. You're not worth my time, you cunt. Have a nice life." He turned and marched toward the front door. He had some difficulty with the knob before he got the door open and went through it.

Stacy looked at me for a moment with tears streaming down her face. Then she went to the kitchen. "Fuck it. I'm drinking." She brought an open bottle of red wine and both of our glasses to the living room couch. "You'd better have a drink too," she said.

"Damn right I'm drinking. That guy could o' beat the shit out of me!"

Stacy rolled her eyes. "Oh, he wouldn't do that. He's really not like that." I was unconvinced and chugged my wine glass. Stacy did the same and then refilled our glasses. We sat down on the couch, side by side. She gave me an angry look and said, "I can't believe you're in love with Sarah. What is it about her?"

"I'm not in love with her. It's pure lust. And I thought we covered that the other night."

"Oh yeah. You told me that she's a gourmet pizza and I'm uncooked. Well I'm gettin' cooked now."

Then, as I expected she would, Stacy had a total meltdown. The only thing I could think about was how much I wanted to leave, but I stayed. "My life sucks," she said, and then she continued with a monologue of how miserable she was and how she continued to make a fool of herself in front of me. She made a sound like "pschhhhh." Then she said, "I don't know why you even talk to me." She finished another full glass of wine and started yet another before she stopped talking. I sat on the couch next to her, feeling helpless.

After her three-quarters of a bottle of wine to my one glass, Stacy lay down on the couch with her head in my lap. She soon was asleep. I sat for a few minutes, feeling helpless, and then I eased her head off my leg and got up. I took a blanket off her bed and put it over her. Then I drove back to the motel. It was nearly midnight and I had to put together my new plan to ask Sarah for a date.

CHAPTER TWENTY-TWO

I slept fitfully in my room the night after dinner at Stacy's house, and in the early morning I had a vivid and startling dream. The details are unimportant, except for this: The beautiful Sarah was in it, and she was naked. I woke up in a sweat and was disoriented for about half an hour. I made some bad coffee in the tiny coffee maker in the bathroom and then stared at the blank TV screen in my 'living room' for awhile. As my head cleared, a feeling of dread came over me. I had to ask Sarah out again. I had no choice after what she said to Jonas. I was forty-four years old and I felt like a schoolboy who had a crush on the head cheerleader, to the point of having pornographic dreams about her. Now I had to face her. I started to get dressed, and then found myself wearing a pair of long black socks. Why did I even pack those? I took them off and put on my flip-flops.

I'd been awake almost an hour before I remembered what happened the previous evening at Stacy's house. I had left her passed out on the couch after her husband nearly killed me. Poor Stacy. This is how adulthood arrives for some people. It reminded me of some of my own pathetic experiences, so I felt sympathetic. I'd better go check on her, I thought. At least I could offer her breakfast. I loaded a fresh syrup bottle into my shorts pocket and headed out. I saw no sign of the head cheerleader as I left the motel, and I was glad for that.

I was surprised to find Stacy awake and alert when I knocked on her door at nine-o'clock Saturday morning. It was July 3rd. "I woke up at three and drank a half-gallon of water and took four aspirin," she said. "I learned that hangover cure a long time ago." Then she said, "I'm not even going to apologize for last night. I'm sure you're used to these disastrous evenings by now. Thanks for not taking advantage of me though." I wasn't sure if she meant that or not.

"Let's go to breakfast," I said. I patted my right cargo pocket. "I've got the syrup, loaded and cocked."

"Not so fast, cowboy. I'm the cook around here. I'm a farm girl and I can make you the best flapjacks you've ever had." She grinned as I said okay and walked into her living room.

I looked in the kitchen and it was spotless. Every dish was put away. "This is amazing," I said. "When I left last night, you were passed out on the couch and your kitchen looked like Beirut."

"I've been up for awhile. I couldn't get back to sleep after I saw that mess." Stacy went to the kitchen to get out her griddle. "And no weapons in the house. Gimme that bottle." I handed it over. Then I sat down on the couch in the living room and Stacy yelled from the kitchen, "So did you ask Miss Hotsy-Totsy out on a date this morning?"

"No I didn't," I yelled back, "and I don't think I will. And don't call her that."

Stacy came to the kitchen door and smiled. "But you have to ask her out, Rob. Your manhood is at stake. What kind of man would turn down an opportunity like that?" I stared at her and didn't respond.

Stacy was right though. I had to do it, even though I'd been obsessing over Sarah for a week and I was sure I would probably be unable to speak when I came face to face with her. "Let's not talk about Sarah anymore," I said. "So what was up with Curtis last night?"

"He's an asshole," Stacy said, now back in front of her griddle. "Let's not talk about him anymore either."

I got up and stood in the kitchen doorway while Stacy worked on the pancakes. "Okay," I said. "I know, we can talk about the big elephant. Do you think it'll still be there when you're Gladys's age? You'll probably be one of the old bitties trying to protect it then."

She laughed. "Probably. Nobody ever wants to change anything around here. I'm sure I'll be the same way when I'm old."

At that moment a chime sounded in my right cargo pocket. I got out my phone and read the new text message. It was from Peter Ellington. "News 4 u. Holly wills EG 2 grlz. Thx 2 pic" That was it.

I stared at the phone with a frown for several seconds. "What's the matter?" asked Stacy. "Did somebody die?"

"No. It's a text from Peter. You know, Sarah's grandfather that I told you about? But I can't make any sense of it."

"Let me see." Stacy came over to the door and read the message while her pancakes cooked. She immediately said, "It says that Hollister McCune is leaving Elephant Gas to the Hockensmith sisters in his will. And then something about a photo."

"Yeah, I should have known you'd speak 'tee-ex-tee'. It's like a foreign language to me." Then I explained. "When I met with Peter the other day, I showed him a photo of Sarah on my phone. He texted it on to Hollister."

"You have a picture of Sarah on your phone?! You are in love with her, aren't you?"

"Gladys took it last week. It was her idea. And no, I'm not in love with her. Well maybe."

"Lemme see the picture." She reached for the phone again and I pulled it away.

"I don't think so."

"OK, fine." She pulled her hand away, but as soon as I relaxed, she suddenly snatched the phone out of my hand before I could react. "You gotta be quicker than that, cowboy," she said with a big smile. "Good thing that wasn't your gun."

When she couldn't figure out how to bring the photo up on the screen, I took the phone back and did it and showed it to her. "Oh what a lovely couple," she said in fake baby talk. "You look so cute in your little pink apron." I told her to shut up and finish breakfast, and then I locked the phone. She went back to her griddle.

"So it sounds like Sarah's going to own the big elephant," Stacy said, as she worked her pancake flipper. "She'll be stuck with it forever, because it's a historic landmark. Serves her right."

"At least she and Andrea will get Jonas's rent," I said. "I'm sure they can use the money. And Sarah can do the maintenance on the garage."

"Maybe we could talk her into blowing the elephant up," said Stacy.

"Yeah, right."

"Seriously. We could build a bomb and put it inside the elephant and then set it off."

"That would be funny," I said. "We'd better do it by tomorrow night though. Otherwise we'll be blowing up a historic landmark. They put people in jail for that, don't they?

"Yeah, I guess you're right."

The subject was dropped and Stacy delivered her pancakes. They were the best I'd ever eaten. They were crisp on the outside and dense and thick and moist on the inside, and they had nuts and fruit in them. And they were hot and swimming in syrup when she served them to me. "Wow!" I said after the second bite. "I just had a pancake orgasm."

Stacy laughed. "At least I can satisfy a man somehow."

We started making small talk. I asked Stacy how her work was going. "What does the Executive Director of a Chamber of Commerce do on a normal day?"

"Listen to people complain, mostly," she said. "I did have an interesting visit this week though." She told me that an optometrist's office in Pendleton was thinking of opening a small office in Elephant. They would have a doctor there one day a week. "One of the eye doctors came in," she said. "He was pretty old, but really cute. And so nice."

"How old?"

"At least your age. Maybe even older."

"Wow, that old. Married?"

"Ring. So I guess so."

"So you gave him the sales pitch?"

"No!" She suddenly looked annoyed.

"I meant the sales pitch for the town, stupid," I said, "not the one for yourself."

"Oh. Sorry."

"You gotta get him here first. Then you can wreck his marriage."

"Very funny."

I left Stacy in a good mood and decided to go to Jonas's shop. I needed to avoid the motel as long as possible, and I wanted to check into what Peter had written in his text message. But as I approached the big elephant, I saw the tall Ford pickup parked next to the garage. Before I could turn around, Jonas and Sarah both waved. I was stuck. Sarah came up to the door of the car before I could open it and said "Hi Rob!" with her beautiful smile. Jonas stood behind her with a big grin and waggled his closed fists in front of him, like he was gripping the reins of a horse. Then over by the garage door in the shadow, I saw that Gus Reimer was standing next to his Plymouth Business Coupe, which was parked in the garage. I asked Sarah how her work was coming. "I'm ready to start painting, as soon as I get some shade," she replied. She said she had to work in the motel that afternoon, and that she was going there now. "You should stop by the office." Her smile got bigger and more beautiful. I told her that I agreed that I should.

After Sarah drove away, Danny stepped out from behind Gus's car. "Did you get a date with Miss Hotsy-Totsy yet?" he asked.

I was getting annoyed at Danny's pet name for Sarah. If she was going to be my wife some day, the world needed to take her more seriously than that. "No," I said. "I'm too chicken."

Jonas shook his head in disappointment. "Your manhood is on the line, Smith."

"Yeah, that's what Stacy just told me. What is this? High school?"

"High school is just life, my boy," Jonas replied. "And life is high school. Don't you know that by now? If you wanna be one of the popular boys, you gotta score with the best looking girls in the school. It doesn't change when you get older."

"Okay, Okay. I'm gonna do it, but that's not why I'm here. I got a strange text from Peter Ellington. You know, Sarah's grandfather? I think he said that Hollister McCune is leaving Elephant Gas to the Hockensmith sisters in his will."

I showed Jonas my phone, and he looked puzzled for a moment. Then he reached into his shorts pocket, pulled out his phone and pressed a couple of buttons. In a moment he said sharply, "Phil. Get out here."

Within seconds, Phil emerged from Jonas's office. "Have you heard any new developments in the Hollister McCune case? Show him the text, Smith." I showed my phone to Phil, and he understood the message immediately.

"News to me, but I'm on it," Phil said, pulling out *his* phone. Now we were all three standing under the big elephant with our cell phones in our hands. Phil walked into the shade and in a few moments, he had an answer. "It's true. They just sent me an email confirming it."

"Forward it to Smith here," Jonas said.

I gave Phil my phone number and he punched at his phone a few times. "Done." My phone chirped, and within five minutes of arriving at Elephant Gas to ask about Hollister's will, I had written proof on the little screen in my hand.

"Now you really have to ask her out, Smith," Jonas said. "She's an heiress."

I looked up at the big elephant. "Great. What an inheritance."

"Well, she gets me, too. As a tenant, I mean." He smiled.

I told the group about Stacy's idea of talking Sarah into blowing up the elephant. "She says we should build a bomb."

"No need to do that," Danny said. "This elephant is a bomb waiting to happen. Remember the Hindenburg? This thing is like a big blimp. Just fill 'er with gas and add a spark. And then kaboom!"

Jonas and Gus laughed. "Let me get my car out of here first," Gus said.

"Well, back to reality," said Jonas. "Are you going to show Sarah the email?"

"Maybe over dinner."

Gus went over to his car and pulled out an envelope and brought it to me. "Mr. Smith, I found something that belonged to my wife that I thought you might be interested in. She wanted to be a writer, like you. She wasn't very successful, but she got a few articles published." In the envelope were clippings from newspapers. Some were obviously very old. We took them into Jonas's office, and Gus spread them out on the counter for Jonas and Phil and Danny and I to examine.

"Check this out," said Jonas, holding up one of Gus's clippings. "She wrote an article for the Elephant Press newspaper when the elephant was unveiled. July 5th, 1960." A barely legible black and white photo showed a crowd of people and several 1950s cars crowded into the parking lot under the new elephant. A row of narrow round-topped gas pumps sat under the elephant's belly. The byline on the article said "By Eunice Reimer."

Another article Eunice wrote was published in the Oregonian in Portland. "That was her claim to fame," said Gus. "She was so proud of that." The article was in the Travel Section in 1973 and gave a list of places to stay and places to eat and things to do. "There was a lot more to do here then," Gus said.

"So how's your article coming?" Jonas asked me.

"Yeah," said Danny, with a grin. "Is it done?"

"Can I make copies of those?" I asked Gus. "They might give me some ideas." Gus agreed.

"You haven't started yet, have you?" Jonas said.

"Well, I've been working on it in my head. Writing's hard. I need some ideas."

"You could write about the wheat," said Danny. "We have lots of wheat."

"And sunshine," said Phil, smiling. "There's lots of sunshine here."

"Yeah, and trees," added Jonas with a grin. "Write about the trees, Smith. Oh, and don't forget about the roads. We have roads. Paved ones and gravel ones. And even some dirt roads. And there are houses here too."

"You guys are hilarious," I said without laughing. "I know. I'll write about a town full of people who think they're a whole lot funnier than they really are."

"Good one," Jonas said.

"Well, right now, I've got to go and get a date with the world's most beautiful handyman. Since you guys are so full of good ideas, where should I take her? She doesn't drink. And she obviously barely eats."

"Invite her to your room," said Danny.

"Nah, Smith's got way more class than that," said Jonas. "Take her for a drive. Then invite her to your room."

"Sorry I asked."

Gus spoke up. "Here's what Gladys and I used to do in high school," he said. "There's an old log cabin at an abandoned mine up on Moss Creek, about 15 miles upstream. I'm pretty sure it's still there. It's a beautiful walk. And there's probably still furniture and other things there."

"Not bad," said Phil. "That could be very romantic."

Gus told me that the trail to the log cabin was on the right side of the road, and just beyond it was a small yellow cottage on the left. "You can't miss that cottage," he said. "If you pass it, you've gone too far." Then he added, "And then come back to Elephant. Sarah can be your date to the Fourth of July Picnic. She won't even have to eat."

"What a cheap date. That's what I like," said Danny.

"Or, you could just invite her to your room," said Jonas.

I thanked the boys and then took the copies of Gus's articles and got into the Beemer and drove to the Motel. And then I sucked it up.

CHAPTER TWENTY-THREE

I drove slowly along Main Street from Elephant Gas to the Moss Creek Motel in my freshly repaired, repainted and detailed 1990 BMW 535i. The interior smelled good – not the formaldehyde smell of a new car, but more like the tangy freshness of strong cleansers. I looked down between my seat and the center console and not a food crumb could be seen. I almost ran off the road as I searched the floor for any spec of dirt. I didn't pass any moving cars or pedestrians on my way to the motel, except for Billy, who nodded as he walked past Guns-N-Things. I entered the motel parking lot and saw three customized Harley Davidson motorcycles parked next to the entrance to the office.

Inside the office, both of the beautiful Hockensmith sisters were behind the counter, talking simultaneously. Across from them were three leather-clad pudgy men in their 50s or 60s. And each bearded biker had a grin frozen on his face. I stood, unacknowledged near the door, and then chickened out and decided to go to my room and return later. But just as I opened the door to exit, Sarah called out, "Hey Rob, don't leave." The three old Hell's Angels turned and frowned at me, clearly annoyed at the interruption.

"Hey there, Sarah," I said weakly. I told her I would come back later, but she insisted that I take a seat in the lobby and wait.

"We're almost done," she said cheerfully. The motorcyclists obviously disagreed, but I waited. One of them got on his cell phone and began an animated conversation. It soon turned in to a heated argument, which he obviously won, because, just as abruptly, he closed the phone with a big smile. He turned to his fellow Angels and told them it was all arranged. Shortly after that the three bikers walked out the door in a happy mood. Sarah looked at me, cocked her beautiful head toward the door behind the counter and said, "Come on back." She went through it and I followed dutifully.

The disarray in the motel's back room was worse than it had been a few days before. The children's and dogs' toys were no longer in one pile, but were now strewn evenly across the floor. Near the entrance to the small office, a box of file folders was spread across the floor. Andrea told me later that a guest from a month earlier had requested a copy of her receipt and the mess on the floor was the result of the ultimately successful search. "Sarah's kids were supposed to clean that up," she had said.

A lively discussion was now taking place between Andrea and Millie. "We have to get the toilet in Room 26 replaced," Andrea said excitedly. Then she glared at Sarah. "Hear that, sister?"

"I'm on it," Sarah replied calmly.

Millie seemed even more agitated than Andrea. "Kenzie and Nick can help Sophia with the housekeeping. But we'd better go shopping for more towels. We have a lot to do."

Sarah looked at me with her smile. "Twenty motorcyclists are coming next weekend. All because we're pretty. Those guys were headed up to Washington with a big group, but we talked them into coming here instead." Sarah was clearly proud of herself. "Now mom and Andie are stressing," she said.

Outside the back door under the patio roof I saw Taver and Nela quietly sitting and playing with some kind of unrecognizable toy. Both of the rat dogs were sleeping in the grass. Kenzie was sitting in a chair nearby reading a book. This time it was only the adults who were in an uproar. Millie and Andrea both talked at the same time. Then Sarah turned and added her opinion about which of the motel's 36 rooms should be set aside for the group.

"They'll want to be downstairs near their bikes," said Andrea.

"We don't have 20 downstairs rooms," said Millie, "but we have exactly

20 rooms in the east wing. We'll put them there."

"The guy on the left had pretty eyes," said Sarah. "Let's put him in room 2."

A yell came from outside. "Taver, get back here." It was Kenzie, who jumped up and began sprinting away from the back door."

"Oh God!" Andrea exclaimed as she headed out the door. She grabbed Nela and then ran after Taver and Kenzie and the dogs.

"When are you going to build that fence, girlfriend?" Millie asked Sarah.

"Maybe when I'm a grandmother."

I stood silently near the door to the office while Millie and Sarah worked in the kitchen area preparing lunch for the group. It was 2:30 in the afternoon. The microwave oven in the corner on the counter was running continuously. I didn't pay attention to what was in it until Millie handed something to Sarah. It was a plastic tray – a frozen dinner, that was now unfrozen. "This is Kenzie's," Millie said. I'll do Andie's next and then yours.

"I'm starving," Sarah said. "We should start having lunch sooner." She peeled the cover from the tray. "This looks good," she said. Actually it didn't.

"Would you like us to heat one of these up for you?" Millie asked me cheerfully.

"I already ate. But thanks so much. It looks good." Lying to women was a skill I had perfected long ago. I hadn't eaten since the pancake breakfast at Stacy's, but the sight of that TV dinner ruined whatever appetite I had. Sarah went out the back door with Kenzie's lunch and Millie pulled Andrea's tray out of the microwave and replaced it with another one. She pushed a few buttons on the microwave, which responded with appropriate beeps, and then it whirred away for a couple of minutes. Kenzie and Andrea returned to the back patio after successfully retrieving Taver and the dogs from the field behind the motel. "Thanks mom!" Kenzie exclaimed with a big smile when she was presented with her lunch.

Andrea and Sarah came back into the office and again I was offered lunch, and again I declined as gracefully as I could. Andrea took her tray back out to the patio and Millie retrieved Sarah's lunch from the microwave peeling off the thin paper. Sarah opened a metal TV tray that was leaning against the wall and set it in the middle of the room. "Grab a chair over there, Rob. You can still join me." I did as I was told and then looked over at her lunch. The peas and mashed potatoes had a gray cast to them and whatever it was that served as gravy was still mostly solid, and even grayer. Encased in that substance, presumably, was some form of meat product. It looked like what I imagined prison food would be.

Millie and Sarah began discussing the Hell's Angels' visit again, while I sat silently. "We should put care packages together for them," Sarah said. "Leave them in each room. You know, cookies and juice. And maybe some flowers. Some of them are bringing their wives."

"We could throw a party for them," Andrea yelled in from the patio. Then she came into the room. For the next five minutes all three women talked rapidly at once, and they seemed to make perfect sense to each other. I was like a spectator at a three-way verbal ping-pong tournament. My head pivoted as I looked from one speaker to the next to the next, as they volleyed their opinions at each other.

There was a short pause, and then Sarah looked at me and laughed. "Are you lost, Rob? It's hard to keep up, isn't it?"

"My husband can't stand it when we get going like that," said Millie. "He just walks away."

"So does Jamie," said Andrea. "That's my husband. He tries a little harder than dad, though."

"This is why we like working together," Sarah said. "This is the most fun we have. Just us girls talking."

At that moment a heart-stopping scream came from the patio. Then Kenzie yelled Taver's name. Andrea and Millie jumped up together and ran out the back door. Sarah smiled at me. "I'm so glad my kids are older." Then she asked," So what did you do last night?"

I was stumped. I wasn't expecting any questions. I didn't know where to start with the whole Jonas and Phil and Stacy and Curtis thing. I began formulating my response, but was spared when Sarah spoke again. "We all had a family meeting last night and we came up with a plan to open a flower shop here in the motel. Do you know that you can't get flowers in

Elephant? You have to go to Pendleton."

I got a rare sentence in. "That sounds like a good idea."

Sarah went on talking. She told me about how the flower and gift displays would be in the lobby of the motel and pointed to where the cooler would be, in the back room. My mind started wandering. I thought about Peter and how much he and Sarah looked alike; especially their green eyes. I thought about asking her about her grandfather, but I'd have to wait for a break in her monologue. I also needed a break in the action to talk about a date for the next day. Sarah must have read my mind, because she suddenly stopped talking and looked at me. "I'm off tomorrow afternoon," she said, and then actually didn't speak for several seconds.

My Big-Boy-Panties felt saggy, but I cinched them up and went for it. "Wanna do something?"

"Yeah, I guess." Now she was shy and not so confident.

I felt the same way, but I proceeded, "I need a guide to show me the countryside around Elephant."

"Okay." She seemed hesitant. "I don't get out there that much, but we could."

I asked her if she was going to the Fourth of July Picnic with anyone later tomorrow."

"My family," she said, almost protectively. I waited for her to invite me along, but she didn't.

I pulled the panties up a little tighter and went ahead and invited myself. "Maybe I could tag along. I don't really have anybody else to go with." This wasn't true, of course, since Jonas would have been happy to have me tag along with him and Phil, and Stacy would probably have been thrilled.

Sarah hesitated. "Well... I guess."

"Okay then."

The conversation had become completely awkward, but thankfully Millie and Andrea returned from the patio, each with a small sobbing child in her arms and a small dog trailing behind. Sarah practically jumped from her chair and ran over to console the babies. The three women, along with Kenzie, who had also come in from the patio, spent the next several minutes attempting to cheer up the younger ones and completely ignored me. I looked over at the metal folding tray, and saw Sarah's lunch. It was only half eaten, and she was obviously done. This might explain how she stayed so thin.

What I was witnessing now was almost like a ritual. Everyone in the room seemed genuinely content, except for me and Taver. I was nervous as hell and Taver was fussing and complaining. But all of the older females in the room were engrossed in playing out their maternal instincts, and Nela was smiling and laughing. I sat watching and said nothing.

After a few minutes, Kenzie grabbed Nela and took her and Taver back out to the patio. Sarah made a joke to Andrea about how much easier Andrea had it as a mother because of cousin Kenzie. Then the three women simultaneously remembered me. They all looked at me without saying anything. It was obviously my turn, so I spoke. "I met someone interesting this week," I said. The ladies pretended to be curious. "His name's Peter Ellington." The room suddenly turned ice cold, and I knew immediately that mentioning Peter's name was a mistake. I thought breaking the news of the inheritance of Elephant Gas would score some points, but I could see now that I had just lost a bunch.

Millie lit into him first. "My ex-father-in-law has been disowned. I don't even want to hear his name spoken here."

"Well, he gave me some interesting news," I said lamely.

"There's nothing that old man could possibly say that would be interesting to me." Millie's face was bright red now. "He and his no-good son pissed away everything they ever had. And he'd better stay away from Sarah and Andie and these kids." Millie was overtaken with anger by the time she finished her speech. Sarah and Andrea looked on in silence, but they obviously both agreed with their mother. It was time to make an exit.

"Don't worry, he's not coming to Elephant," I said.

"Let him come to Elephant," said Sarah. "We don't care. We have guns. And we'll use 'em."

"That man is not welcome here," said Andrea.

That was it. There was not even a tiny shred of curiosity about Peter or what he was doing. They weren't even curious about how I came to meet him. There surely was no point in talking about inheritances. I had started to pull my phone out of my pocket so I could show the ladies the letter from the lawyer on the screen. I discretely slipped it back into my pocket.

At that moment, Kenzie yelled from the Patio. "Grandma!" Millie and Andrea both jumped up and headed out the back door. I stood up and Sarah smiled at me weakly.

"Well, I'd better head out," I said. "I'll pick you up tomorrow around two?"

She smiled and acted like the last five minutes hadn't even happened. "Yeah. Sounds great. That'll be fun."

I went to my room and lay on the bed for twenty minutes. I got the date I wanted. My visit was a success, and yet I felt depressed. I wondered what would happen when the Hockensmith women found out that they were inheriting Elephant Gas. With their attitude, they'd probably burn the place down, including all of Jonas's stuff. And it would be my fault. Gus and Gladys, I thought. Hollister and Peter. Stacy and Curtis. People in this little town seemed to get along so well on the surface, and yet there was so much hostility lying just beneath it. Eve at Guns N Things had told me there hadn't been a murder in Elephant in 42 years. At the moment, I was having a hard time believing it.

With all of this churning in my brain, I got up and changed clothes and took the Beemer to Pendleton. It was time for another break; and for some decent restaurant food.

CHAPTER TWENTY-FOUR

A lot of things were starting to go right for me now, which was making me nervous. I was less than a week away from a big commission for the sale of Doris's apartments, and I would actually have money in the bank. My run-down old car had been transformed into a restored classic – free of charge. And I was about to go on a date with a woman who would take her place at the top of my "all time best looking dates" list. But I had an article to write, with a deadline four days away, so I spent the evening in Pendleton stressing out over that. I was feeling carnivorous and went to a steakhouse. This was Pendleton, after all – home of the "Roundup." I sat in the dark, nearly-empty dining room, at a table under a dim light, with my notebook. I stared at it but nothing came to me. Except for Jonas's cars, and of course the beautiful Hockensmith sisters, I couldn't think of a single good reason why anyone would want to visit Elephant. It was a nice little town with nice people, but the world is full of those. And right now, I didn't want to go back to Elephant either, thanks to a case of nerves over my upcoming date with the beautiful Sarah.

I ordered the most expensive steak on the menu. The waitress was friendly and asked me where I was from and what I did. I told her I was a writer from Seattle, and it felt strange to say that. After a little more conversation I asked her if she'd heard of Elephant. She screwed up her face and admitted she'd heard of it, but she'd never been there. Then she said, "I hear it's a hillbilly town, and it's kind of a joke around here. They say that half the people in Elephant are married to their cousins." When I told her I was writing a travel article about Elephant, she rolled her eyes and said, "Well good luck with that!" and then walked away with a laugh. My writer's block turned into a big block of ice. I made no progress in my notebook, but the steak was delicious.

* * *

Back in Elephant, after another restless night in my room and another lurid dream about you-know-who, I got up late on that Fourth of July Sunday morning and saw the brilliant sun. Everything outside was still and silent, and I went for a walk, sneaking around the fence so I wouldn't be spotted by any Hockensmiths. The town was quiet and everything seemed better. The streets were vacant, but I could see clusters of cars huddled around the two churches visible from Main Street. As I walked, I reminded myself that the world was full of beautiful women, so if things went wrong with one of them, it wouldn't matter that much. I was near the Chamber of Commerce office when Gus's pickup passed me. He gave a short honk and kept going. His truck bed was piled high with tables and chairs. He turned into the city park, where I could see a large canopy being set up. As I walked past Guns-N-Things, on the opposite side of the street, I saw Eve pulled up in her green Ford pickup. She smiled and waved, so I crossed over to visit. It felt like such a small-town thing to do.

I asked Eve if she was opening her store, which was a dumb question. "Oh no," she laughed. "It is big holiday. I am proud American on Four July. It is like Bastille Day, but better. I have French tablecloths. Red, white and blue. Same colors in France. I will take them to the park for the picnic." I asked Eve what the Fourth of July picnic would be like, and she told me it was the best day of the year in Elephant, at least for her. Then I asked her what she thought a visitor would most want to see if he came to Elephant. It turned out to be a hard question for her. After thinking for a few moments, she said, "Visitors come here to hunt. And to fish. Fish in spring. Hunt in fall." It hadn't occurred to me to write an article about fishing and hunting. But a person can fish and hunt near almost every rural town in America, so this didn't seem much better than Jonas's advice to write about the roads and the trees. When I pressed her to think of something else that would draw visitors, she said she couldn't. "It is just nice place," she said. I told her that I agreed.

I walked over to the city park and found the four hysterical ladies all gathered around a table piled high with small boxes. Ruth saw me and waved me over. "Mr. Smith, we're so glad to see you," Gladys said when I got there. "We're decorating the park for the Fourth of July picnic." That was obviously what they were doing. The four ladies wore various outfits of red, white and blue. Gladys's was actually pink, white and blue. The boxes on the table held small paper American flags with wood dowels serving as flag poles. Beverly was wearing a straw hat with two of the flags stuck in the hat band.

All four of them stared at me awkwardly. Even Gladys seemed at a loss for something to say. The article I needed to write was on my mind, so I asked for ideas. "So ladies, what do you think a visitor from Seattle or Portland would want to see most if they came to Elephant?"

"Our history," they all said, almost simultaneously.

"This is a very historic town," Bea said. "We have many homes over 100 years old." I smiled and nodded and decided not to mention that almost every city and town in America has many homes over 100 years old.

"What about hunting and fishing?" I said.

"Oh, we get many outdoorsmen here," said Gladys. "Maybe you should write about that. Do you hunt and fish?" I replied that I preferred to buy meat at the store, but that little joke seemed lost on all of them. About a dozen people were working in the park, setting up canopies, tables and chairs. A group of men was setting up a small wooden stage under one of the canopies. Gus's pickup with the tables and chairs still in it was parked nearby. I could see Gus among the group of men, and occasionally Gladys would glance toward them and then look away.

As I stood with the group of ladies, I was startled by a tap on the shoulder and I jumped. Then I heard a high-pitched homosexual voice say, "Oh, sorry Rob. I didn't mean to scare you."

"Hello Phil," I said. He giggled in a squeaky, girlish way. He was standing with a piece of paper in his hand. It was a formal letter to Sarah and Andrea from one of Phil's fellow attorneys in Los Angeles. His client, Hollister McCune, wanted the ladies to know that he was putting the Elephant Gas property in trust for them, and they would eventually inherit it.

"You should give it to them," Phil said.

I considered trying to explain to Phil the reaction I got when I brought up Peter's name to the Hockensmiths, but then I got a more selfish idea that maybe this could make me the hero. I would give it to Sarah on our date and explain carefully what it meant, and how she and Andrea would be able to earn rental income. Perhaps then she would apologize for the angry reaction I got when I brought up Peter's name before. "I'll do it," I told Phil.

I could see Gladys trying to overhear us and read what the letter said, so I took it from Phil and rolled it into a tube. It was time to finish my morning walk. I told the hysterical ladies that they were doing a fabulous job decorating the park, and Phil echoed my compliments even more exuberantly. It was early afternoon now, and more people were arriving at the park as Phil walked back to Jonas's office and I walked back along Main Street toward the motel.

While I walked, I planned my date with the beautiful Sarah. We would go for a drive and search for the trail to the log cabin that Gus had told me about. I wondered if she would know about it. We would go for a walk along the wooded trail. Maybe I would reach out and take her hand when we came to a particularly treacherous spot in the trail. I wondered what she'd wear. The Daisy Duke outfit, I hoped. Maybe with pink running shoes and little pink ankle socks with fuzzy balls on the back. She'd be nervous about being alone with me, and yet also very trusting. My mind raced on and on, continuing to get carried away with its fantasies. I couldn't help thinking about the city park and the evening festivities, and Sarah and me arm-in-arm, staring sweetly into each others' eyes as the fireworks exploded. As I walked, I tripped on a curb and nearly fell down. I looked down and saw that I had gripped the rolled up letter so tightly that it was now shaped like an hourglass, wadded in the center. I said "shit" a couple of times as I unrolled it and tried to smooth in on my leg, which didn't help much. Back in my room I unrolled the letter and flattened it on the table. I got the Pendleton phone book out of the little drawer and set it on the letter, which was face down. I put the lamp on top of the phone book for good measure. Then I decided to drive out and try to find the trail to the cabin.

* * *

I got in the Beemer and headed out of town. And quickly got lost.

The foothills of the Blue Mountains were stunning as I curved and climbed into thicker and thicker forest. I had no idea where I was, but I was going uphill, so I knew that when I turned around I had to come out of the mountains eventually, and hopefully funnel my way back into Elephant. I saw a couple of trails head off into the woods, but there were no signs or markings. And no sign of any log cabins.

Then, at the top of a long, straight hill, I spotted a double-rutted dirt track to the right. On the left, up ahead, was a small yellow cottage, just as Gus had described it. This had to be the spot. I parked in the wide spot next to the beginning of the trail and walked down the double path. I was in the mountains now – there were no wheat fields or desert landscapes, and the temperature was several degrees cooler. Cottonwood trees mingled with the tall pine trees that were prevalent in these arid mountains. White daisies and purple and blue wildflowers that I didn't recognize gave beautiful color to the sunlit edges of the path. I followed it as it curved to the left and then to the right; then down a bit and then up. I walked for at least five minutes before the path crested and opened up into a small green meadow full of wildflowers. To the right, under a stand of tall pines, was the cabin. It was much more forlorn than Gus had described it. The center part of the roof was caved in and litter was strewn around it. It had obviously had visitors recently. I walked toward it, stepping over shotgun shells that littered the ground. A campfire area surrounded by a circle of large rocks sat a few yards away from the cabin. It was filled with ashes that couldn't have been more than a few days old. Tall pine forests surrounded three sides of the meadow, but its far edge was open, with blue sky above it. I walked in that direction, and soon I could faintly see the plains of eastern Oregon in the far distance. A soft blue haze looked like smoke settling over the wheat fields and desert. It was like the view from a plane, but with rolling pine forests spreading out in the foreground.

The cabin had been well scavenged, but it still had some old broken cabinets in it, and lots of intricate woodwork. I wondered how it had lasted this long without somebody burning it down − it seemed like a bonfire waiting to happen. I looked around the meadow and I knew that Gus was right − this was the ideal romantic spot for my picnic date. It just needed a little cleaning up. I found an old plastic grocery bag in a rubbish pile, and I filled it with trash and some of the old shotgun shells. A large cardboard box was stuck between a tree branch and the side of the house. I un-wedged it and began filling it with trash.

I thought about Jonas's comment about the roads and the trees. The drive up into the mountains and the walk down the wooded path to this beautiful meadow with the incredible views made me think that maybe he was onto something after all. I had discovered a hidden gem − with Gus's help. These were possibly the most beautiful roads and trees I'd ever seen.

After 20 minutes I had the meadow mostly clear of litter. I straightened out some of the rocks around the fire pit and then started looking for a good picnic spot near the open end of the meadow with the view. A few trees had been cut at some point near the left side of the opening and I spotted one large stump that would make an ideal table. I just needed a place for us to sit.

Near the cabin was a short thick log, about six feet long and at least two feet in diameter. I decided it would make a perfect bench for my picnic with the beautiful Sarah. I began rolling it in the direction of the stump, which was at least 50 feet away. Most of the distance was slightly downhill, and at first the log rolled easily. But it reached a bump that stopped it. When the log refused to budge, I turned around and pressed my butt against it and lifted with both hands as hard as I could. I gritted my teeth and pulled up, straining every muscle in my arms and legs. When the log suddenly gave and lurched over the bump, my butt dropped into the soft dirt, and the back of my head struck the log − not hard, but in exactly the spot that was almost healed from the cowboy boot incident a week before. I lay down in the dirt and let the excruciating pain lessen. Then I slowly got up and brushed myself off. My clean tan shorts were trashed and my hands and legs were stained with dirt. The log rolled freely now, and I got it next to the stump and in a perfect spot to view the eastern half of Oregon.

The beautiful wildflowers in the meadow were calling out to be arranged in a vase. I had seen some old jars in the cabin earlier, and I found one that looked like it once held peanut butter and wiped it clean with some leaves. There was no water here, but we'd be back soon, so the flowers should make it until then. I walked around the edges of the meadow and picked a fistful of all different sizes, shapes and colors of flowers. I put the jar on in the middle of the stump and spent a few moments arranging the flowers. When they were as perfect as I could make them, I stepped back and admired my work. If this didn't cause Sarah's heart to fill with romance, I thought, something was wrong with her.

As noon approached, I finished cleaning and organizing my date spot and walked back down the path to the Beemer. I turned the car around and headed downhill in the general direction of Elephant. Danny had fixed the faulty odometer on my car, so I made a mental note of the mileage reading to calculate how far I would need to drive with Sarah. After three miles, I came to an opening in the trees and I could see the town of Elephant in the distance. I drove happily on down the hill and made it to town without a missed turn. The car felt luxurious and handled perfectly, and the pounding in my head was going away. At the grocery store I bought a cheap foam cooler along with some fresh vegetables and fruit, snacks, chips and soda. I found napkins, a bag of ice and, sure enough, a red-white-and-blue plastic tablecloth. With the cooler stocked and iced in the trunk, I drove back to the motel. The coast was clear as I parked below my room and then I went up and took my second shower of the day.

After scrubbing the dirt stains off my arms and legs, I toweled off while I whistled Bruce Springsteen's "Born in the USA." I was in a positive mood and I knew I had come up with a failsafe date plan. I was very proud of myself and feeling much more confident when I heard a knock on the door. A young female voice yelled, "Rob, are you there?" I wrapped myself as best I could in the skimpy motel towel and then opened the door a crack and peered around it. Sarah's daughter Kenzie stood a foot away from me. "Hi Rob," she said in her businesslike voice. "Mom says to tell ya she has to cancel on ya. She's too busy. See ya." She turned around and ran toward the stairs with no further explanation. I stood frozen in the doorway and watched Kenzie run back toward the motel office. Then I closed the door and yelled obscenities at it.

I lay face down on the bed, naked and clean for no reason. She got me again. I felt like a dog whose owner pretends to throw a stick but then doesn't. And he keeps falling for it, running off into the woods trying to find it. "My god, what a fucking chump I am," I yelled into the mattress. My phone rang and I looked at the caller ID. It was Stacy. "I hate women and I'm not talking to you," I yelled at the phone. Eventually it stopped, but the pounding in my head was back, and it was worse. After about half an hour, I put on an unwashed pair of cargo shorts and an unwashed T-shirt. On this beautiful Fourth of July Sunday afternoon, I kept the door and the curtains closed and turned on the television. I looked at the lamp on the table. It was sitting on a phone book, and under the phone book was the wrinkled letter to Sarah and Andrea from some attorney in southern California telling them that Elephant gas was going to be theirs someday.

I decided not to think about it. A NASCAR race was on TV, so I spent the next half-hour watching two dozen colorful rolling billboards go around in circles in a big pack. I hit the mute button and had no idea who was winning. It was just as clear and sunny wherever the race was being held as it was in Elephant, and occasionally I saw older gray-haired men in bright baseball caps and giant headphones being interviewed. Then I could see a camera view from the inside of one of the cars, with other cars very close by. A sponsor advertisement was placed strategically on the dashboard.

I thought about Charles's computer project – Corvettes racing around his basement on old computer screens. I had thought that that was a pretty pointless game, but it wasn't a whole lot different than what I was watching now, except I only had one screen. Maybe he could sell sponsorships for his Corvettes.

I finally decided it was time to get up and do something. I removed the lamp and the phone book from on top of the letter. Then I went to the motel office to give it to the Hockensmiths. Andrea greeted me with a smile from behind the counter and I asked her if Sarah was there. "She's pretty busy right now," Andrea said, sounding protective.

"It's kind of important."

Andrea paused for a moment and then went to the back room. She reemerged a few seconds later and said, "Okay, she'll be out in a minute."

Sarah was beautiful as usual, but now she was nervous. She obviously assumed I was going to confront her about standing me up. I tried to hand Andrea the still-crumpled letter. "Jonas's friend Phil asked me to give you this. Your grandfather convinced their client to leave Elephant Gas to the two of you in his will."

"Well we don't want it!" Sarah barked, before I even finished my sentence. "If that man gave me a million dollars I wouldn't take it."

"Sarah!" Andrea exclaimed, looking at her sister.

Sarah wouldn't let up. "We don't want nothing to do with him or his sperm donor son!"

"They're giving us that property?" Andrea asked.

"I guess you can talk to Phil if you have questions about it." Then I said "We'll see you later," and walked toward the door.

"I don't want it!" Sarah declared one last time. "Not if it's from that jerk."

I stopped and turned around and decided that I might as well get pissed off. It didn't matter what she thought at this point. I looked directly into those beautiful green eyes and yelled, "That's ridiculous. You haven't seen him since you were four! You have no idea if he's a jerk or not." Sarah and Andrea stood in stunned silence and stared at me as I continued. "He was a really nice guy when I talked to him. I think you're the one being a jerk!" Then I threw the paper toward Sarah and it fell to the floor halfway between us.

At that moment Millie walked into the office from the back room. "What's going on?" She looked at me threateningly. "Is there a problem?"

Sarah and Andrea stood silently. I glared at Millie and said, "Nope. I was just leaving."

"They're just giving it to us?" Andrea asked again. She reached down to pick up the letter and I walked out the door and went back to my room.

CHAPTER TWENTY-FIVE

"We need to talk about the elephant," Stacy's voice said in the message she left. "Jonas and Danny have an idea. We're at the park. Hope your date's going well." Then there was a giggle before she hung up.

It was about three o'clock and the TV was still on. Within five minutes the phone rang again. "DEATH," said the caller ID. "No fucking way, Doris!" I yelled at the phone. "It's the Fourth of July!" I didn't answer.

Another voice mail message: "I'm concerned about the plumbing at the apartments. You need to go over there and make sure the plumber got the work done. Call me back and let me know what you found out." Click. Apparently Doris's lapse into being almost human was over.

The NASCAR race had just ended on the muted TV and a lot of men in bright red and blue coveralls were jumping up and down and celebrating the winner's victory. A beautiful young blonde, who reminded me of Sarah, kissed the winning driver as they stood on the podium. I turned the TV off and called Stacy back. "I've got a cooler full of food here," I told her. "Have you eaten?"

"No, and I'm starving. I'm at the park, waiting for them to start serving hamburgers, but it's going to be awhile. What happened on your date? You didn't eat?" Another giggle.

"It's a long story. Meet me in the parking lot."

"I think I'd rather have a burger and potato salad," Stacy said a few minutes later, as she looked into the cooler in the trunk of my car.

"This is a lot better for you," I replied. She dug around in the cooler while I told her my story of being informed by a 12-year-old that her mother was standing me up, and how Sarah had refused to take the letter about Elephant Gas when I tried to give it to her. Stacy looked up from the cooler with a fake smile. "Gosh, Sarah doesn't know what she missed."

"She eats frozen TV dinners."

"Well she definitely wouldn't want this. It's mostly vegetables." Stacy looked disgusted as she said it. I pointed out that the cooler also contained fruit and some other healthy snacks, and then I agreed to leave it in the car and go have a burger and potato salad. We went to the end of the hamburger line. "They're serving apple pie too," Stacy said

The park was decked out in red, white and blue decorations and it was filling with people now. Dozens of large American flags on eight-foot poles were stuck into the ground around the park. The stage and the canopy above it were surrounded with flag banners. A large banner with red, white and blue lettering that read "God Bless America!" hung behind the stage. A big canopy with three rows of long tables under it was set up to the right of the stage. Another canopy next to that one was the serving area for the picnic. Both were adorned with flags and banners. Stacy told me that many businesses in the area had donated food for the picnic, which was free and "all-you-can-eat." The Chamber of Commerce had organized the meal. "Meaning me," she said. She told me she came to the Fourth of July picnic every year when she was growing up. A long line had already formed at the serving table. There were probably a hundred people in it when Stacy and I joined it, but no one was serving food yet. I recognized several people from the gymnasium a few days before.

On the stage, the mayor was standing at a microphone, trying to get it to work. The city clerk, Marla, stood off to the side, waiting to step in and help. At the back of the stage a group of people dressed in costumes waited. "Those are the founding fathers," said Stacy. "And their wives, I guess."

"So they'd be the "Founding Mothers?"

"Can you hear me?!" The mayor's voice suddenly blasted across the park. It hurt my ears. Marla rushed over to him as he kept talking. "Testing,

testing."

Someone in the crowd yelled "I hope you pass your test!" It was Hector, the heckler from the gym on Monday.

Marla turned off the microphone. This was obviously the same sound system that had been used in the gym the Monday before. The mayor stepped away and Marla turned down the volume, which was still too loud. The mayor was wearing white dress slacks and white shoes, along with a bright blue dress shirt and a bright red tie with blue and white stripes. Nearly everyone in the park was wearing red, white and blue clothing. Even Stacy had on a red, white and blue blouse. I was wearing tan cargo shorts and a green and white Hawaiian shirt. But my flip-flops had red and white straps, and I pointed that out to Stacy when she questioned my attire.

As we waited in the hamburger line, the mayor welcomed everyone in the park, and far beyond, to the 82nd annual Elephant Fourth of July picnic. He thanked all of the businesses that had donated food and money for the picnic and he thanked all the volunteers who helped set up the tables and canopies and decorate the park. He also thanked Stacy for her hard work in organizing the food donations. She smiled and waved. At each mention of a name, a scattering of applause floated across the park. Then the Mayor smiled and looked over at me and said, "And please, everyone, keep your shoes on today. I'm sure our special guest, Mr. Smith, from Western Oasis Magazine, would appreciate it." I nodded and waved and heard a couple of chuckles. The mayor then introduced the "special guests" behind him.

George Washington, Thomas Jefferson and Benjamin Franklin stepped forward. All three were wearing tight red, white and blue clothing meant to resemble what people might have worn in the 18th century, if they wore red, white and blue. Each also had on a white triangular shaped hat. George and Benjamin wore running shoes, and Thomas had on cowboy boots. He also had on a large fake Rolex watch. Each founding father, and two of the founding mothers, carried a twentieth-century rifle or, in Thomas's case, what appeared to be a double-barrel shotgun. The wives, wearing red white and blue dresses that looked like they belonged on the Hee Haw television show, stood behind them. I told Stacy that I was pretty sure the founding fathers' wives weren't around when the Declaration was signed in 1776.

And Ben was a widow. "Must be their girlfriends," she said.

"It is an elephant tradition to welcome three of our most notorious founding fathers," the mayor announced. Marla winced. "As they do every year, they will read the Declaration of Independence. We'll start with George here."

"Wait a minute, wait a minute! I wrote it and I should read first," whined Thomas. It was a well-rehearsed line.

The mayor gave out a loud chuckle and then said "Okay Thomas, I guess you're right. Why don't you go first?"

Thomas approached the microphone. He was about five foot seven and well over two hundred pounds. His bright blue corduroy vest had obviously been let out at the sides. "When, in the course of human events, it becomes necessary..."

After Thomas finished the first paragraph, George stepped up and announced, "OK, my turn. After all, I won the revolutionary war." The mayor chuckled again and agreed. Thomas stepped back and George's harsher baritone took over. In an overly theatrical voice, with his arms waving vigorously, George said. "We hold these truths to be self-evident, that all men are created equal." At that moment the explosion of a large firecracker could be heard, and George paused and looked out beyond the crowd. Then he continued, with an annoyed expression: "...that they are endowed by their Creator with certain unalienable rights, that among these are life, liberty and the pursuit of happiness."

George was well over six feet tall and had dark hair cut short under his triangular paper hat. "He's the minister of the Lutheran Church," Stacy said. "I think he used to be an actor."

"Bang!" Another fireworks explosion rang through the crowd at the park.

The crowd in the Elephant city park stood in rapt attention as the rest of the Declaration was read, with each founding father taking turns. Their wives and/or girlfriends stood behind them, silently smiling. "I've seen them do this a thousand times, and it's still moving," Stacy whispered to me. I looked over at one of the tables and saw that Jonas, Danny and Phil were deep in conversation and ignoring the whole scene in the park.

Gladys and the other hysterical ladies were standing front and center, frozen, taking it all in with pride. Each of them was holding a small flag in her hand. When the founding fathers finished their recital of the Declaration of Independence, the mayor stepped back up to the microphone and led the crowd in singing "God Bless America." Two more firecrackers exploded during the song. Then the mayor started talking about something relating to Elephant's history, and the crowd quickly lost interest. People began moving around, and the hamburger line inched forward.

"So what about the elephant?" I asked Stacy, as we took a couple of steps.

"What about the elephant?"

"You said you wanted to talk to me about the elephant. In your phone message."

"Oh yeah. We're gonna blow it up."

"Who's gonna blow it up?"

"Danny. And Lindsay. And me and you."

"Lindsay?"

"Yeah, she was here earlier. Danny says he knows exactly how to do it. Lindsay says she's in. I said I'd help too," Stacy said.

"What about Jonas?

"He said he'll be glad to watch. After he moves his cars out of the shop. Phil said he'll watch from a mile away. He thinks we're all crazy."

"So why do I have to be involved?" I asked.

"Well, since Miss Hotsy-Totsy is gonna own the building soon, I figured you'd want to be involved too."

"You just love that name, don't you."

"Yeah," she said with a big smile.

"I think I'm with Jonas. I'll watch too."

"You big chicken. Somebody needs to go talk to her and tell her what we're doing. We elected you."

"Not a chance in hell. I'm done with her."

Stacy grinned. "We'll see."

We moved a little closer to the hamburger table and both announced how hungry we were. She asked me if I liked the city or the small town better. I told her I needed more time to think about it. "Good answer," she said. Then I asked her what it was like growing up in a little town like Elephant. She told me about going to mass at the Catholic Church every week.

"So that would explain the slutty behavior in high school and college," I said.

"Yup, that pretty much sums it up. The Catholics scarred me for life." Then she told me a story about going to confession when she was a little girl. "The priest took confession when he was here," she said. "Even the kids did it."

"Little kids give confession?" I told her I knew nothing about the Catholic Church, other than the child molestation.

"Yeah, there's that," she said. "Anyway, when you're a kid, what do you really do that's a sin? Back then I was a good girl. I did what my parents said. They made me go to confession. Since I didn't ever really do anything that would be considered a sin, sometimes I just made things up."

"That's pretty funny. But it makes sense," I told her.

"So one time, in the confessional, I couldn't think of anything. So I told the father that I'd committed adultery. I was nine. I didn't even know what it was. I had just heard somewhere that that was a popular thing to admit to in confession. Probably on TV."

The woman standing in front of us in line had been listening to Stacy's story. She started laughing and turned around. "Stacy, that's hilarious."

"Yeah, I could hear the father laughing in the booth, Mrs. Olsen."

"So what did he say?" Mrs. Olsen asked.

"He just did the 'father' thing. He said, 'Bless you my child, for you have sinned.' Then he told me to do a bunch of 'Hail Marys', or whatever."

"That was probably for lying," I said.

Stacy and I sat in the shade of a large maple tree in the park and ate our burgers and potato salad. In the opposite corner of the park, a large group of Hockensmiths sat off by themselves. Sarah was on a blanket with Taver on her lap. Millie and Andrea and the rest of the kids sat in a tight group. A man I hadn't met – obviously Andrea's husband Jamie – was sitting next to

Andrea with Nela on his lap. I asked Stacy if she'd heard from Curtis anymore. She said she hadn't. She was surprised how much she was okay with being single and living alone. "I talked to Lindsay on the phone last night," she said. "We got all caught up. She says she really happy with Rick. She likes older men." Stacy gave me a sly smile when she said that. Just as we were finishing our lunch, I saw Gladys motioning to me wildly. She was standing near the stage with the other hysterical ladies. Stacy and I took our paper plates and plastic forks and knives to a garbage can, and then went over by the stage.

"Wasn't it just wonderful?!" Gladys gushed. Stacy and I simultaneously agreed that it was wonderful. Gladys began telling us the history of the Fourth of July picnic in Elephant. "I was two when they had the first one," she said. "My father played George Washington."

"That's amazing, Gladys," Stacy said, actually sounding amazed.

"Yes dear. The stage was in the same place, but there were no tables and no, you know, roofs."

"You mean these canopies?" I asked.

"Oh my, I never know what to call them." A couple of times, while she was talking, Gladys looked nervously off to her left. I looked over and saw Gus sitting at a table less than 20 feet away. He caught my eye and smiled. Stacy waved and motioned at him to come over. Gladys looked horrified as Gus got up. Stacy looked at me with a huge grin.

Gladys started to walk away, and Gus called out, "Hello Gladys. Don't leave." Gladys stopped and froze. She was paralyzed. And speechless.

Gus greeted Stacy and me. "Beautiful day for a picnic." Then he looked toward Gladys. "Don't you agree, Gladys?" Gladys stared at him, but didn't reply. She was shaking.

Stacy was totally into it now. "You know, Gladys," she said with her grin in place, "Gus tells me he hasn't been very happy with his barber in Pendleton."

"That's right," Gus said.

"And having to drive there, just for a haircut is such a hassle," Stacy continued, in an overly dramatic voice.

"I was thinking," Gus said. "It would be nice to find someone right here in Elephant to cut my hair. Maybe you could fit me in?" Gladys stared at Gus, but didn't say anything. Her face was as pink as her dress. "I've been admiring Mr. Smith's haircut here," Gus continued.

"Well then it's settled," Stacy announced. "Gus will stop in and make an appointment on Tuesday."

"Th-that would be fine," Gladys finally stuttered.

"So, Mr. Smith, are you enjoying our picnic?" Gus asked, making no sign of leaving our little group.

Before I could answer, Gladys exclaimed, "Oh, there's Ruth. I'd better go," and marched off toward the other hysterical ladies.

"That woman," was all Gus could say. He was smiling.

"That was awesome, Gus!" Stacy exclaimed.

"I think I ruined her day," replied Gus.

"Are you kidding? You definitely made her day," Stacy said. I agreed with Stacy.

Just then, Jonas and Danny approached us. "What's going on?" Jonas asked. "Gus, did I see you talking to Gladys? That's a breakthrough."

"Just a little business arrangement," said Gus.

"It's more than a haircut," laughed Stacy. "This could be a new phase in your life."

"My life isn't having any more new phases," replied Gus. "I'm just getting a haircut."

"Okay, we need to talk about the plan," interrupted Danny. I asked Danny what plan he was talking about. He told us he had figured out how to fill the big gray elephant with propane gas and then ignite it. "Kaboom!" he said. "We'll do it at the end of the fireworks show. It'll be the grand finale."

"Tonight?" I asked.

"It's gotta be tonight," said Stacy. "It's the fiftieth anniversary."

"What about the new owners?"

"You've gotta tell 'em," said Jonas, looking at me. "Now that you're back up on that horse, you da man!"

"No, I'm not 'da man'. I got bucked off big time," I said. Jonas started laughing when I repeated my story of being stood up for the second time."

"You gotta stay in there," Danny said sternly. "You can't let women intimidate you."

"So you're elected Smith," Jonas said. "You've gotta go talk to them."

Just as Jonas said that, I felt my pants vibrate. I had forgotten about Doris's message. "Oh Shit!" I said.

Jonas laughed. "Oh come on Smith, it won't be that bad." I explained that I was responding to another conversation I was dreading. This one on my phone. I let the phone go to voice mail.

At that moment I looked over and saw Andrea walking toward us. Danny froze. "Hi Rob," Andrea said to me. Then she looked at Danny and smiled. "Hi Danny, how's it goin'?"

Danny nodded and blushed, but didn't say anything. Stacy started laughing. "Boy, this is one stressful picnic for some people," she said.

Andrea looked puzzled, but then turned to me and said, "Rob, can I talk to you for a minute?"

"Sure." I looked at the rest of the group. "Carry on," I said. Then Andrea and I walked toward an open space near the corner of the park. Behind me, I could hear Jonas tell Danny not to let women intimidate him.

Andrea had an intense and angry look on her face. "When did you talk to our grandfather?"

"I met him in Seattle. On Wednesday. He was really nice."

"Why are you looking for our relatives?"

"I wasn't. I know his sister-in-law. She's my client. I found out that he lives near me in Seattle." I told Andrea that I went to talk to Peter about the Elephant. It was just research for my article. I tried to sound cheerful, before she chewed me out even more. "Small world, huh?"

"Oh," she said. She seemed satisfied that I wasn't up to anything evil, and she was stumped for something else to say. She looked up at me inquisitively and asked. "So what's he like?"

"Peter?"

"Yeah."

"He was totally cool," I said. She smiled. "He looks a lot like you and Sarah. Well, especially Sarah."

"Oh."

"He said he hasn't seen you since you were a baby."

"My biological father was a jerk. Mom says Peter was too."

"He wasn't a jerk to me. He's really into computers. He's like the world's oldest computer geek," I said. She laughed. "He showed me how to use Bluetooth."

"What's that?"

"It's a thing where computers and phones and other gadgets can talk to each other without wires."

She shrugged and rolled her eyes. "So he told Mr. McCune to give us the gas station?"

"I think he suggested it."

"Mom and Sarah say there has to be a catch. They don't believe Peter would do that. Is it contaminated or something? Does he owe money on it?"

"I don't think so. Jonas said he checked it out before he rented it."

Then Andrea smiled and relaxed, "I think it's nice that he did that. I never thought Peter could be as bad as they said."

"He said he's really sorry he didn't get to see you and Sarah grow up. Your father's in prison you know."

"Yeah, I know." Then we stood there awkwardly for a moment until she said, "Well thanks Rob. I gotta go." She sort of laughed and gave me a quick wave and then walked back to the Hockensmith group. I could see the beautiful Sarah give her a quizzical look as she sat down.

I walked back toward the other group, who were deep into their plotting for the demise of the big gray elephant. "Are they on board?" Jonas asked.

CHAPTER TWENTY-SIX

Dealing with women is like car maintenance. It's unavoidable, and the longer you put it off the more unpleasant it is. So off I went. I had two women to deal with at the moment: I needed to call Doris back and I had to walk over to the other corner of the park to ask Sarah if she would have a problem if we blew up the big elephant tonight. A group of people sitting at a picnic table behind me were watching to make sure I followed through with the second one. But first I got out my phone. "I'm out of town, Doris. It's a holiday," I said, after announcing my first and last names.

"Well, I don't know what I'm going to do. You shouldn't have left."

"Where's Manuel?"

"He's in California. He needed the holiday weekend off." As if I didn't. I told Doris I would check on the apartments one last time before we signed the closing papers on Wednesday. Then she said, "Robert, I've been thinking. I'm not sure I'm going to go through with this."

I paused to consider that statement for a couple of seconds before replying. "You know what Doris? I gotta go. We'll talk about this tomorrow." I hung up. Now on to uncomfortable situation number two. I looked over and saw the entire Hockensmith family happily sitting in their group with hamburgers and salad and pie spread over a large area. Children were laughing and running, and two dogs, who were smaller than dogs ought to be, were following them and barking annoyingly. Adults were laughing and talking as they watched the children and the dogs. Everyone seemed happy and content, except for me. I cinched up my big-boy panties one more time as tightly as I could and headed in their direction.

Sarah greeted me with a big smile when she saw me. "Hey Rob, how's it goin'?" She got up and gave me a hug, which I accepted. "Isn't this picnic fun?" I agreed that it was. Sarah was wearing her cutoff shorts that seemed even shorter than before, along with a red, white and blue bikini top. I took a deep breath as she continued to talk. "We were just discussing our new inheritance. We were thinking that it would make a great location for our flower shop; or maybe a cute little café."

All I could say was, "Really." I said it as a statement, not a question. It was as if the events of earlier in the day hadn't happened. Had I dreamed the whole thing? Sarah sending her 12-year-old daughter to break her date with me and then telling me she wouldn't accept anything that "that jerk" her grandfather gave her? And then me calling her a jerk? Now, four hours later, she was totally friendly and seemed happy to be part owner of Elephant Gas.

She continued: "Question for you."

"Shoot."

"Do you think the hysterical committee (she used the word 'hysterical') would get really upset if we got rid of the elephant?" I tried not to look surprised. Better to just follow this and see where it went.

"I'm sure they would," I told her. "And they could stop you from doing it, too; at least starting tomorrow."

"What if we just did it anyway? What could they do to us?"

I told her that destroying a historic landmark might be considered a crime, although I had no idea if that were true. "I don't think you'd enjoy jail," I said.

"So I guess we'll have to blow it up tonight," she replied, laughing and obviously meaning it as a joke. "I guess that won't be happening."

"Hey, the night's still young," I said. She looked at me and I shrugged and gave her a grin.

"What are you two plotting?" It was Millie, leaning over from across the group.

"We're going to blow up the elephant tonight," Sarah said with a laugh.

"Just kidding."

"Hah!" Millie said. "I think that's a great idea."

"Yeah right. We don't even own it yet," Andrea pointed out.

"I don't know," I said. "Peter told me he and Hollister would have no problem if that elephant went away." I made that up too, but I was sure that was how they felt. "Besides, what if it were an accident?"

"But how are we going to do that?" Sarah asked. "Do you think we could find somebody to ram into it with a truck in the next two hours."

"I think those concrete legs could handle just about any truck," I said.

"Do you have any other ideas?"

"Well…hmmm. Let me think," I said, stroking my chin. "Okay, here's an idea. What if we filled it with flammable gas and then lit it?"

Sarah tilted her head and gave me a look that showed that her brain was working hard. "Do you think that would work Rob?"

"Jonas has that big propane tank behind the shop," I replied.

"Of course it would work," Millie exclaimed. "Remember the Hindenburg? Well of course you don't."

"Exactly," I said. Then I repeated Danny's words as if they were my own. "That elephant is like a big blimp. Fill it with explosive gas and then, kaboom!"

"Boy Rob, that's pretty smart," Sarah said, smiling at me.

"You guys are out of your minds," Andrea said, with a mortified look.

"You go girl!" said Millie. "I'm with ya a hundred percent." She pumped her fist.

"Okay," Sarah said. "Do you think we should tell Jonas and Danny our plan?"

Andrea interrupted us. "There's no way you're going to pull this off."

"We'll see," Sara replied. Sarah and I agreed to go talk to Danny and Jonas about helping us with "our" plan at around 5:00, after the group was done with their dinner. "They'll be really surprised by our idea, won't they?" Sarah said excitedly.

"Oh yeah. They'll be surprised all right."

"Do you think we can talk them into doing it?

"We might. Danny seems like the kind of guy who likes blowing stuff up."

"This is so exciting," Sarah finally said, grabbing my arm and practically hopping up and down.

I left the Hockensmiths as they continued making plans for their newly acquired gas station, minus its giant historic landmark. I walked back toward the stage, greeting people that I vaguely recognized. A couple of older farmers that I remembered from the chicken fried steak episode at the Elephant Inn came up to me and told me how much they were looking forward to reading my article in Western Oasis. I thanked them and said that I'd try not to disappoint them. On the stage, a group of mostly overweight middle-aged men and women with guitars and drums, and wearing cowboy hats and red, white and blue plaid shirts, were setting up sound equipment. It turned out that the Elephant Fourth of July picnic included a sort of barn dance, only without the barn.

I spotted the ladies of the hysterical committee, along with two of their husbands, so I went over to ask them how they were enjoying the picnic. When I got there, Ruth immediately spoke up. "Right after the fireworks we want to present the historic preservation plaque for the historic elephant," she said. "Do you think Jonas will agree to accept it on behalf of the owners?" I told Ruth I was sure Jonas would be very honored to do that. "And we'd like you to help present it," she added. Before I could object, the country and western band broke into an explosively loud song. All conversations in the park ended at that moment and many people covered their ears, including me and the four female members of the Elephant Historic Preservation Commission.

As soon as the group's first song ended, Marla, the city clerk, ran up onto the stage and spoke excitedly to the lead singer. They argued for a moment, and then the singer reluctantly huddled with her band-mates, who then reluctantly turned down the volume on their amplifiers. The music improved for the next couple of songs, and we all sat at the table, still unable to hold a conversation. Now, several couples began dancing in an open grass area in front of the stage.

I looked up just in time to see Gus walking up behind Gladys. I motioned to Gladys and she turned around. "Care to dance?" Gus asked her. Gladys had a look on her face like she was being carjacked, but she agreed. She stood up on wobbly legs and walked with Gus through the grass toward the stage. As soon as Gus and Gladys started dancing, Bea and Beverly both got up to dance with their husbands. Ruth and I sat awkwardly at the table, until I reached out my hand and said "Shall we?"

When we joined the group on the grass, I saw that Gladys had relaxed a little. She was talking to Gus with a smile spread across her face. "I don't know what Gladys is going to do," Ruth said to me, as we danced at arms' length.

"I know," I said. "Being mad at Gus is a big part of her life, isn't it. She'll have to be mad at someone else now. And after tonight, I can think of a few people who might qualify." Ruth looked puzzled and then I said, "Never mind." While Ruth and I were in the middle of dancing to our second song, Stacy cut in. "Sorry," I said to Ruth. That was mean of Stacy, but I have to dance with her now. It's the rule." Ruth walked slowly back to her table.

"So where did you go this afternoon, since you didn't have a date?" Stacy asked. While we danced in the grass to the bad country and western music, I described to Stacy my drive into the mountains and then my walk down the path the little log cabin. "It's a very romantic place," I told her. "You should take a date there sometime."

She gave me a funny look and said, "Maybe I'll just do that."

"You'll know when you get there, because you'll find an old peanut butter jar on a stump with a bunch of dead flowers in it."

Stacy laughed and then said, "You're quite the romantic. But you're a terrible dancer." I explained that I wasn't very good at dancing to music I liked, and since I didn't like country music, there was no hope. The band moved on to a bluegrass-sounding song that they did a better job with. Stacy told me they were from Pendleton and they were pretty well known there.

"The lady playing the fiddle is good, but boy is she ugly," I said.

Stacy laughed. "That's not very nice. She's visually challenged."

"Look at her nose, I went on. She looks like a dolphin. I'm surprised that thing doesn't get in the way of her bow."

Stacy stopped dancing and started laughing out loud. "Does she have any teeth? I can't even tell. Of course, you know what they say about women with no teeth," she said with a big smile.

"You're awful," I said. "And yes I do."

"Look, I think she's checking you out," Stacy said.

"Yeah, I seem to be a magnet for ugly women."

Next the band played a slow ballad with a twangy guitar. The fat woman who had sung the previous songs gave way, and the skinny male bass player, who had long stringy hair that looked like it hadn't been washed in a year, moved up to the microphone. Stacy grabbed my arms and pulled me closer for a slow dance. She put her head on my shoulder and said, "You're just the right height."

"Thank you. I always thought I was."

"Here, let me lead," she said then. "I'll show you how to do it." I let Stacy lead and our dancing immediately improved. "Do you think you can do that?" I told her it would be better if she continued leading.

The ballad was a long one and the sun was just setting over the flat western horizon. We turned so that I was facing the giant elephant across the street from the park. The pink light on its hind quarters brought out the contours of the sculpture. It almost looked majestic. "Look at that," I said to Stacy, stopping our dance and pointing to the elephant in the fading sunlight.

"Oh my god, it's beautiful," she replied. "Why did you have to show me that?"

"So now you don't want to blow it up?"

"When I was a kid, I loved that elephant," Stacy said. "They had candy machines lined up in front of the gas station. I saved my lunch money and rode my bike over there after school. My parents never knew." She said she was about ten when the gas station next to the big elephant finally closed for good. "I never thought much about it after that, until I got this job and started hating it." She looked over at the elephant again and said, "It is pretty amazing, isn't it. And the fact that it's lasted 50 years."

We slow danced for awhile without talking, and Stacy's head remained on my shoulder. Then she looked up at me with pretty brown eyes that I hadn't really noticed before and asked, "Do you think I could visit you in Seattle? You could be, like, my tour guide." Her eyes remained fixed directly on mine.

This is the kind of situation that always turns into disaster. There's only one correct response to a question like that in a situation like that, and it has to be instantaneous and enthusiastic. Stacy's reaction to my slightly delayed "Uh sure, I guess," was to let go, drop her shoulders, look down at the ground and say "never mind. I'm sure that would be a problem." Then she turned around and walked back toward the group at the picnic table.

"No, really! You can come to Seattle, Stacy," I said, walking behind her. "It would be really fun!" I put every ounce of effort I could into sounding enthusiastic and welcoming, but the damage was done.

"C'mon, we have an elephant to destroy," she said grimly. I stood there by myself for a second in the middle of the park. It was about five o'clock, so I walked toward the Hockensmith group. I saw that Gus and Gladys were back at her table, along with Bea and Beverly and their husbands, and Ruth.

"Shall we break the news to Danny and Jonas?" Sarah asked me as I walked up. "I can't wait to see the looks on their faces."

"Me neither."

I walked behind Sarah as we approached the table where Danny, Jonas, Stacy and Lindsay were sitting. I put my index finger up to my mouth before they could ask how things went. "Sarah has something she wants to ask you guys," I said. "She has an idea."

Sarah sat down at the picnic table and looked at the four puzzled faces. "I know you guys are gonna think we're nuts," Sarah told them, "but Rob and I came up with this crazy idea. And we'll need your help, Danny. And everybody, we have to keep this really quiet. No one else here can know about it."

"What are you talking about," Danny replied, sounding annoyed. "We already…"

I waved my arms frantically behind Sarah, trying to get Danny to shut up. Jonas caught on and grabbed Danny by the arm. "Let's hear the lady out," Jonas said. "She might have something very interesting to suggest."

Danny stopped and stared at Sarah.

"Our family was talking" She continued, "and if we're going to own the old gas station, we don't want that big ugly elephant. But Rob here explained that after tonight, it'll be a historic monument or something, so we'll be stuck with it. I thought there was no way we can get rid of it by midnight. Then Rob...he's so smart." She looked up at me with a grin. "He came up with the idea that we could fill it with gas and blow it up. Like the Hindleberg, or something. We could do it tonight!" Now Danny was visibly pissed.

"Aw shucks, it was nothing." Those words actually came out of my mouth.

Jonas laughed. "Damn, Smith. You really do have a sense of drama. No wonder you're a writer."

Stacy stared at me and shook her head, but said nothing. "Hindenburg," Danny growled.

"Whatever, but we need to get our plan together," Sarah said, in total seriousness. Now she gave Danny a hard look, with her lower lip extended. "Danny, will you help us? I know we couldn't do it without you."

Danny was silent, his face bright red. Jonas intervened. "Of course Danny will help you." Then he turned to Danny with a disappointed look. "I don't know why you didn't think of this yourself, Dan-O." Lindsay and I laughed out loud. "I guess Danny just doesn't have that sense of drama that Rob has," said Jonas.

With a defeated look, Danny spoke up. "Okay, fine. We'll need a garden hose, a ladder, some duct tape and a rope," he said as he glared at me. "I know there's a long hose at the shop. You got the rest of that stuff, Sarah?"

"That's the spirit," said Jonas.

"I'm on it," Sarah said with a grin. She got up and headed toward the parking lot.

Now Danny glared at me even more angrily, while Stacy refused to even look at me. "Sorry Danny," I said. "I just thought our chances would be better if she thought it was her idea."

"She doesn't think it's her idea. She thinks it's your idea. You'll do anything to get laid, won't you."

"Hey, look at it this way," I replied. "If things go bad and we all die in the explosion, at least it'll be my fault."

CHAPTER TWENTY-SEVEN

"Okay fine," Danny said again. He got up and headed across the street to Elephant Gas. When the rest of us arrived there at six, Danny had a long stretch of green garden hose laid out in the driveway in front of the shop. "It's a good thing Jonas just had the propane tank filled," he said.

The big 500 gallon tank behind the shop was used to power heaters in the paint booth Danny used to paint cars. Jonas also used it for the little stove in the kitchen. "Gas is much better to cook on," he had said. Elephant had no natural gas service, so gas cooking, or heating paint booths, required propane in storage tanks.

"We need some way to ignite the gas," said Danny.

"I thought you'd have this all figured out by now," Jonas said.

Danny got even more annoyed and pointed to me and said, "Talk to the big hero over there. Why didn't he figure it out?" I suggested that perhaps we needed a long fuse. We talked about finding someone who used blasting caps to see if they had any kind of fuse.

"Wait a minute," said Lindsay. "Rick went to the Indian reservation last week and bought a giant box of firecrackers."

"So?" Danny barked. He didn't see how that would help, and neither did I.

"They come in long strings," replied Lindsay. "You know how you can light a string of them at once and they go 'bam-bam-bam-bam-bam'?"

Danny's eyes lit up. "Fuck. How cool would that be," Danny said.

"Okay, that's your job." Lindsay proceeded across the street to her car. "We need Sarah's ladder," Danny said then. He was getting into it now.

"How's it goin', MacGyver," Jonas asked Danny as he walked out of the office.

Danny gave him a serious stare. "It's gonna work."

Jonas gave him a fatherly smile back. "Yes, I know it is, Daniel." Then he looked at me and said, "Smith, you gotta help me get some chairs out." As I walked over to help, Sarah's big Ford pickup pulled into the driveway.

Danny gave Jonas an exasperated look. "What do we need chairs for?"

"We're gonna want front row seats."

"I don't know, Jonas. That could be dangerous."

Then Jonas said, "Okay, we need hard hats, or helmets."

I looked over at the local contractor as she walked up. "Sarah, you got any hard hats?" I asked.

"We've got a big box of motorcycle helmets at the motel," she said. "For our ATVs."

"Perfect. And we need your big stepladder," said Danny.

"It's on the truck. Anything else?"

"Yeah," said Jonas. "Flashlights. It's going to get dark."

"What about head lamps?" Sarah asked. "Dad uses them for hunting. We've got a bunch of them."

"You're a genius," said Jonas. "Go!" And off she went again in her giant truck. "Come on, Smith. I'll show you where the chairs are. You too, Stacy." I followed Jonas and Stacy, who refused to look at me, into the Elephant Gas building. The shop area was empty of cars. Gus's Plymouth had been moved to a spot at the far edge of the property and covered with a tarp. No Corvettes were in sight. I asked Jonas how he had gotten the cars out. "Oh, shit," he said. "Phil is up at Gus's, waiting for a ride.

"I'll get him," Stacy said, obviously looking for an excuse to get out of there. She ran toward the parking lot next to the park to get her car.

Danny dragged the end of the long garden hose around the building. "This is going to take some improvisation," he said. "And duct tape." I followed Danny behind the shop building. He explained how he would take an old pressure hose and cut it off a foot from the fitting at the tank. "I'll slide the garden hose over the top of it and tape it up good. It won't be under pressure. We'll just release the gas into the elephant." Danny looked up at the elephant. "I have no idea how much to put in there. I guess we'll just wait until we smell it." Up to this point I had had some doubts about this whole operation. Now I decided it was completely nuts.

Just then I heard Sarah's voice excitedly behind me. She had returned quickly from the motel with helmets and headlamps. "Oh Rob, I'm so glad you thought of this." Not only was this plan nuts, but it was going to be my fault.

Before I could respond, Danny said, "Sarah!"

She froze, like an army private. "Yes sir."

Danny played the sergeant, totally in charge now and relishing the mission. "We need your long stepladder up inside the elephant on the platform." Then he looked at me. "You go help her, Mr. Hero."

"Aye, aye, sir," Sarah said. Okay, maybe she was a sailor. She gave me a grin and said, "Let's go, you big hero." We went to her truck and she climbed into the bed, unstrapped the ladder from the rack and slid it down toward me. We were barely able to fit it through door in the lower right leg of the elephant and stand it up in the little closet-sized room. "I'll climb up and you feed it up to me," Sarah said. With the light on above her, I watched her lovely ass and beautiful bare legs go up the vertical ladder attached to the wall. I tried to keep my mind on the task. When she was on the platform looking down, I pushed the stepladder up toward her.

Danny appeared in the door behind me. He was holding a long piece of nylon rope about the thickness of a clothesline. "You've got to tie this to something on the frame, he shouted up to Sarah. We'll attach the hose to it. And the firecrackers." Sarah was struggling to pull up the stepladder, so I took the rope and started climbing the fixed ladder, pushing the stepladder ahead of me until she could get hold of it. When I got to the platform, she already had it set up.

Even from the top of the ladder, it was impossible to reach any of the framework inside the elephant. "We'd better tell Danny this isn't going to work," I said. "Maybe we can just tie the rope to the ladder."

"You're going to blow up my ladder?"

"Okay, what's your suggestion?"

By the time I said that, Sarah was already tying knots in the end of the rope. She tied about five. "There, that gives it some weight. Now we can throw it."

"Good thinking," I said.

"Is it tied yet?" Danny shouted from below.

"Almost," Sarah yelled down. Then she smiled at me. "This'll work. Relax."

After three tries from halfway up the ladder, Sarah couldn't quite get the rope over the truss. "Here, you try, you big strong man."

"Fine." I took the knotted end of the rope halfway up the ladder and gathered about 20 feet of it in my left hand while holding the wad of knots in my right. I gave it a heave and the knot went well past the truss but fell straight back down to the platform. Sarah picked up the knotted end and said, "Get down and move the ladder off to the side. Then you can throw it at an angle." It worked. On the first try, the rope sailed over the truss dropped about three feet down on the other side. But I couldn't reach it. I shook the end of the rope I was holding, but I couldn't get the knot to drop. Finally I pulled the rope off the truss and it fell to the platform again. Sarah handed it to me and I gathered a little more free rope in my left hand.

Danny appeared at the top of the elephant's leg with the end of a garden hose in his hand. "Don't you clowns have that tied yet?"

"One more try and I'll get it," I said. With a couple of extra loops in my hand, I gave the knotted end a huge heave and it sailed clear of the truss and swung back down. It would have hit me in the head if I hadn't grabbed it with my left hand.

"Right on," said Danny. "You should be in the rodeo, Hero."

"Yee haw," I said, and climbed down the ladder, pulling the knotted end down with me. Sarah clapped her hands. Then she untied the knot, made a loop in that end of the rope and pushed the other end through it. She pulled the rope so the loop slid up to the truss and tightened around it like a noose.

"Good to go," she said, and then held her hand out to Danny. "Duct tape?"

"Shit," he said. "Be right back."

I looked at Sarah. "This is cool. It's like Mission: Impossible."

"Yeah, the Tom Cruise movie."

"Well, I was thinking of the TV show, but same difference."

"There was a TV show?" I ignored the question. Danny reappeared with the duct tape. Sarah took it and then took the end of the garden hose and held it up next to the rope. Reaching above her head and pointing the hose upward, she started wrapping the tape around the hose and the rope.

"Put a lot on there," Danny said.

"I know," Sarah replied, sounding annoyed. Peeling tape off the roll, she wrapped and wrapped it around the hose and rope, until about two feet were completely covered.

"That should do it," Danny said. "Now you guys stay here until we get the firecrackers set up.

We stood silently for a few moments, and then Sarah sat down on the platform. She looked around at the inside of the elephant and said, "This is amazing."

"Yeah," I replied. Then we sat silently for another minute or two. Finally I asked what she thought about owning the old gas station.

She looked at me with a serious face. "I've always wanted to open a little café," she said. "This would be the perfect spot." This seemed like an odd idea coming from someone who ate TV dinners and bragged about how she couldn't cook. I smiled and told her it sounded nice. "Yeah, we've got it all planned out. Kenzie and I picked out the dishes and the tablecloths. And the colors for the walls. It'll be the cutest café in Oregon." I asked her what she would serve in her café. She laughed. "I guess I'd have to learn how to cook. But I've got the whole place designed."

"What about pancakes. You could serve pancakes. And really good waffles and French toast."

"Nah, no breakfast," she said. "I can't get up that early."

"Well, Elephant could definitely use a nice café," I said.

I had almost gotten up the nerve to ask Sarah why she kept backing out on our dates when Danny popped up through the elephant's leg again. He said, "This is going to take awhile. You guys can come down." We climbed down the inside of the right rear leg of the big elephant. When I stepped out the door, the sun was low in the sky. It was just after eight o'clock and the fireworks were scheduled to start at nine.

Stacy's car pulled up and Phil got out looking peeved. "My phone didn't work up there," he said. "At least I got to spend some time with Gus's dogs. They get treated better than some people's partners." Phil's face was as red as Stacy's blouse, but Jonas ignored him. Then Phil looked at the group of chairs set out in front of the shop doors. "What's going on here? You're not really going to do it?"

"Oh we're doin' it." Danny said.

By this time, Jonas was sitting in one of the eight lawn chairs that had been set up next to the rollup door. He was wearing his helmet with a headlamp wrapped around it, and he had a lit cigar in his hand. He reached another helmet out to Phil, who took it reluctantly. "Keep that thing away from me," Phil said, pointing to the cigar. Phil's helmet was red, white and blue, like the helmet Peter Fonda wore in Easy Rider. Jonas's was black.

Gus appeared suddenly from out of the darkness under the big elephant. "I'm here to check on you young people," he said. "What are you up to?"

We all immediately started giving Gus a hard time about Gladys. "Well, aren't you the ladies' man?" Jonas teased him.

"I was just being neighborly," Gus said. "That's it." Then we explained to Gus our plan to turn the elephant into a giant bomb. He shook his head and rolled his eyes, and then sat down next to Phil. Jonas reached under his chair and pulled out a box of cigars and handed one to Gus, who now laughed out loud. "This is to celebrate the end of the elephant," Jonas said. "Not your hot date."

Stacy and Lindsay emerged from inside the shop. They were also wearing helmets. Pink ones. Lindsay carried another red, white and blue one in her hand. "Here, this is for you, Rob. You seem like a patriotic guy." She handed me the helmet and another light. Stacy was carrying another pink one, which she tried to give to Sarah.

"No way," Sarah said. "I don't do helmets."

"Come on," Danny urged her. "We're in this together."

"Uh Uh."

"Oh, but you'll look so cute in it," Lindsay tried to persuade her.

"Oh no. I'm not putting my hair in that," Sarah said firmly. "I have my priorities."

"Well, at least your hair will look good in the coffin," I told her.

She just smiled. "That's important." I was pretty sure she was serious.

"Smith! You and Stacy help Danny with the firecrackers," Jonas said. Stacy wouldn't look at me as we went into the shop where the Corvettes had been parked before, and there Danny was on the floor with dozens of strings of firecrackers.

"Sarah, you got a tape measure?" Danny yelled out the door.

"Yes sir," came the reply from the helmetless blonde.

"I need to know the distance from the top of your ladder to the ground."

"I'm on it." Sarah ran toward the lower right leg of the elephant. Then she looked back and called to Lindsay, who ran over to help in her pink helmet over her jet-black hair."

"I figure it's about 20 feet, so we'll need about 15 feet of firecrackers," Danny said. "Each of these strings is ten inches, I think, so we'll need to tie about 20 of these together." I looked down at the firecracker strings. Each string had two rows of firecrackers, with their fuses facing each other and wrapped in a long line down the middle. A length of fuse stuck out of one end of the joined line of fuses. "So the way this works is you have to tie the free end of the line of fuses into the ass end of the next string," Danny said calmly to me. "Like this." He carefully threaded the fuse end of one string through the first pair of firecrackers on another string. He looked up at me to see if I was comprehending him.

"Twenty-seven feet," Sarah yelled a couple of minutes later.

"Shit," said Danny. "That means we'll need more like 25 strings."

"Okay, I'll get another pair of hands," I said. It was time to try to talk to Stacy. She was standing around talking to Jonas, Phil and Gus. "Come on. This is all your fault," I yelled. "You're the one who hated the elephant so much." She finally looked at me, but it was an angry look. Then, without speaking, she walked into the garage.

Over the next 10 minutes, the long string of firecrackers slowly came together. Sarah and Lindsay came into the shop and helped pair up strings. Then pairs of strings were joined to make sets of four. Many times, the pairs came apart and had to be reattached. "These have to hang over twenty feet guys," Danny said. "You've got to tie them better than that." Then he said, "We need something stronger to support these. Smith, get some string." He told me exactly what shelf in the shop I could find it on.

Suddenly Stacy said, "I'm sure this isn't going to work, but what if it does?"

"It's going to work," said Danny.

"We're going to have to call the fire department, you know. Then we'll have cops all over the place."

At that point, we all looked at Sarah. "Don't worry," she said. "I've got law enforcement covered. He's over in the park right now, dancing with some disgusting skank."

"Do what you gotta do," Danny said, looking at Sarah with a smile.

"You guys about done?" Jonas asked through his cigar. "Fireworks are about to start. We're ready for some entertainment." It was nine o'clock and just at that moment a loud boom shot across the park, like a cannon going off. The wall of the shop had a momentary red and blue cast and the sparkler sound of fireworks could be heard behind us.

"Okay, we're almost there," said Danny. The show lasts about 15 minutes, so we've got to get this thing tied up on the rope. Everybody line up." Danny, Stacy, Lindsay and I each grabbed a length of the string of firecrackers in both hands and we carried it carefully over to the elephant. Stacy was in front, with Lindsay behind her, then me and then Danny in the back. "Sarah, onto the platform," Danny commanded.

"Yes sir." And up into the elephant's leg the beautiful Sarah went.

Danny directed Lindsay to start up the fixed ladder and hand the end of the string up to Sarah. The fireworks filled the sky every few seconds now. The large crowd in the park gave a loud "ooooooooh" as each bomb burst and filled the sky. Jonas, Phil and Gus cheered and whistled as loudly as anyone. Jonas and Gus had lit their cigars, and the ends glowed in the dark. I stood under the elephant as Lindsay called to Danny that they needed help. "It's falling apart," she said.

"Smith, we need more short lengths of string," Danny said to me. He told me where to get a pair of scissors. "We gotta hurry and get the gas turned on," he said.

In about three more minutes, Danny had the strings of firecrackers tied to the cloth string, which was tied to the nylon rope just below where the hose was duct-taped. The long line of firecrackers dangled down into the elephant's leg next to the fixed ladder. The stepladder had already been brought out and Lindsay and Sarah emerged. Sarah came out last, saying, "Goodbye Mister Elephant. It's been a great fifty years." Lindsay laughed.

"Okay, I'll attach the hose to the tank now and turn it on," Danny said, and he disappeared behind the shop building. "Everybody stay away," he yelled. Soon he reappeared, now much more relaxed. "We'll let 'er go until the fireworks end. We all took our places in our chairs – all but one of us wearing helmets and headlamps. A few of us puffed on our cigars as we watched the grand finale begin in the park. "Boom, boom, boom, boom, boom." Successive bursts of fireworks followed, one after another. Flashes of red, white and blue filled the sky. Between the explosions we could hear the faint rush of gas flowing through the long garden hose. Danny went back and checked the gauge on the big tank. "We need to give it about three more minutes, I think," he reported.

"This isn't going to last that long," Jonas said.

"Shit, said Danny. "What the hell, it'll take a minute for the firecrackers to reach it. Let's go."

At this point I couldn't smell any gas. Sarah said, "I wanna light it. It's my elephant."

"You got it," said Danny. He handed Sarah the barbeque lighter he had retrieved from the shop. "Be careful."

"Goodbye elephant," Sarah said again. The fireworks were over and the crowd in the park was still cheering, as people started moving around. Sarah lit the fuse on the bottom string of firecrackers. She jumped away, and almost immediately a machine-gun burst came from the string and about twenty firecrackers exploded. Then they stopped. "What do I do?"

"Be careful," Stacy and Lindsay yelled simultaneously.

Sarah tiptoed back to the door and reached up and relit the string, stretching her arm out as far as she could.

"It better go this time," Danny said.

The machine gun burst started up again and Sarah sprinted back toward the chairs. This time it kept going. "Here, at least hold this over your head," Phil said, as the machine gun rattled on. He handed Sarah a magazine, opened in the middle, that he had retrieved from Jonas's office. It was a copy of Western Oasis.

"Thanks," she said, as she draped the magazine over her beautiful blonde hair. I could see the cover photo with the million-dollar house overlooking Half Moon Bay. The machinegun bursts continued, and people in the park started clapping and cheering and looking our way.

Then, in an instant, the big gray elephant became a fireball. A huge "whump" accompanied by a loud "crack" replaced all other sounds. The entire town lit up, and immediately we heard the crackling of breaking fiberglass and wood. In another couple of seconds, the sky went dark again and we could hear the sound of debris hitting the ground. "Get in the shop!" Jonas yelled, and we all knew that the motorcycle helmets weren't enough. The rain of debris stopped after a few seconds more and then everything was eerily quiet. A few flames emerged from the tops of the elephant's legs. We could see the shadow of burned framework of the former elephant above the flames.

A couple of cheers came from the park. Then it suddenly became the roar of a crowd, like the home team had just scored a touchdown. Many voices cheered and yelled, and the group in the shop came back out into the driveway. "We did it!" yelled Sarah.

Pandemonium continued in the park, and many in the crowd began walking slowly across the street toward the burning elephant. Suddenly Billy appeared right in front of me. He stopped, looked up at the remains of the elephant and uttered the only words I ever heard him speak. "Right on," he said in a calm voice, and then he continued walking toward downtown.

Just as suddenly, in the parking lot across the street, blue lights flashed. A police cruiser blasted out of the driveway, spinning its wheels. "Sarah, you're up," Jonas said with a smile, as Carl screeched the cruiser to a halt in front of us and jumped out. His right hand was poised over his gun as he looked up at the remains of the big elephant.

Sarah jogged up to him with a big grin. I had never thought of her as a dumb blonde or a bimbo, but she gave an excellent impression of both now. "It was an accident, Carl." She shrugged those beautiful shoulders, put her arms straight out and cocked her head in a demented way. "We were trying to wash out the inside of the elephant," she said in a perfect air-headed voice. "But the hose got attached to the gas instead of the water. Just a little mistake."

That was probably the lamest lie I'd ever heard, but it worked. Carl looked at Sarah for a moment in disbelief, and then looked up at the smoldering remains of the big elephant and shook his head. He got on his radio and called for a fire truck. Then he stepped toward the shop. "Everybody stay back!" he commanded, attempting to take control. "The Fire Department is on its way."

Sarah walked back toward the helmeted group sitting in chairs. I was now seated with my lit cigar. She wore a huge smile as she sat down next to me and we all applauded. I looked at her and thought about how amazing it was what beautiful women can get away with.

CHAPTER TWENTY-EIGHT

Ms. Pemberton was very patient while Doris lost it. "Seven hundred dollars?! You're charging me seven hundred dollars to spray those trees?!" Then Doris looked at me and said, "I told you not to spray those trees; that I wouldn't agree to that. You're supposed to represent me and you violated my trust!" She was visibly shaking as we sat in the small, spare conference room in the Bothell Title Company office.

Ms. Pemberton spoke calmly. She was surprisingly professional and composed for someone who looked like she could still be in high school. "Ms. Ellington, the purchase and sale agreement you signed for the sale of your apartments contained a clause that specified that the trees would be sprayed. You did agree, in writing, to spray the trees." Doris gave her a frozen stare for at least five seconds.

My 75-year-old client was about to receive around a million dollars for an apartment building she owned with no debt, and she was quite comfortable financially even before selling the building. But this seven hundred dollar expense she felt she shouldn't have to pay was about to make her head explode. I expected her to drop over dead at any moment, which would have caused me a lot of financial hardship.

Then Doris clenched her teeth and looked at me coldly. "This is coming out of your commission," she said. Ms. Pemberton shook her head.

For most of my real estate career, I would have agreed to eat that expense, just to get out of the room. My commission was going to be twenty-nine thousand and change, so the seven hundred dollars would have been a relatively small nick for me too. But today I held out. "I explained to you about the trees when the offer came in," I told Doris. "If you had a problem with it, you should have objected then." I could tell that Doris was very close to walking out without signing. She could have called my bluff, and in the end I would have paid it. But she didn't. She signed, paid for the spraying of the trees, and stalked angrily out of the office without saying a word to me or Ms. Pemberton.

"I owe you one," I said to Ms. Pemberton after Doris was gone.

"Not at all. It's part of my job. I'd say you earned every penny of your commission." With that, Ms. Pemberton smiled and handed me a check for $29,754.83.

* * *

Two hours later I was sitting in Ugly Al's Coffee Emporium telling Jennifer the story of Doris's meltdown. The envelope containing my check was lying on the table in front of me. It was Thursday, three days after I returned to Seattle from Elephant. "Wanna buy a coffee shop?" Jennifer asked with a smile. I shook my head. "At least you could buy a gal dinner." Two weeks earlier, this would have been a surprising request, but now it somehow seemed normal.

"Why not?" I said. "What are you going to tell mister Chris?"

"That I'm having dinner with you, and that he gets to watch Christopher tonight. And that's all. Don't get any ideas Mr. Big Shot. I could be bought, but it would take a lot more than thirty grand." Then she smiled and then asked me what Fourth of July was like in Elephant. I told her it was definitely the strangest Fourth of July I'd ever experienced, and then I started the long version of the destruction if the big gray elephant. About five minutes in, my cell phone rang. I had already deleted "DEATH" from my phone, but I knew it wouldn't be Doris.

"Where the hell are you, Robbie boy? We gotta talk." It was Charles. I told him where I was and he said he'd be there "in five." I continued telling Jennifer my story, and it was nearly fifteen when Charles finally walked into Ugly Al's. He was holding a blank white envelope in his hand. "How's that article coming?" he asked as soon as he sat down.

"It's not. Tomorrow's the deadline, right?"

"Yes it is, mister procrastination." Charles had a strange smile on his face.

I explained to Charles and Jennifer the progress I'd made so far. During the five-hour drive home from Elephant on Monday, I tried to write the article in my head. But I figured out that that doesn't work. On Tuesday I spent an hour reading all of the copies of the articles Gus gave me that Eunice had written over the years. Then I went to the library in downtown Seattle and looked through at least three dozen lifestyle and travel magazines, reading every article about a small town that I could find. Every one of those towns was far more picturesque and inviting than Elephant, or at least my memory of it. All towns have nasty parts, I thought to myself, and these writers just pick and choose the good parts. But I couldn't think of any good parts of Elephant, except that I liked the people, and they were friendly and nice. I decided that would have to be my angle.

"I'm going to write it tonight," I told them. "After I take Jennifer to dinner."

"Hold on there," Jennifer said. "Maybe we'd better take a rain check. It sounds like you have something more important to do."

"So what's your angle?" Charles asked, still smiling mysteriously.

"The people. Those are the friendliest and nicest people I've ever met."

"That's a great idea." Jennifer said.

"It's a terrible idea," countered Charles. "Every small town in America has nice friendly people. That's why people live in them. You've been living in the big heartless city your whole life and you never knew that it's possible for people to actually be nice to each other."

"Okay mister wise guy, what's your idea?"

"It doesn't matter," Charles replied, "because you're off the hook."

"Huh?" Charles handed me the white envelope. "What's that?" I asked.

"It's your money. Three hundred clams. Angela said to tell you to turn in your expenses. They'll reimburse you and you're done. They don't want your article."

"What are you talking about?"

Charles said he had been working at the Western Oasis office that day and Agnes, or Angela, or whatever her name was, had called him into her office. "Remember the old man who wanted them to do the article on Elephant?" Charles asked me.

"Yeah, he was some relative of the big boss," I said. "He was going to his high school reunion, and he wanted to impress his old classmates. His name was Ralph, or something like that."

"Yeah, Ralph. Well…" Charles said, and then paused. "It seems that on Sunday night, during the fireworks show at the Space Needle, old Ralph got a little too excited and had a stroke. He's in a coma, and he's not expected to come out of it." I stared at Charles for a second. He was serious. "Therefore, as I said, they no longer want your article. In fact, they wouldn't run it even if you wrote it."

I took a moment to process this new information. "The old man had a stroke. Fuckin'-A! That's fantastic news!"

"Rob!" Jennifer was appalled, but Charles grinned.

"I thought you'd like hearing that," he said. "Here." He shoved the envelope at me. I opened it and looked at the $300 check, and then put it in the other envelope with my commission check.

"Cool. That puts me over 30 grand," I said. "And my work is done. Dinner and drinks are on me."

* * *

The three of us rode in the restored Beemer along Lake Union toward downtown and a little bistro that was one of the most expensive and exclusive restaurants in Seattle. None of us had eaten there before, and we all felt totally out of place as we waited for our French wine and tiny plates of the most beautiful food I'd ever seen. I resumed my story about the aftermath of the explosion of the big gray elephant.

When I checked out of the motel early Monday morning, the beautiful Sarah gave me a bear hug, and held on for several seconds. She seemed genuinely sad when she made me promise to come back for a visit "real soon." I could have a free room in the motel for as long as I wanted, she promised.

Jennifer's eyes got big. "You gonna do it?"

"He's dumb enough, of course he will," Charles said. "And she'll stand him up again."

I nodded. "You're right. I probably will, and she probably will." Then I continued.

When I went to say goodbye to Jonas at his office, the area within 50 feet of the stumps of the elephant's legs was blocked with yellow tape. There was a narrow space to fit the car through and I parked behind the shop building. Jonas told me he had hired Gus's son, Charlie, to bring his excavator over and finish what we started the night before. "By next weekend no one will know there was ever an elephant here," he said. Jonas and Danny shook my hand and told me I had to return. Then I drove out of town.

I got almost to the interstate freeway, but the impasse with Stacy was eating at me too much. I turned around and retraced my route up the beautiful winding country road back to Elephant. When I opened her office door, Stacy gave me a big smile. "I'm so glad you stopped by before you left," she said. "I was sure you wouldn't." I didn't tell her that I actually didn't stop by before I left, but came back. She started in on a big apology for her forwardness when we were dancing the night before. I stopped her and said I'd forgotten all about it. I told her I really did want her to come to Seattle for a visit, even if I'd been hesitant before. She told me she'd think about it, and then said, "But you have to come back to Elephant." She didn't seem too surprised when I said I'd promised the beautiful Sarah yet another date. "You're such a boy. You'll end up on a date with me, you know. Just like the other dates you had with her."

"I hope so," I said. Then I held my arms out in the Elephant hugging posture, and she got up from her desk and came over for what started out as an awkward hug. It became less awkward after a couple of minutes.

Jennifer and Charles had been silently picking at their gorgeous food while I told my sorry. Jennifer spoke up now. "Did you kiss her? Please tell me you kissed her."

Then Charles broke in. "I don't care about that. Did you take her back to her house and, you know…" Then he pounded his knuckles on the table five times.

Jennifer gave Charles a disgusted look and I said, "Yup, I kissed her. And it lasted a good long time, I'll have you know." Then I looked at Charles. "And that was it."

Now Charles gave me a disappointed look and Jennifer smiled. "That's so romantic," she said.

"Well, thirty grand and a new paint job," Charles said, as he held up his coffee cup like he was toasting me. "Not bad, even if you struck out with the babes."

Jennifer scrunched her face up and looked at me and said, "You know Rob, my sister's going to be in Seattle next week."

"You have a sister?" Charles and I asked at once.

"I've told you about her, Rob. Mary Ann."

"Oh yeah," I said. "Mary Ann. In Ohio. The one with the perfect husband, who's cute and funny and takes her traveling and does all the things Chris doesn't do. You're totally jealous of her, as I recall."

"They're getting a divorce," Jennifer said. Charles and I both laughed as she explained: "It seems that somebody else found him cute and funny too, and he was also taking her traveling. Mary Ann found out. You wanna meet her?" she asked me.

"Uh, I don't think so. I'm done with women. I'm thinking of proposing to Charles."

Charles slid his chair away from me. "I'm spoken for," he said.

"She's drop-dead gorgeous," Jennifer said. "Way better looking than me."

"That's impossible," I said. "And besides, I'm not dating based on looks anymore. The uglier the better, as far as I'm concerned. Beautiful women are highly overrated."

"I've got a picture of her on my phone."

"It doesn't matter."

Jennifer pulled out her phone and tapped the keyboard a couple of times. Then she showed the screen to Charles and me. We both coughed. "Fuck," said Charles.

"Yeah, you wish," said Jennifer. "What about you, Rob? Is that what's on your mind too?" Based on what I saw on Jennifer's phone screen, Mary Ann would bump the beautiful Sarah from the top spot on my best-looking dates list — if she were on it.

"We could double date," said Jennifer, with a big grin. "We'll take your fancy BMW. That'll impress her."

"Tell you what. Let me sleep on it and I'll get back to you."

* * *

I got a couple of emails from Stacy over the next week. In one she said she started the divorce process with Curtis. She also told me that someone else had asked her out. It seems the eye doctor who started coming to Elephant one day a week was also getting a divorce. "He's fifty, but he's really cute," Stacy wrote. "And he's so nice to me. But he's fifty. I told him I needed to sleep on it, and I'd get back to him."

I replied and told her that men over fifty are always nice to cute women half their age. I also told her that she was still invited for a visit to Seattle. And that I meant it.

A week later I got another email from Stacy that was more than chatty. "I have giant news!!! I couldn't wait to tell you. You're gonna be heartbroken." Stacy wrote that the group of motorcyclists had come to Elephant the weekend after the Fourth of July and stayed at the motel. One of them didn't leave. "He's six-four and full of muscles. And tattoos. He moved in with Sarah. And the kids. He's a truck driver and she's totally in love. Everybody in town's talking about it. That's all the news I got." I could see the grin on Stacy's face without seeing it. She ended her email with, "I'm thinking about your offer to visit Seattle. I'll let you know."

Within minutes of Stacy's email about the beautiful Sarah and the tattooed biker, I received a text from Peter. "call owen s. wants 2 sell." This was followed by a phone number. And so I had a new client. Peter's fellow Tall Pines resident, Owen Stringfellow, had three large apartment buildings in north Seattle he was ready to put on the market. Other than being about the same age as Doris, he was the complete opposite. He was friendly and considerate and actually listened to my suggestions. My struggling little real estate company was soon to become a thriving business.

The next day I sent Stacy a reply to her email about Sarah's new situation. For some reason I resurrected my pizza analogy from our dinner at Melville's. "I guess my taste in pizza could use some improvement," I wrote. "Sometimes those gourmet pizzas that look so good don't have any substance. But I'd say that you're cooked to perfection and about ready to serve." Then I put in one more pitch for her to visit me in Seattle.

Stacy wrote me back with a newsy email about some of the other recent goings-on in Elephant. Gus had a goofy old-fashioned looking haircut now, and he and Jonas and Danny were hard at work on the old Plymouth. The whole west end of town looked different with the elephant gone and Jonas's shop having a new paint job, thanks to Sarah and her new boyfriend. Stacy even got a small bonus from the Chamber of Commerce board of directors.

"I'm usin' it for a plane ticket to Seattle," she said.

* * *

It was just after 8 a.m. when I rolled the shiny Beemer along the long, never-ending curve outside the arrival gates at Seattle-Tacoma Airport. Stacy had taken the earliest flight out of Pendleton on a Saturday, three weeks after the Fourth of July. The weather in Seattle had turned cool and cloudy. I spotted her under the Horizon Airlines sign, and she looked different. She wore a gray hoodie sweatshirt with the word "PINK" in giant pink block letters across the front. She had on tight jeans and pink sneakers, and she was noticeably thinner. Her hair was cut shorter, and it was redder.

I pulled to the curb, got out and gave Stacy a long Elephant hug. Then I opened the trunk and put her small pink roller bag into it and told her how great she looked. I think she could tell I was actually surprised.

"I got out some of my college clothes," she said. "This is the first time they've fit in three years."

"Damn, girl." I stepped back like I was admiring a work of art.

She beamed. "I discovered the secret to weight loss," she said.

"Divorce."

I noticed a security guard walking toward us and staring at my car. He was about twice my size. "We better go," I said. "Get in."

As we headed out onto Highway 99 toward downtown Seattle, I told her, "It's about time you stopped dressing like a 50-year-old."

"I brought you a present," she said. Then she pulled something out of her pink handbag. It was a small bottle of maple syrup. "Let's go use this."

In the restaurant at the Edgewater Hotel on the Seattle waterfront, we enjoyed the opposite end of the spectrum from the Moss Creek Inn. "I guarantee you won't find chicken fried steak on the menu here," I told Stacy, as I handed my car key to the valet. "But they'll have real syrup. You can leave the bottle in the car."

We sat next to one of the giant windows looking out over Elliot Bay. I ordered walnut and blueberry pancakes. "And I'd like extra syrup with that," I told the waitress.

"Absolutely, sir," she replied.

Stacy rolled her eyes and then looked at the waitress and smiled. "I'll have the same," she said.

While we ate, I told Stacy about Owen's apartments in North Seattle that I was getting ready to sell. Then she told me that Gladys and Gus had been seen having dinner together at the Moss Creek Inn. "They look so cute together!" she said.

"And speaking of people who look cute together," Stacy went on. "Are you sad about Sarah and her new stud?"

"Of course I'm sad. But what else is new? I've been disappointed by women my whole life." Stacy gave me a big smile, like she didn't believe me.

Our waitress was friendly and attentive throughout our meal, and she didn't once chew gum. She cleared our plates quickly when we had finished and then refilled our coffee cups. Stacy wrapped both hands around her cup with her elbows on the table. She stared directly into my eyes and gave me a smile. Suddenly, for the first time since I'd met her, I wanted to see Stacy naked.

Then she spoke: "You know that last email you sent me?" she asked. I must have looked puzzled as I snapped out of my daydream, because she went on. "You know, how I'm a cooked pizza, ready to eat?"

"Kinda stupid, huh?"

"Yeah, and kinda insulting too," she replied. "You know, now that I'm sober..." She paused and smiled. "I'm thinking that maybe writing isn't your thing. You should probably stick with real estate." I just stared at her, and then she gave me an incredibly sexy smile and said, "Come on, it's time for you to take me home."

And so my writing career ended just as it began: with the encouragement of a woman.

ABOUT THE AUTHOR

Ken Graham is owner and publisher of The Times newspaper in Waitsburg Washington. He lives on a mall spread in the Blue Mountains of southeast Washington with his wife and several random animals.

www.ingramcontent.com/pod-product-compliance
Lightning Source LLC
Chambersburg PA
CBHW070553130626
46556CB00001B/134